Restored

Tanya Eavenson

"*Restored* was an amazing read! It was heartbreaking at times, but also very inspiring and filled with lots of hope. I didn't want to put it down and read it as fast as I could. It's a great reminder that nothing is impossible with God." ~Ashley

"In *Restored*, Tanya Eavenson brings back several of the characters we found in *Unconditional*. Tanya's writing strength lies in characterization. She takes us deep into the thoughts and emotions of Dr. Steven Moore and Elizabeth Roberts. Throughout the novel, we walk alongside the characters pulling for them, even when the future seems bleak. If you want to read a deeply romantic love story, this is the book. The novel kept me turning pages until The End." ~Virginia

This book is dedicated first to my stepfather, Gary Barnard, and my father-in-law, Charles Eavenson. Both have faced the realities of melanoma cancer and know how life-changing cancer can be. They are my heroes. I pray they both know how deeply they are loved.

Secondly, this book is dedicated to anyone whose faith is shaken. To anyone who is searching. To anyone who needs to believe in the impossible.

"For with God nothing shall be impossible." Luke 1:37

Elizabeth ran her fingers down the wooden handrail along the stairs, glancing at the ornate clock on the mantle. "Not much longer now." Her heart pounded with excitement as her gaze moved to the framed picture beside the clock and settled on her husband's handsome face. Warmth flowed through her as she lifted the portrait with its silver frame. Chris had just tackled their son, Luke, with the football in the front yard when she snapped the picture.

She touched the glass over Chris's blond hair. His hazel eyes peered up at her. She smiled. It still amazed her how their lives had changed throughout the years, coming back from the brink of divorce to discovering what unconditional love truly meant. What they meant to each other.

"Two hours and you'll be home," she breathed. This mission trip to Goma, Africa, kept Chris away for several weeks this time, but now it was time for him to come home to stay.

She closed her eyes, envisioning Chris's arms

around her. Tonight, she'd drink in the words of love she'd missed before she fell asleep every evening, the feel of his body next to hers.

She smiled and pressed a hand against her flat belly. "Yes, Daddy will be home soon. Won't he be surprised?" The chime of the doorbell broke through her thoughts.

She set the frame down and hurried to open the front door. Elizabeth smiled at her sister and brother-in-law. "Hey, why did you ring the doorbell? You could have come right in." She halted. Something in their expressions made her heart race. "Where's Luke?" she asked her sister.

Sam's mouth opened, but no words came out. She grabbed Phillip's arm as if she needed support.

Moisture filled Phillip's eyes. "There's been an accident. They tried to call. We tried to call."

"Lizzy." Her sister moved to her side.

Elizabeth couldn't breathe. No, God, no. Please, God, I can't take losing another child. "Where is he, Sam? Where's Luke?"

Phillip cleared his throat. "Luke is fine. He's with Mom."

Elizabeth glanced between them, not understanding. "But you said there was an accident...they tried to call—"

"My brother..." Phillip's voice broke and a tear ran down his face. "Elizabeth, there's been a plane crash."

Chapter One

Four Years Later

Sweat beaded on Dr. Steven Moore's brow as he thumbed through several medical files. Where was…? Frustrated that he couldn't recall the simplest things, he stood, picked up the receiver, and pressed the nurses' extension. Shrugging out of his white coat, he threw it onto the back of his leather chair.

"Hello. Nurses' station."

"Mike there?" He switched the phone from one hand to the other, raking his tie from the desk. His hand shook.

"Yes, sir. Hold on a minute."

Steven slung the tie around his neck, catching the telephone cord. Unraveling the knotted mess, he exhaled and glanced at his watch.

"This is Mike."

"Hey, do you have the file? I can't find it."

Mike chuckled. "You must be on edge. You gave it to me an hour ago and I gave it to George. Are you sure you want to go through with this?"

"Positive." His gut wrenched.

"All right. We have thirty-five minutes until we need to be at the church. I'll see you in a few."

Steven hung up, walked to the bathroom, and flicked the light on. He studied himself in the mirror. He'd been tying his own tie ever since his wife died eighteen years ago, it came as natural as breathing, but today was different. His fingers fumbled anything he touched.

He stood to his full height, cutting off half the view of his head, but the silver streaks through his hair were still visible as he leaned down. Who was he kidding? At forty-two, he was graying and life had passed him by.

Straightening his shirt, he glanced at himself one last time and took a deep breath. Steven tapped the light switch off and strode through his office. He yanked his suit jacket from the couch and shrugged it on when there was a knock.

"Come in."

The door swung open and Mike turned toward him. "You ready?"

"As ready as I'll ever be…considering." Steven locked his office door, anxiety not only kicking him in the stomach, but making it gurgle as he made his way to the garage.

Mike patted his shoulder. "I'll meet you there. And hey, you'll make it through."

Steven slipped his key ring out of his pocket, pressed the unlock button, and climbed in the driver's seat. Mike took the lead exiting the hospital garage. He was thankful for his friend because if Mike hadn't been going with him, he didn't know if he could do this…seeing Elizabeth after all this time. Twelve years. It felt like a lifetime ago.

Twenty minutes later, they pulled into the church parking lot. Steven cut the engine and stepped out of his car. People milled around the front door. He strode a few steps, then stopped and tugged on his collar. This was a mistake.

Mike came up behind him and spoke over his shoulder. "If you don't want to do this—"

"That's not the problem. I want to be here." He glanced at the church entrance and the bustle of activity.

"Then what is it?"

Steven exhaled. "Should I be here?" His phone vibrated in his pocket. He yanked his cell out and glanced at the caller. "George. I need to call him back. Nine-one-one."

Mike nodded. "All right. I'll save you a spot."

Steven frowned as he palmed his cell and pushed recent calls. "Hey, George, I saw you called." A groan answered him.

"Where are you?"

A nerve pulsed in Steven's jaw at the sound of George's impatience. "A friend from college is getting married. It's about to begin."

"I'll make this quick. The board has planned an emergency meeting."

"When?" Steven glanced at his watch.

"In ten minutes."

Steven's arm fell to his side. "I won't be able to

make it. If I left now—"

"We need you here at the hospital. I still don't agree with you quitting like this, but with you being so determined to resign, what choice do I have?"

Steven ran his fingers through his hair. "George, I have to do this. I can't be a liability to my patients or to the hospital. I can't do my job."

"Take some time off."

"I've made up my mind." Steven glanced toward heaven wishing for.... What? Things to be different? His health to be restored? A dream?

Elizabeth walked through a row of cars toward the church. Steven's heart lurched. Her blonde hair shone like satin in the midday sun. Dare he continue to stare? Yes, he was compelled, not only by the deepest desire he'd clung to most of his life, but by the dream that also haunted him, teased him. Even after all this time.

"Steven?" George sighed. "Your diagnosis. It doesn't mean—"

"I'll be there as soon as I can." He hung up and shifted his gaze. Elizabeth must have entered the church because she was nowhere to be found. His mind tried to recapture the memory of only moments ago. Instead, he shook his thoughts away and refocused on the problem at hand. He needed to find Mike before the wedding started.

Steven followed a small group inside, eyeing the crowd until he found his friends. He slid into the pew next to Mike.

"What did George say?" Mike mumbled as the

wedding march began. Everyone stood and turned toward the aisle. The doors opened and the fragrance of flowers, perfume, and melted wax stirred in the air.

No matter how much he tried to direct his attention to the happy couple and their special day, uneasiness over his decision to leave the hospital still tore at him. He loved being a doctor and always felt God had called him to help others. But how could he help others now when he couldn't help himself?

He perched on the edge of the pew and glanced around, searching for one person. Elizabeth sat toward the front. He would never forget the last time he saw her at the airport, and how soft her chin felt in the palm of his hand. When he told her she would always hold a place in his heart, he meant every word.

Memories of them together were what he'd clung to over the years and those same memories would help him overcome the battle he'd soon be facing. She was the reason he came. He needed to see her one final time no matter how fleeting the moment was, no matter how his dream of her was dying with him.

But no matter how deeply he longed to stay, he realized it was better for them both if he left. There was too much history between them, too much pain, and not enough time to start over.

Steven leaned into Mike. "I've got to go. The board might have found my replacement."

"You should stay," Mike whispered, eyeing him.

"It's better this way."

Steven hurried though the hospital corridors in search of George. He had already checked his office, but when he circled back around, raised voices caught his attention from beyond a closed door.

A familiar voice argued, "This isn't right. If Steven had been there, none of this would be happening."

"What can we do?" another man's voice asked.

Silence. Steven straightened, then knocked, but it took a moment before the door swung open. George was alone.

"Come in." George closed the door and crossed to the far side of the room to sit in a chair, drumming his fingers on the conference table. "I have a headache." He rose and bolted into the bathroom, came out with a bottle. Yanking the lid off, he peered in before he threw it in the trash and reclaimed his seat. "I work at a hospital and I can't get pills when I need them."

Steven couldn't sit. Instead his eyes darted to the only other door in the room. "I overheard you talking to someone. What happened at the meeting?"

George pounded his fists on the polished mahogany table. "The board didn't like the way you're leaving regardless of your heath, and without an official replacement or enough time to find one, they're letting you go by the end of the week. They'll require you to be on call for three weeks to help out or to assist in any way." George shook his head. "I'm sorry, Steven. Since you've been here, the hospital has grown. This place has helped more children than we ever imagined with the millions you've raised. I think they're just upset at losing all that."

Steven flopped into the nearest chair, stunned, numb. At the end of the week, everything he'd worked for would be gone, but in one way, he was relieved. He looked over to George. "It's hard not to look back over one's life. You know what I've concluded?"

"What?"

"Solomon from the Bible was right. Everything is meaningless."

"I don't believe that for one second. As I just mentioned, the millions you've raised to help dying children means something. The programs you've implemented mean something. Without you, this apnea wing wouldn't have been added to the hospital. Your name on this building means something. Steven Moore, the man, means something."

Steven couldn't listen to this. He rose and walked to the door.

George followed him. "Where are you going?"

"I don't know any more."

"Steven, I wish—"

"Me too." Steven threw open the door and hurried down the corridor. As he made his way to the front of the hospital, Mike came through the automatic sliding doors.

"Steven, what happened?"

"Not now, Mike!" Steven continued past him and went out the entrance. He needed to think.

Needed to pray, but lately, no matter how hard he tried, he couldn't. What would it matter if he begged God? His fate had been sealed. He headed toward the fountain in the center of the architectural grounds and sat on a bench, burying his head in his hands. What was he going to do? There was a touch on his shoulder, and he lifted his head to his friend. He had no right to speak to Mike the way he did. He had always been there for him, when Elizabeth left before their wedding, when his wife and child died, years later when he found Elizabeth again—married. And now. "Sorry, Mike."

"What's happened?"

"Life happened." After explaining the board's decision, Steven became lost in his thoughts and an overwhelming feeling of lonesomeness grew inside him, in his heart. But when the name Elizabeth cut into his thoughts, he looked to Mike. "What did you say?"

"You should visit Miami. See Elizabeth."

"No." Steven shook his head and met his friend's gaze. "You of all people know I can't. Why would you even suggest it?"

Mike remained quiet so Steven studied the hospital grounds. Dogwoods encircled them. White petals rained through the breeze and shook the tips of the branches. He inhaled the sweet aroma, once again recalling how beautiful Elizabeth looked at the church. No matter how brief it was, he gathered the memory and filed it with the others. "How is she?"

"She looked great. Nicole was the only one that talked to her. She has two boys. I didn't stay for the reception or I would have found out more."

Steven stood. "Ready to go back?"

"Sure." They walked a few steps before Mike slowed. "Why can't you be honest with yourself?"

"About what?"

"Living."

"How can I when I'm dying?" His strides increased as yellow particles of pollen edged his shoes.

Mike caught up to him. "I've watched you, Steven. You're living like you've already died. Who knows when the Lord will call you home, but you're alive now. Act like it. Go see her."

Steven lowered his voice. "Leave her out of this."

"Why?"

"This conversation is over."

Mike called after him. "Chris died, Steven. Almost four years ago."

As if a knife stabbed him in the back, Steven stopped cold. He mourned the day he heard about Chris's plane crashing as it returned from a mission trip in Africa. It had nothing to do with him, yet a part of him perished right along with Chris. It was Chris who should have grown old with Elizabeth. The only man she truly ever loved.

Mike stood in front of him. "You took yourself out of her life—completely. You're an honorable man, but maybe it's time to step back in."

Steven shook his head. "I...I can't see her." Didn't Mike understand he was a broken man and couldn't be fixed? "Besides, she wouldn't want me there."

"You might be surprised. Don't let fear rob you of what God may have in store. Step out in faith and live while you still can."

Steven left Mike and headed into the hospital. He'd worked his shift before the wedding so he could very well leave, but being alone right now was too much. He needed to focus on something, anything besides Elizabeth.

Yet Mike's words filtered through his mind.

Chapter Two

Elizabeth rushed to her purse, lifted her wallet, and pulled out thirty dollars. "Luke, when the pizza guy comes, give this to him." She waved the money in the air. "I'll set it on the foyer table." Christopher ran past her in his birthday suit.

"Christopher, what did Mommy say? Go potty so I can give you a bath." The white-cheeked little boy paid her no mind. She slapped the money down and glanced out the window for the pizza man. Maybe she could have the bath done before the food arrived. How wonderful would that be? Then she wouldn't have to rush to the bookstore.

"Come on, Christopher. Let's get into the bath so we can have pizza then go to your favorite place, Mommy's work. We can see the fishies." She sang the last word for emphasis as she made her way to the bathroom. Hazel eyes peeped around the corner.

"Movie? Pockcorn?"

"Only if you take a bath." She turned the nozzle on.

"I weady."

She bit her lip, he reminded her so much of

Chris. Elizabeth lifted him into the tepid water when the doorbell rang.

"Sweetheart," Elizabeth hollered. "Can you get that?"

"Yeah," Luke yelled back.

Elizabeth hurried. "Lean your head back while Mommy rinses your hair." She filled a cup with water and poured it over his head and face. Christopher laughed.

"Mom! It's not the pizza guy!"

Great. She couldn't leave her little boy in the tub unattended. "Tell them to wait outside. I'll be there in a minute." After towel drying Christopher, she walked him to his room. "Since you're getting to be a big boy now, I want you to try to get dressed. Here are your clothes. Okay?" She heard the doorbell again.

Elizabeth expelled a tired breath as she walked into the foyer. Luke handed the pizza man the money, and she joined him in the doorway. "Thank you." She reached for the pizza boxes, but beyond the deliveryman, she glimpsed Steven gazing at her. The boxes tumbled from her grip.

"I'm sorry about that, ma'am." The pizza man tucked his carrying bag under his arm. "I thought you had it."

"No. No. It's my fault. Thank you again." She bent down and snatched the boxes from the ground, then stood and shielded her eyes, taking a deep breath as the man left. She spun and shoved the boxes into Luke's hands. "Take these and set them on the table. I'll be there in a minute."

"Sure." Luke lifted one of the box lids. "Look! They must have glued the toppings down with cheese."

Elizabeth waited until he walked out of sight before stepping through the doorway toward Steven who still waited by her white hydrangeas. "What are you doing here?"

He took a few steps toward her. "I was in the neighborhood."

Neighborhood? "I didn't realize Atlanta was around the corner."

"I hope you don't mind." Steven focused on something behind her and smiled.

Small fingers slipped into her hand and tugged. She looked down at Christopher and exhaled. Her youngest stood naked with his underwear on his head.

She knelt with a moan. "Go in your room and Mommy will be there in a minute, okay?"

Christopher climbed her knee and swung his arms around her neck. "Dwessed."

"Yes, sweetie." She pressed a kiss on his soft cheek. "Dressed."

Christopher slid down and ran toward his room. Whether he actually made it there was another story. Elizabeth stood. Should she invite Steven in? What would they talk about?

Steven pointed down the driveway. "I should go. You're busy."

"If only you knew." She tucked a few flyaway

strands of hair behind her ear, feeling self-conscious for the first time in—she couldn't remember when. "Would you like to come in?"

He hesitated for a moment, indecision playing out in his features. "Sure."

She moved from the doorway to allow him to enter, noticing his scent of soap and wind, as if he'd stood along the beach before coming. She touched his arm, stopping him in the foyer. His dark eyes caught hers and she seemed lost for a moment. She drew her hand away. "I have to warn you. You're entering at your own risk."

He leaned toward her and whispered, "Will I be attacked?" A smile played on his lips and she smiled in return.

"You might. I'm not making any promises." She led the way into the living room where Christopher was still wearing his underwear as a hat. She excused herself, lifted him up in her arms and carried him to his room.

She planted him on his feet. "Sweetie, what did mommy ask you to do?"

"Get dwessed."

"And are you dressed?"

He nodded furiously.

Shaking her head, she swiped the underwear from his hair and helped him put it on, along with the clothes still folded on the edge of the bed. "Christopher."

He looked up at her with Chris's eyes. He was Chris made over as a child.

"Go play."

He ran out of the room.

Standing, she looked around at the messy floor and walked over several toys toward the mirror. She patted her hair down then straightened her wet shirt. She was a mess, but what did it matter? A mother raising two boys on her own, and running a bookstore took all her strength and time.

Luke rushed into the room. "Mom, you okay?"

"Of course. Why wouldn't I be?"

"Good! Don't worry! I called the cops!"

Elizabeth stared at her son. "What are you talking about? What cops?"

"That guy from outside… he came in."

It took seconds before Elizabeth understood what her son was saying. Her breath caught. "Luke. You didn't."

"What?"

Elizabeth hurried into the living room and Steven was nowhere to be found. She went to the front door and swung it open in time to see the green and white Miami-Dade police car pull up. Then she saw him, standing by the driveway. "Oh, Steven." She dashed past him to the vehicle.

A young officer climbed out of the car. "We got a call about an intruder."

She looked him directly in the eye. "Officer, there's been a misunderstanding. My son thought…he'd never seen him before."

Steven's hand briefly touched her elbow.

"Sorry, Officer. Her son doesn't know me. Elizabeth invited me in. All Luke saw was a stranger standing in his living room. When he told me to leave, I left. I assure you, I was waiting outside until Elizabeth realized what happened."

The officer pointed to her. "I take it your name is Elizabeth? The one he is referring to?"

She nodded. "Yes. Elizabeth Roberts."

He took out a pad and pen from his pocket and scribbled something. "Is this true?"

"Yes," she said again, swallowing the knot in her throat.

"What's your son's name?" He continued to write.

"Luke Roberts."

The officer met her gaze. "May I see him?"

"Of course." Elizabeth led him into the house. "Luke, come here please. The officer wants to speak with you." She scanned the living room. Christopher was nowhere to be seen. Where is he? *Please, Lord, help him not to get into anything.* She took a deep breath.

Luke came around the corner and ducked his head. The officer met him halfway. They spoke for a few minutes before the policeman turned and nodded in her direction.

"Everything checks out." He commented, exiting the house. "If you need us, don't hesitate to call." He tipped his hat before sliding back into the car. As he pulled out of the drive, she looked toward Steven. "I need to find Christopher, but will you come in? I'll introduce you to Luke."

Steven entered the house in time to see Christopher lunge for Elizabeth's legs, and his heart grieved for the son he once had. In a blink of an eye life could change and no two people were more aware of that fact than him and Elizabeth. One minute they held life within their arms, the next it was stripped from their grasp.

"Mommy, home. I miss uo."

She lifted the little boy into her arms and pressed her face against his. "Mommy would never leave you. I stepped outside for a minute. I have a friend I want you and your brother to meet. Go find Luke and tell him to come here." She set the little boy down and he ran from the room. She turned to Steven. "Would you like to sit? With your height, it would be easier for them to see you, relieve the intimidation factor."

Intimidation factor? He'd never heard that one before. But when the pitter-patter of small feet slapped against the hardwood floors, Steven quickly sat on the edge of the couch. Christopher ran to him and tapped on his leg. "Fit."

Steven looked up at Elizabeth and smiled. He plopped the little boy on his knee.

Elizabeth turned a smile on Luke as he came in. "Steven, this is Luke. Luke, this is my old friend from college." Luke's shoulders slunk forward.

Steven felt for the boy having to confront him. He held out his hand. "Hey, Luke."

Luke stared at him for a moment, then finally shook his hand. "I'm sorry."

"Don't be." Steven turned his attention to Christopher. "Now who's this young man in my lap?" He poked his finger into Christopher's stomach. The little boy giggled.

"This is my little brother. He likes to run around with no clothes on."

"I noticed." Steven chuckled. "And how old are you both?"

Christopher held up his hand and waved his fingers in the air.

"I'm eleven," Luke said, pulling down two of his brother's fingers. "You're three now, Christopher. Three. His birthday was yesterday."

Steven's gaze flicked to Elizabeth. Did Chris know before he left for Africa that he was to be a father again? As if she had read his thoughts, moisture filled her eyes and she looked away.

He returned his attention to the boy sliding from his knee. "Well, happy birthday, Christopher. So what do you boys like to do?"

"We both like to fish. I play ball. First base. Outfield some. We win a lot."

"I'll have to come and see you play sometime. I like to hit the ball around a bit myself."

"Um. Thanks." Luke turned without another word and headed upstairs.

"Will you excuse me for a minute? I won't be long." Elizabeth followed her oldest son. Her shoulders slumped slightly as she made her way to the top.

Steven glanced around. Her mahogany furniture with its deep rich colors reminded him of his office and the hospital, a place he'd soon never return except as a patient.

With a deep breath, he stood and walked to a shelf near the stairwell that held family photos. It seemed odd being in Chris's home. His eyes narrowed in on the pictures, the happy faces, and his stomach wrenched. He had no right to be here.

"I'm sorry for calling 911." Luke's voice seemed to come from one of the pictures.

Steven peeked behind one of the frames and spotted a monitor that now broadcast Elizabeth's soft voice.

"It's okay, Luke. I'm not upset. I'm thankful to have a son who wants to protect his mother. What you did was brave."

"If Dad were here...."

"I know. If he were here, things would be different. But God loves us and he's taking care of us."

"If God loved us so much, then why did He let dad die?" The boy's pain came through the monitor loud and clear. Steven understood how Luke felt. He'd felt the anguish too when his sister died in the orphanage where they both were raised, when his wife and son died in the car accident. He hurt for Luke, but also for Elizabeth knowing what she and Chris had gone through together. It was wrong to have come. Nothing good could come of it, only to bring more hurt and pain to a family that needed healing.

"Honestly, sweetheart, I can't answer that. But don't ever think God doesn't love you."

"Stop calling me sweetheart. I'm not a baby anymore."

"If you'll do me a favor. I want you to come back downstairs."

"We've already met, remember? I'm the one who called the cops on him."

"Please, Luke. He's a very kind man. I know he understands."

Steven's attention landed on a silver frame of Elizabeth swinging on a tire-tube. His heart skipped a beat. Her turquoise eyes twinkled as the picture captured her mouth parted in mid-laugh. He glanced up the stairwell during the long pause to make sure no one was coming down and caught him listening.

"Are we still going to work?"

"Oh no. I completely forgot. Get your shoes on. Hurry."

The monitor picked up movement and he started back to the couch when Elizabeth rushed down the stairwell, but before she reached the bottom, Steven stood ready to meet her. "Please…don't hurry down the stairs."

It was an impulse to rush to her, but a foolish impulse to say the words he'd spoken, taking her elbow in the process. He could see it in Elizabeth's eyes, a flashback to her terrible fall down a set of stairs while pregnant, resulting in a premature delivery while she was in a coma. And the loss of this infant daughter six months later—the only child Steven and all his medical training hadn't been able to save.

Luke came down the stairs with a bag in hand. When he saw them, he headed in his mother's direction. "Mom?"

Steven released her arm.

Elizabeth looked up at him, but spoke to Luke. "I'm fine. I just need to be careful on the stairs."

"Dad used to tell you that all the time."

She glanced away. "He did."

How easy it was for him to fall back into the role as being her protector. Mike was right—Steven had stopped living after his wife and child died because the only other woman he ever loved was Elizabeth. The realization hit him hard. He didn't want another family without Elizabeth in it, so he gave up. And once again Mike was right. Without this woman in his life there was nothing to live for, to fight for.

"Steven, I hate to cut your visit short but I lost track of time. Do you remember my sister, Sam—Samantha?"

He nodded. "I do."

"We still own the bookstore Books and More. I'm running a little late." She paused and glanced around, the crease on her forehead deepened. "Where's Christopher?"

"I'll go find him." Luke set the bag down at their feet and left the room.

Elizabeth turned back to Steven and met his

gaze. Her turquoise eyes seemed to search his for answers as to why he'd come. How could he explain? But her hesitation brought memories of the last time they were together, how close they stood to one another like they did now, and how soft she felt as he cupped her cheek so long ago.

"When do you travel back to Atlanta?"

"In a few days." She continued to regard him until pitter-patter of small feet hurried in their direction.

"It was nice to see you again, Steven. Say hello to everyone for me. It was nice seeing the gang from college at the wedding. Hopefully it won't be so long until we see each other again." She led him to the door and opened it.

He stood silent for a moment, then took a step into the moist air. "Good-bye, Elizabeth."

"Bye Steven." The door closed behind him.

How he wanted to stay, but he was a stranger, staring through frosted glass at someone else's life. A life he'd dreamed of for so long.

Shortly after nine that night, Elizabeth's last customer exited the double doors from Books and More. She turned the lock and checked the latch to make sure it was secure before heading to the office where her children slept. It had been a long day for them, homeschooling, swimming at Chris's parents in the morning, then home in the afternoon to rush to the bookstore a few hours later. Although she was just as tired, constant thoughts of Steven energized her throughout the day, and questions rose to her mind.

Why had he come to see her? He just popped in and stayed for an hour, never mentioning the reason for his visit. It was odd, to say the least, since she hadn't seen him in twelve years. Why now? He could have seen her at the wedding.

She leaned against the doorframe to the office and looked at her children. Both slept on the king size mattress on the floor, Luke with his mouth open, Christopher sucking his thumb. She smiled. "Oh, how I love you both. Thank you for my children, Lord. Thank you for letting me have them in my life to love...for keeping them safe, for providing for us these last four years without Chris. Thank you for staying by my side."

Elizabeth glanced at her desk. A stack of bills in the to-be-paid pile needed her attention. She covered her mouth with her hand to stifle a yawn but failed. Her eyes grew heavy. The bills could wait.

She turned off the light and crawled between her children. Luke never moved, but Christopher snuggled closer. She closed her eyes and inhaled.

Soap and chlorine.

A lazy smile crossed her lips. Luke could take a bath tomorrow.

Chapter Three

Indecision plagued Steven as he made a few calls to find out where Luke was playing baseball, but now as he set his soda down on the metal bleachers and leaned forward, he didn't want to be anywhere else. The ball flew out to midfield and number five bent to scoop it up but missed. Number eleven from the backfield ran, grabbed the ball, then threw it to home plate, but not before the runner crossed it. Safe.

If Steven remembered right, Luke would be up next to bat, number twenty-four. The boy strutted out to the plate in his blue and red uniform, planted his feet, and held his bat up over his shoulder. With a practice swing, Luke smiled. With his next swing, he made contact, dropped the bat and ran to first base. "Safe!" The umpire signaled. Steven stood to his feet and cheered. Luke's team won.

"Are you a friend of the Robert's family?" A feminine voice asked behind him.

Steven turned to a cute brunette with short hair. "Yes."

"I hope you don't think I'm being terribly nosy, but I've noticed you've cheered for Luke several times, and I haven't seen you here before."

"I'm an old friend. If you would excuse me." He turned and made his way to the bottom of the bleachers as the boys finished shaking hands. "Luke." Steven stood against the chain link fence.

"You came?" His forehead creased.

"I did and you were awesome! That was a great hit. I wanted to tell you good-bye since I didn't get a chance a couple of days ago."

"Thanks." The boy jabbed his cleat into the ground.

Somewhere behind him, someone called "Luke."

"Bye." Luke ran to an older woman in her sixties. She glanced at Steven. No recognition had shown in her eyes as she looked away and escorted her grandson down a paved walkway.

Steven headed for his car. It would be a long drive home.

Luke jumped from the boat onto the dock and ran to Chris's father's truck. With a deep breath, Elizabeth put the boat in reverse, then pushed the throttle forward and headed for the boat ramp. Chris's father asked her, begged was more like it, if he could come with them. When she reminded Henry of her promise to take Luke fishing three months ago, just the two of them, the last thing he asked was if she would be able to drive the bass boat onto the trailer. She reassured him, but now she wasn't sure. It had been so long since she tried.

She guided the boat onto the trailer, giving it one last push of speed. "I did it." She laughed as Luke gave her a thumbs-up signal from the truck's rear window.

She grabbed the key from the ignition, walked to the front of the boat, and steadied herself as she climbed onto the maroon trailer. Cranking the winch, her muscles tensed and exhaustion overtook her. She'd come this far. "Please, Lord, help me get this boat on here so I can drive back." Using every ounce of strength, she cranked. The tip of the boat rose and rested securely.

After finishing the rest of the steps Chris taught her, Elizabeth sank against the side of the truck, her breath heavy. The aching in her body weaved its way through her as she got into the vehicle. "Have you decided what you want to do with the fish?" She yanked the door closed, muscles burning in her arm.

"I want Grandpop ... I mean, Henry, to see them."

How she wished Luke didn't feel the need to grow up so fast, but to be the child he still was. Even calling Chris's father "Henry" was another reminder of what they all lost. "All right then, I'll let the two of you take them to the pond." Elizabeth started the engine and drove to Chris's parents' house. She was certain Linda was waiting for them.

Luke touched her arm. "How's your finger? Is it still bleeding?"

Thankfully the treble hook hadn't gone in too far when it snagged her earlier. "No. You did a great job with that lure."

"Did you see the size of that bass? I wonder how much it weighs. Grandpop has a scale. He'll know." Luke stared out the window. "I can't wait to show him."

Elizabeth smiled. Moments like these brought her contentment no matter how much her muscles ached or head pounded.

Happiness. She was afraid she'd never feel it again when all she could do was survive. But God's help and her children gave her focus. There were still those nights she longed for Chris's embrace. At times the loneliness was maddening, but God had been faithful, staying by her side through every tear, pain, doubt, and fear. Both she and Luke were healing. The look on his face was proof. It had taken a while for Luke's tears to stop falling after Chris's death, even from the mere sound of his name, but today, she'd made him happy.

Luke sat on the edge of his seat most of the hour's ride home. His hand gripped the door handle as they parked in Henry and Linda's driveway. The garage door rose and Luke climbed out.

Henry came to the truck and opened her door. "Don't worry about anything. I've got it."

Elizabeth placed the keys in his palm and smiled. "Thank you."

"Grandpop! Look at what I caught!" Luke waved at him from inside the boat.

"I'm coming." Henry met her gaze. "Grandpop. I miss that." He helped her out of the truck, holding onto her arm when her legs threatened to collapse. "You okay?"

She nodded and almost laughed. "Just tired."

Henry shut her door, strode to the trailer, and climbed up.

Elizabeth stood in amazement at the ringing in Luke's voice. She drank in the moment. A door closed behind her and she turned to find Linda holding two glasses of tea. "I figured you might need something after your long day."

She nodded and accepted the glass, slipping an arm around Linda's stout waist. "Thank you for today. Luke needed this."

"Come inside and let me fix you something to eat. Christopher's already in bed and an extra room is ready whenever you are."

"Sounds wonderful." Elizabeth stepped through the kitchen doorway and her stomach growled at the smell of fried chicken wafting through the air. She washed her hands at the sink. "Chris would have been so proud of the fish Luke caught today. He caught a big one and wanted Henry to weigh it."

Henry ran through the house, eyes round. "Where's my camera?" He huffed.

"Over here." Linda swiped it from the small desk in the kitchen and handed it to him. "What's the hurry?"

"My grandson caught a six pound, two ounce

bass." He rushed back outside.

Linda laughed and scooped potato salad onto a plate.

Elizabeth sank into a chair.

"You look exhausted, dear." Linda set the plate down in front of her and pushed several strands of hair out of her face, then took a seat across the table. "You and Samantha are the daughters I've never had, so I hope that if something is bothering you in some way, you feel comfortable sharing it with me."

"I know." Elizabeth reached over and cupped the older woman's hand. "I think I've worn myself out is all, and you know, both you and Henry mean everything to me and the kids. Thank you for letting us stay for the night."

Linda inhaled a heavy breath. "We were talking. Henry and I…" She sat a bit taller and leaned in. "How would you and the kids like to go to the condo? We can talk to Samantha and see if she can fill in for you at the bookstore? I know how much you like the beach."

"Linda…I can't." Elizabeth picked up the chicken leg and took a bite. Potato salad and cornbread brightened her plate, but not her thoughts. Not with the mention of the condo.

"Sure you can. The two of you own the store." Linda got up from the table and brought her a piece of chocolate pie.

Elizabeth swallowed the lump of food in her throat. A few times since Chris's death, she'd wanted to visit the condo they owned, but she couldn't. There were too many memories, especially their last night together, the night she conceived Christopher. How could she go back?

"Then will you stay with us for a few days? You can work all you want and we'll keep the kids."

Elizabeth set her fork down.

Linda rushed on. "After you lock up the bookstore, you come here and let us take care of you and the children for a change." Linda collected her hands. "Please. Let us do this for you?"

Elizabeth smiled. Linda's constant concern warmed her. A few days might be nice. Elizabeth did feel tired lately, more than normal, and she had promised they'd come stay sometime. "All right. A few days. I'll let you know when it would be a good time with Luke's games."

"Wonderful!" Linda's pleased expression changed suddenly. Her brows furrowed. "That reminds me. You need to make sure you keep an eye on Luke. There was this man speaking with him after the game."

A man? "What were they talking about?"

"I'm not sure." Linda released her hands and rose from the table. "All I know is Luke and this man were on opposite sides of the fence talking. I thought you should know. Times are different than in my day."

"What did he look like? I can ask my friend Beka if she saw him."

Linda returned with her own slice of pie and sunk into her chair. "I couldn't tell his height because he sat on his heels, but he had dark hair and dark eyes. Not a good combination in my book. Too mysterious." She sliced a section of pie with her fork and took a bite. "Although something about him did look familiar."

The door flew open and Luke burst into the kitchen. "Can you believe how big that fish was, Mom? Hey, I want some of that pie." Luke searched the counter.

Linda laughed. "It's in the fridge. Help yourself."

"Now that doesn't mean eat the entire pie." Elizabeth stabbed her last piece of potato salad and savored it as she placed her dishes in the sink. "Luke, I need to get washed up and you do the same when you're done. I'll come say goodnight before I head to bed." She kissed his head before he could protest.

"Mo-o-om."

She smiled, catching Linda's glance, and headed to the bathroom for a shower.

Once she finally slipped into bed, Elizabeth lifted her cell from the nightstand and called her friend.

Beka answered on the second ring. "Hey, how was the fishing trip?"

"We had such a great time. Luke caught a six pound, two ounce bass."

"That is awesome! It's a fish, right?"

Elizabeth chuckled. "Of course. I'll bring the pictures to practice. I wanted to ask you something. Linda told me someone was talking with Luke after the game. Did you see anyone?"

"He wasn't only talking with him, but rooted for him throughout the entire game. When Luke saw the guy, he came to the fence to talk like he knew him, so I didn't stick around after that."

"Can you tell me what he looked like?"

"Well, I was sitting behind him for most of the game, but each time Luke made a play, this guy would clap, cheer, or even stand up. Me being the nosy person I am, I asked if he knew Luke's family so I got a good look at him."

"And?"

"Tall, dark, and handsome. A touch of grey, but very handsome. And broad shoulders. He definitely works out." She laughed. "He was kind of hard to miss and I wasn't the only woman who noticed."

Oh, Steven. Why have you come back?

"You're too quiet. Elizabeth, are you still there?"

"Umm, yeah. That helps. Thanks."

"Hey, I gotta go. Don't forget the pictures when you come to practice."

"I won't. Goodnight." Elizabeth ended the call and stared into the dark room.

<h1 style="text-align:center">Chapter Four</h1>

Steven entered through the hospital's sliding doors. A draft of air blew his hair and ammonia assaulted his nostrils. He bit back his breath and hurried down the corridor. He caught stares as of late, which wasn't unusual since his picture had been removed from the board of trustees, but his still being head of the apnea center also gave more fuel to the gossip circulating. He never expected to hear the whispers over his decision to leave so suddenly, or that it could affect his reputation, with some saying he was let go.

Nothing made sense to him anymore. One of the main reasons he accepted the job in the first place was to help others. The other reason involved the woman with turquoise eyes. God led him to distance himself from Elizabeth.

Shaking those irises from his thoughts, he unlocked his office door and entered. This had been his home for twelve years, a safe place where he met with God. But not for much longer.

Steven walked to his bookshelf and lifted his family's photo. He missed his wife and son, but as the years passed, the pain's sharp edges no longer lingered. He'd forgotten what it was like to feel his loving wife's arms around him at night or his son's soft cheek against his face. He ran a finger along the glass.

A buzzer went off out in the hall. *Code blue.* Steven sprinted to the door out of habit, but paused in the hall. The light above one of the rooms flashed. His friend and colleague John rushed into the infant's room. Steven said a silent prayer for the child. This had been his life, preserving other precious lives that teetered between life and death. Watching others carry on the struggle without him made leaving surreal. And the waiting to hear about the child nearly killed him.

At last, Claudia from the nurse's desk caught his eye. She came to him and touched his sleeve. "You have such a tender heart. The little girl is fine."

Steven glanced toward the patient's room in time to see John leaving. He made some notes on a chart and handed it to a nurse at the station. As soon as he'd left, Bethany brought the chart to Steven.

"How are you tonight, Dr. Moore?"

"Doing well, Bethany. How about yourself?" He flipped through the chart, reading each note and scanning several readings from the child's monitor. *Apnea. A severe case. Oxygen levels low. Reflux.*

"Good night, Dr. Moore."

Steven's eyes rose from the file. Bethany headed down the hall. He looked to Claudia. "Where's she going?"

Claudia smiled. "You have no idea what she said, do you?"

He shook his head and handed Claudia the chart to add the information to the computer.

"She said Dr. Thomson needs you to evaluate his patient. She mentioned she was off the clock and was going home before someone convinced her to stay another twelve hours."

"I caught the last part."

Claudia gave him a sweet smile then turned and ambled toward one of the rooms.

Mike clapped him on the shoulder and chuckled. "I saw that. Ready to go to lunch?"

"John asked me to see one of his patients. Probably trying to convince me to stay. I'll be back in a minute." Steven weaved around the desk and headed for his first visit to an apnea patient, or any patient, since informing the board of his intention to leave.

The door was ajar as he pushed through and offered his hand to the parents. "Hi, I'm Dr. Moore. The doctors will be checking on Ashley throughout the night." He strode toward the crib and took out his stethoscope. He stared down at the sleeping child, lifted her shirt, and listened around the white patches attached to her chest. *Normal right now.*

Pulling her shirt down, he noted her lips and mouth. *A bit pale, but not blue or purple.* He turned to face the child's parents. The husband cuddled his wife in his arms as tears flooded the mother's eyes. "Right now we are keeping an eye on her and they'll be in every so often to give you an update from the readings we're receiving from the monitors. Do you have any questions?"

They both shook their heads no. They had already been here for eight hours and Steven assumed they knew the drill from what happened not long ago. "Have you eaten anything since you've been here?"

"No. But it's okay. Can we get a blanket for my wife? She's cold."

"Of course. If you need anything else, let us know." Steven closed the door behind him and walked to the nurse's desk. He pulled out a blanket and pillow from the cabinets. Opening the small fridge, he grabbed two turkey sandwiches and drinks, laying them on the counter. "I need someone to take this to room 230."

"I'll do it, Dr. Moore." The nurse hesitated. "Should I add this to their bill?"

He frowned at her. She wasn't a new hire. In fact she'd worked with him long enough to know the answer to her question. Still, her gaze flitted between him and the head nurse.

The supervisor turned to them. "Yes. Didn't you get the new memo? It says we charge for everything now. No free food or drinks. We keep a tab of what they use." She turned with an ECG cart and headed toward one of the rooms down the hall.

"Yes, keep a tab," Steven spit the words out, "but add it to my bill. I'm covering any food or drinks the patient or families want until I walk out the hospital doors for good. Does everyone understand?"

"Yes sir, Dr. Moore." The nurses at the station answered in unison.

His name was on this building and he'd run this apnea wing as he saw fit, whether people liked it or not. And if he had to pay out of his own pocket to make it happen, so be it.

Fourteen hours later, Steven carried his hospital tray to a booth and sat staring at his food.

"Are you up for company?"

Steven looked up and his friend John slid into the seat with today's lunch special—hamburger. "I never did tell you, you did a great job yesterday. You saved that little girl's life."

John lifted his cup and drank a few sips before setting his cup down. "You know for a moment there...."

Steven nodded. He knew too well. "I know."

"You're referring to Elizabeth's daughter?"

"I tried to save Katherine. It's something I'll never forget, holding her limp body in my arms. I did all I could...but I wish I could have done more. She's the only child I ever lost. I've prayed for Elizabeth to have another daughter. Not to replace Katherine but..."

John lifted his napkin off the tray and wiped his mouth. "You never told me about your visit with Elizabeth. How did it go?"

Steven leaned forward and smiled. "I haven't

told this to Mike because he'd have too much fun with it. I was kicked out of the house for being an intruder. The police were even called."

John's mouth hung open. "What? Elizabeth called the cops on you? And you're smiling?"

"Of course not." Steven chuckled, recalling his visit. "Luke, her oldest, didn't know she'd invited me in. So when she left to take care of her youngest, Christopher, Luke told me to get out and he called the police."

"What did Elizabeth say?"

"Oh, she apologized. Luke did as well, but I told him it was wonderful to meet the man of the house. He seemed to take pride in protecting his mom and he should." Steven's thoughts lingered on Elizabeth and Luke. How hard it still must be without Chris. From what Steven heard through the monitor, Luke still missed his dad greatly. Steven remembered what it was like to lose his parents early in life—the hole in his heart never filled. In fact, it grew with his sister's death…until he met Elizabeth.

"Are you okay, Steven?"

"Honestly, I'm afraid of the future and the time I have left. I'll miss this place but I don't want to be here any longer."

"And where do you want to be?" John took a bite of his burger.

Steven thought about his time watching Luke and how proud he was of him, and his heart warmed. "Sitting on smothering hot bleachers cheering for an eleven-year-old boy named Luke."

"Then go. There's nothing to stop you."

"That's not true and we both know it. I'm not a fighter anymore, John."

"Go see her, Steven. Tell her how you feel before it's too late. You need this." Steven opened his mouth but John's hand rose in protest. "I know you've mentioned you're not a fighter, but that's not true. I've seen you fight for what you believe in. Maybe the real fight is going to be within yourself." John scooted from the booth. "Think about it."

Chapter Five

Steven sat in the same bleachers as he did three weeks ago, but this time, Luke wasn't on the field. He overheard the coach talking about playoffs and making sure the parents had the correct times and dates. Steven listened closely. Glancing around, he caught the attention of the woman who'd questioned him last time.

The brunette tucked her short hair behind her ears. "Still rooting for Luke?"

"I am." Steven smiled, then turned toward the movement at the corner of his eye. Luke, in a blue and red jersey, ran toward the field. He fisted his bat to his side with his mitt in the other hand. His white gloves fell to the pavement.

Steven jumped from the bleachers and hurried to retrieve the gloves. He swooped down and snatched them from the concrete, then stood to find Elizabeth a few feet away.

She halted when she saw him. "What are you doing here?"

"I think you asked me that same question the last time we met." Steven chuckled. "I wanted to see

Luke play. Hope you don't mind?" Steven turned, scanned the field for Luke, and headed to the fence. "Luke!" He held up his gloves.

Luke ran over to him and took the gloves. "You're back."

"Yep. Wanted to see you play. Have a good game."

Luke nodded then ran back. Steven sensed Elizabeth standing close. She had always liked the scent of vanilla body lotion and he inhaled it now.

"You just happened to be in the neighborhood?"

He nodded. "Just happened to be."

"Elizabeth." A feminine voice called from behind them.

Steven glanced over his shoulder to see the brunette he'd spoken to earlier waving in their direction. "I guess I should find a seat."

"I guess we should." Elizabeth headed toward the woman calling to her. Steven stood at the end of the bleachers, never forgetting Elizabeth sat a few feet away. Luke came to bat and missed. Steven walked to the chain link fence.

Swing and a miss.

"You can do it, Luke." Steven's fingers itched to angle Luke a little more to the left. When he missed the third time, his slender shoulders slumped forward. Something squeezed within Steven's chest. It wasn't only the thought to tell number twenty-four it would be all right, but how easy it would be to love this boy as his own. Was he willing to fall in love with a family he could never have?

Steven leaned against the fence and planted his elbows over the edge. Luke ran out to the field with his team. With legs spread apart and knees bent, number twenty-four slammed his fist in his glove. Steven chuckled at his intensity.

Through the rest of the game, Luke had several outs but struggled to hit. After the teams shook hands for a good game, Luke headed straight for Elizabeth.

Steven waited for Elizabeth's friend to leave before going to her and Luke. "Good game. Great job on those outs."

Luke glanced at his glove. "Didn't hit anything though."

"Maybe just a little more practice will do the trick."

Luke's mouth tightened into a fine line as he looked up at Elizabeth. He pushed past them and headed toward the parking lot.

Elizabeth's gaze followed him. "I should go. Thank you for coming, Steven."

He reached out and gently caught her arm. "I was only trying to help."

"I know." She turned back to him. "Chris would take him to the batting cages after every game. It was their time together."

"I'm sorry." Steven shoved his hand in his pocket and pulled out his keys. "I should be going. Bye, Elizabeth."

Steven headed toward his car. Coming to the

game was a mistake. He didn't belong here. They didn't need him or want him in their lives. He reached the end of a row of parked cars and lifted his head to survey the lot. Where did he park?

"Bye, Elizabeth."

Elizabeth watched Steven weave his way with purpose through the parking lot. Why had his words seemed so final and why had it struck her so hard? She heard a car remote chirp in his direction and it sent her forward, following after him.

She caught up with him as he slipped the key ring from his pocket. She gently touched his shoulder then pulled back before he had time to turn around. Elizabeth cleared her throat. "I wanted to thank you for coming."

Steven ran his fingers through his hair. "I'm not sure it was a good idea. I didn't mean to upset Luke."

She looked up at him, meeting his clouded gaze. Once, so long ago, she'd been able to read the dark orbs as clear as crystal. But now, what were they trying not to tell her? What was he hiding? "Why did you come?"

His gaze held hers, but intensified as something passed across his features. Her pulse rose. She took a step back in response. "If you've come for any other reason except for friendship, I have nothing to give, Steven. Chris has my heart."

He paused and dipped his chin. "I'm not

entirely sure why I came back. When I'd seen Luke play a few weeks ago, I had such a wonderful time, I couldn't wait to see him play again. But I would enjoy your friendship while I'm in town."

Her mouth turned up into a grin. "Always."

"Mom!" Luke hustled toward them with Beka's son, Austin, at his heels. Beka, four car lengths behind, also headed in their direction. Luke and his friend huffed, palming their knees as Beka caught up. "I'm taking Luke and Christopher with me to the pizza shack. Tom's already got Christopher buckled in. I wanted to let you know so you weren't worried."

"Thanks." She turned to him. "Steven, this is my friend Beka. Her husband is the coach of the team. Beka, this is my friend, Steven."

"It's nice to finally be introduced. So where are you from, Steven?" Beka flipped her hair from her eyes and met his gaze with a raised brow.

Elizabeth elbowed her friend. "Don't mind her if she gives you the third degree. She's a private investigator. It runs in her blood." She leaned against Steven's car, a cold sweat washing over her.

Beka's eyes narrowed. "You okay?"

She frowned, standing straight. *Please, Beka. Don't make a big deal over this.* "I'm fine. Still a bit tired from my fishing trip with Luke is all."

"Well, if you took better care of yourself, I wouldn't need to be so concerned."

Elizabeth lifted her chin and jammed her fist on her hip.

Beka shook her head. "I'm going. Come on

boys. It was nice to meet you, Steven. See you in a few minutes, Elizabeth."

Elizabeth's arms fell from her sides as her gaze trailed her friend and their children, the nausea lightening, thankfully. She took a breath and turned to Steven. His focus roamed over her face and she blushed under his scrutiny. "Beka worries too much."

"I like her."

"She's married."

Steven chuckled. "Not what I was thinking. But she was right, your skin paled and moisture formed on your face for no apparent reason. Now your cheeks have a tint of pink. Have you been feeling ill lately?"

"Only a bit tired, but that's normal, Dr. Moore. If you're done with your evaluation, I'd like to invite you to Luke's next game. It's Monday night under the lights. You're more than welcome to come if you're still in town."

"I'd like that. They're in playoffs, right?"

"They are. Luke's so excited." She looked in the direction of her car. "I should probably go."

"Let me walk with you." He locked his car with a beep.

Arriving at her van, Steven held out his hand. She had forgotten what a gentlemen he'd always been, opening the doors for her, helping to carry whatever she needed without having to ask. It felt strange now. Wrong in a way, but she slowly released the keys into his palm. Steven opened the van's door and it let out a long squeak. *Nice. You wouldn't hear his beamer let out a sound of fingernails running down a chalkboard.* She scooted in and turned the key. It took a moment before the engine came to life.

"I want you to know, Steven…you're not obligated to stay in town."

"I know." So he said, yet it seemed like there was more to his visits, so much more, and she wondered what it meant. As if he read her thoughts, he said, "I've never been on a vacation so it's nice to experience what one feels like."

She chuckled. "All right, I guess I'll be seeing you."

Steven closed her door and she drove without looking back. Memories she'd tucked away were beginning to resurface as she headed toward the pizza shack. Dreams she and Steven shared, the life they so desperately wanted, almost had.

That dream, though, was nothing like her life with Chris. A marriage she still missed.

She missed feeling Chris's arms around her, telling her how much joy she brought him. The taste of his lips and the smell of his breath now lingered in her memory. Elizabeth's heart ached and moisture filled her eyes. She bit her lip in determination and glanced at her wedding bands.

Chris…Steven's here.

Chapter Six

Elizabeth rushed through the church's door and found a few seats open on the back pew. The children in the church were already heading down for the pastor's sermon. "Luke, take Christopher's hand and walk him down to the front. Let him sit in your lap, okay?"

"Come on, Christopher." Luke held his hand, but he wouldn't budge.

"Christopher," she whispered close to his ear. "Please don't make Mommy go with you in front of the church. I forgot to brush my hair." Elizabeth ran her fingers through her tangles. He shook his head.

With a deep breath, she stood from the pew and strolled down the aisle. The pastor began reading scripture. She pulled Christopher a little faster and took her seat quickly on the front pew, missing the pastor's illustration of the message.

"God has said, 'Never will I leave you; never will I forsake you.' This verse is telling us how much God loves us. Now children, how can we show those around us we love them?" The pastor waited for only a second before hands flew into the air.

"Tell someone you love them."

"Buy some food for someone that's hungry."

"Take care of them."

"Pray for them."

The pastor smiled. "I like that one. Praying is very powerful. Let me ask you, what good is it if we can help someone but do little to help their physical needs? We need to put our faith and love into action. How do we do that? Like Johnathan said, if someone is hungry, feed them. If someone is thirsty, give them a cup of water. Let us pray."

Elizabeth closed her eyes. Chris left on the mission trip to provide food and clean water to families and children in need. He put his faith and love into action. He'd done what scripture had said to do. A knot caught in her throat.

The prayer ended, and with a heavy heart she led Christopher out of the sanctuary to his classroom. A few minutes later she reentered the church and slid next to Luke. She clasped his hand and covered it with her other one. He tried to pull away, but she held him tighter. He looked at her for a moment then tightened his own grip and leaned into her arm. Did he understand her grief? She wanted to collect him in her arms and hold him for all eternity. To protect him from any more pain this life might cause. To cloak her love around his shoulders so he would never doubt he was loved. She couldn't, of course. Only God could, and that simple fact wove a thread of peace through her soul. God's love was greater than any others, even now as she clung to her son. God's love was perfect for Chris, for their children, and for her. Part of that understanding helped her to acknowledge Chris was with her in her heart and they were forever part of each other through their children. Their love would carry on through them.

But on days like today she missed Chris, and she couldn't stop the tears.

After the service, Luke gave her hand a squeeze before releasing it. He scooted into the aisle in front of Steven and Eric, Chris's friend, both in conversation. Steven saw her, smiled, and then continued out the front doors. *How did they know each other?*

For a brief time during the service she'd forgotten about Steven, but as she gathered her children and headed toward the car, uneasiness settled in the pit of her stomach. Would Chris mind Steven being here?

Buckling Christopher in his car seat, she planted a kiss on his cheek. "Ready to go to Grandma's?"

Christopher raised his hands in the air. "Eat!"

"Yep, time to eat. Luke, you buckled?"

Luke nodded as he read a letter their Sunday school teacher had copied from their class missionary. He was fascinated with missionaries and traveling to different countries just like Chris and his brother, Uncle Phillip. After each one of Chris's trips, he brought back a souvenir and told them all they had done.

She stepped to the driver's door and wiped

her sudden tears. What souvenir had Chris bought that last time and never had the chance to give to Luke? Her hands trembled as she opened the door and slid in. She couldn't let her children see her like this. She wiped at her tears again. That pressure in her chest she'd noticed lately began to build while her breaths became shallow. Inhaling several deeper breaths, she could hear her heart beat within her ears. It was pounding much too fast.

Elizabeth glanced around at the near-empty parking lot, and once they piled into the van, she headed down Main to the interstate. She said a silent prayer to stop crying and settle down before she made herself sick. She couldn't become ill with her children in the vehicle.

As she neared Linda and Henry's, her breathing had quieted and the animal trying to escape against her chest finally calmed as her heart rate returned to normal. Maybe she'd think a little more about Linda's offer to stay with them for a few days. She didn't have the money right now for a doctor's visit, but resting for a few days would be what a doctor would order, right?

"Here!" Christopher yelled when they pulled into the driveway. Linda came out of the house and Henry followed. Luke jumped from the car as soon as it stopped.

"I've been waiting for you." Linda opened her door.

Henry took Christopher from his car seat and carried him. "*We've* been waiting for you," he corrected.

Elizabeth noticed a rental car next to the drive. "Did Phillip and Sam get back safe from Goma?" She asked, pointing to the car. "Are they here? Was their adoption approved?"

"Come inside and see for yourself." Henry smiled. "Christopher, you have a new cousin."

"They did!" Elizabeth grabbed her purse from the front seat and rushed toward the house.

Steven pulled up to the Red Fish Grill where he was meeting Eric for lunch. Seeing his friend made him think about Elizabeth's expression when he and Eric had passed her in the church aisle recently without stopping to talk. Should he have? Maybe, but he didn't want Eric asking questions he couldn't answer. Mike and John were bad enough.

Steven stepped out of the car and met Eric. "I love this place. It's been so long."

Eric held the door open. "Want to dine in or out?"

"Out. The scenery is great here." Steven led the way, stepping up on several rocky tiles covering the main floor. Passing through the narrow dining area, then to the back of the restaurant, they stepped outside and watched the world open up. Lights scaled each palm tree, and behind them white sand. The sea stretched to the heavens. Elizabeth would love this place. Would she agree to come with him if he asked?

After the maître d' seated them and took their order, Eric turned to Steven. "I hope you don't mind me asking, but I saw the smile you gave a woman at church. Do you know Elizabeth Roberts?"

Steven gazed out over the ocean. Did he wear his emotions on his sleeve? Did he care any longer? "Elizabeth and I dated in college. We were to be married." He turned to his friend and saw Eric's amazement.

Eric leaned back in his chair. "Really. What happened?"

"Her parents died and we fell apart. She left two weeks before our wedding."

"And you kept in touch all this time?"

"No. We hadn't seen each other in years, and then one day she came to the hospital with her and Chris's daughter. I had no idea we lived in the same area. It was the only time I wasn't able to save a child. Katherine died in my arms. That was about the last time I'd seen her. Twelve years ago." Eric gave him an odd look, brows furrowed. "What is it?"

"They separated shortly after that."

Steven shifted in his chair, uncomfortable with the way the conversation was headed. "They did. How did you know?"

"I'm their lawyer, their friend, but I also became Chris's accountability partner."

An accountability partner. Of course. To keep Chris on the straight and narrow. To think that a man might have a need outside of Elizabeth was... It was... Well, unthinkable.

Steven felt his blood pressure rising, straining against his temples. He sat back against his chair to allow the waiter room to place two salads in front of them. After saying grace, he forced himself to eat a bite. "How much do you know?"

Eric took a sip of water, then set his glass down. "Most of it, I believe, and how a man saved Elizabeth's life. Twice. But Chris always called him Carrington, meaning *you*."

Steven's throat grew tight. *Carrington?* He hadn't heard that name in years.

"You seem surprised."

"I rarely hear or say that name myself so I'm sure you can understand my shock. 'Carrington' was the name given to me in the orphanage where I grew up. Elizabeth knew me as Steven Carrington in college. I changed my last name before graduation so that when Elizabeth and I married, I could give her a name I chose for us…for our family. A loving family." Steven wiped his mouth with his napkin. "And about Elizabeth, it was God who saved her. He only used me to rescue her."

"So why are you really here in Miami?"

"At first, it was to see Elizabeth. Then when I went back to Atlanta, all I wanted to do was to sit and watch Luke play ball. But now I have another reason for being here."

"What is that?"

Steven glanced around at the red flowers blooming on the hedge surrounding the restaurant and took a deep breath. "I asked you to lunch because

I need you to write me a new will." He glanced at his friend. "I have cancer. Stage four. I'm not sure how much time I have."

A server with a tray set Steven's pan-fried red snapper down, then Eric's. It had been years since he had yucca, and even though his mouth watered, his appetite had vanished. Both men ate in silence, Steven recalling all they'd spoken, and why Chris called him Carrington. He took a few more bites, then set his fork down. "I want to take care of Elizabeth."

"What do you have in mind?"

"When I see you on Wednesday we can discuss the details and how I can help her financially now, but I want to leave everything to her. I want her and the children taken care of for the rest of their lives."

Eric nodded in agreement, his eyes darting in thought. "Are you going to tell her about the will? The cancer?"

"No. I couldn't leave this earth without seeing her again. I had to know if she was happy and she is, so no, I'll be leaving in a couple of weeks and I won't be returning."

Elizabeth held Jeremiah, her new nephew, within her arms. The rocking motion from the chair soothed his cries and lulled him to sleep. She lifted his soft hand to her cheek and kissed his dark skin. Lavender wafted in the air. He was beautiful in every way, and now her niece Juwonya had a brother, also from Goma, both sets of parents having died in the war. She ached for the people of Goma, the same country Chris never returned from. She ached for herself.

"You're safe now, little one. God has brought you to a loving family. They've waited a long time for you to come." *A son to call their own.*

She also ached for her sister and Phillip having never been able to have children. But the tears in their eyes when they recounted seeing their son for the first time, then holding him in their arms, brought tears to her own eyes and thanksgiving to her lips.

Elizabeth leaned back in the rocking chair and closed her eyes against the dull pressure climbing her neck and head. She released a breath.

"That's a heavy sigh, even coming from you." Her sister came into the room and sat on the couch next to her, leaned over, then gingerly ran a finger down her son's jaw. "Handsome little thing, isn't he? Almost eight pounds. We had to stay longer since he was a preemie and his lungs weren't fully developed, it wasn't safe for him to travel."

She knew all about preemies, the hard way. There wasn't a day that had gone by she didn't think of her daughter, Katherine. "He's perfect, Sam. Chris would have been so happy for you both." She wiped at the moisture in her eyes before the tears slid down her cheek.

"Is everything all right, Elizabeth? You seem...I don't know. Do you want to talk about it?"

Did she want to talk about it? With Steven's

return, her emotions were topsy-turvy and no matter why he said he was here, she wanted to push him away. Yet, she was afraid if she did, she might never see him again. "I'm not sure. Besides, I wouldn't know where to begin."

Sam smiled. "From the start is the best place. So I've heard."

"All right, you asked for it." Elizabeth took a deep breath and pressed on. "Steven's here." Her voice quivered and silence filled the room. Did Sam feel she'd been thrown back in time as much as Elizabeth did from saying the words?

"Have you spoken with him? Of course you have. He wouldn't have come all this way and not sought you out. Did he say why he's here?"

"Only that he's on vacation. He's been to Luke's game a time or two. I invited him to the playoff game tomorrow night."

"How are you feeling about him being here?"

She shrugged. "It was odd when he came to the house. He stayed for about an hour and then left. Since then we've barely spoken. Mostly at the games."

"You never answered, Elizabeth. How do you feel about Steven being here?"

She glanced down at the sleeping form in her arms, trapped under her sister's watchful eye. "I don't know. It frightens me."

"What do you mean? Has Steven done anything to make you uncomfortable?"

"Not at all. It's just...Chris. You know my

history with Steven. How would Chris feel with him here? Would he disapprove of me talking with Steven?"

Sam reached over and covered one of her hands. "Chris is gone, Elizabeth. There's no reason you can't speak with Steven unless you feel uncomfortable."

Phillip entered the living room with a baby bottle. "Why do you both look so serious?" He sank into the couch next to Sam.

"Steven's in town," her sister answered and held out her arms for their son. Elizabeth relinquished the child and the warmth within her arms turned cold, bare.

"How's he doing?" Phillip handed Sam the bottle. The little child's mouth latched on quickly, though his eyes never opened. His cheeks narrowed as sucking noises joined their conversation.

"We really haven't had a chance to talk much. He came to town about three weeks ago, went back home, then returned a week later. All I know is he's on vacation. He'll be at Luke's game tomorrow."

"I'll make it a point to say hello," he said, running a tender finger down Jeremiah's cheek. "I overheard Mom say to Dad you're staying over tonight. Everything all right? Nothing with Steven, is it?"

Elizabeth grinned. Phillip was like the big brother she never had, and what a blessing he was to her sister. "No, Steven's been a complete gentleman. Like I said, we really haven't seen much of each other.

While you were gone, your parents insisted we stay for a few nights, but I declined until now. I've been a bit exhausted lately so I'm taking them up on their offer. You know that fishing trip I promised Luke a while back? I kept it while you were gone. I just haven't recovered with work and the games."

"I'm back now." Sam pointed at her. "Don't you try to carry the burden of the bookstore all by yourself. We didn't realize we'd be gone for so long. I'll be there first thing tomorrow morning."

Elizabeth glanced at the child in her sister's arms. "We'll split the shift. I'll take the morning and you relieve me for lunch. After lunch I'll work on paying the bills before I go to Luke's game. How's that sound?"

"And how is that relaxing, paying bills?"

She shrugged her shoulders. "At least they'll be paid." Bookkeeping for the store had been her and Chris's job, now it fell on her shoulders. If things were short, she'd cut here and there hoping to turn whatever profit she could. Although Phillip and Sam were well off financially, she needed the store to succeed. She had mouths to feed and a mortgage she was already behind on to pay.

She rose from the rocking chair and the room tilted. She needed to head to the house for their things if she and the children planned to stay for a few days. But right now getting to their room was all she would be able to manage. "I'm a bit tired so I think I'm going to lie down. How long will you be here?"

"We'll be heading home shortly."

"I'm glad you're both back and congrats on this little one." She kissed Phillip and Sam goodnight then glanced at Jeremiah's small hand wrapped around Sam's pinky finger. "So sweet." She smiled, hiding her increasing discomfort and the nausea that followed.

Chapter Seven

Elizabeth tossed and turned, unable to sleep with Steven close to her thoughts. She rubbed her temples but the constant pounding in her head had yet to subside. She rose before dawn and padded down the hall. She needed someone to talk to, share the burden on her heart. How she wished Chris was here. They'd talked about everything, including Steven.

Linda stood at the kitchen counter cracking eggs into a bowl when she entered. She smiled. "How did you sleep?"

Elizabeth tilted her head. Now the pounding against her skull grew faint as she and her children sat around Henry and Linda's table for breakfast. Exhaustion still claimed her, but not her appetite or her thirst. She downed half her glass of water and picked up her fork. "Linda, would you mind taking the boys to Luke's ball game today?

"Are you going to the bookstore? I thought Samantha told me she was working today?"

Elizabeth swallowed the bite in her mouth and peeked sideways at Luke for his reaction. "I'd like to visit Chris and Katherine's graves before taking the morning shift. Sam will work this afternoon."

Luke sat straighter in his chair. "May I go with you?"

"Not this time, sweetheart. You have the playoffs and you can't be late, but I'll take you the next time I go, all right?"

Luke nodded, though disappointment showed clearly on his face.

"This fits perfectly for what I had planned." Henry said. "Luke, before the game I wanted to make an ice cream cake to celebrate your team and you being a winner. How about it?"

"But we might not win, Grandpop."

"You and your team have worked hard. It doesn't matter if you win or lose as long as you do your best. In my book that's called a winner."

"Dad would tell me that before each playoff." A hint of a smile shone on Luke's face. He nodded his head in agreement. "Your ice cream cakes were his favorite. Can we start now?"

Henry glanced at Elizabeth with a quick smile as he rose from the table. "I think we're done eating. Let's take our plates to the kitchen and start putting out the ingredients."

An hour later, Elizabeth found herself standing between her two loved one's graves. She'd never expected her life would turn out like this, her child and husband taken from her so early, so young.

She stepped to Katherine's headstone and

knelt. "Oh, sweetheart. How I've missed you." Moisture filled her eyes. Her fingers traced the words on the headstone. *The Lord is my Shepherd, I shall not want. He makes me lie down in green pastures. Psalms 23.* She tried to swallow past the lump caught in her throat. "Are you and daddy having fun in heaven with Jesus? I know you are, my precious little girl."

Tears slipped down her cheeks and she wiped them away. "I can still see your features in Luke, they haven't faded as he's grown and I'm grateful. I'm able to picture you in my mind as an older sibling to your brothers. You would have had your hands full with Christopher getting into your things. I have a feeling it might have bothered you from time to time, but you would have been close." She bit her quivering lip. "I love you, Katherine. Mommy loves you with all her heart."

She stood and walked to Chris's grave. Where did she begin? How did she convey all that she felt to someone she loved and still loved so deeply who was now in heaven? All she had left of him were her children, his grave at her feet, and the memories she clung to. But memories weren't enough right now. She needed him, flesh and bone, just for moment, one last moment to feel his touch.

Loneliness she hadn't felt in so long lunged at her from both sides. She wrapped her arms around her waist in an effort to hold herself together. She wouldn't allow her sadness to push her toward what she'd vowed to never go to again. She wouldn't drink or break her promise to Chris or to the Lord, no matter how hard it was from time to time.

She knelt and something stuck in her leg. She reached into her pocket and unstuck one of the treble hooks from her pants. "I brought this for you." She laid the black fishing lure next to the headstone. "You'd have been so proud of Luke. He caught a six-pound bass with this lure. Actually, it was a little bigger, but your dad would know how much it weighed exactly.

"Would you believe I took him fishing—all by myself?" She chuckled through her tears. "I know what you'd be thinking. I handled the trolling motor just fine. It still works great. You taught me everything I know…you did good Chris."

Elizabeth looked toward the heavens. "God, can Chris hear me in heaven? I hope so because I have a lot to say and I miss him dearly."

She touched his name, carved within the stone. "Did you hear me when I said I miss you? If not, I hope you caught it this time. It's not the same here without you. I wish you could've held Christopher in your arms like you held Luke. Christopher is growing into a spitfire like you. I knew the name suited him when he came from the womb kicking and screaming."

Her eyes blurred from tears and she wiped them again. "Thank you for loving me. Thank you for giving me another part of you to love." She ran her fingers across his name once again.

"Chris, I need guidance, I wish you were here to pray with me. It's been weeks since I spent time with the Lord. I'm confused right now and I don't know how to pray. You remember Steven? He's here on vacation and though he says he only wants my friendship, I feel like he wants more. How can I be near him when you have my heart? How do I not feel guilty when he's so caring to our children and they smile when he's near?

"Last night I thought about sending him away, after Luke's playoff game is over, but I can't shake this feeling God brought him here. How do I pray when I'm afraid of the future?"

Whether Chris heard her from heaven or not, she knew the Lord heard every word she said. She bowed her head. "God, I'm so weak right now, physically, mentally, and spiritually. Help me be strong in You and give me wisdom so when You guide me I'll follow You wholeheartedly. Heal whatever is going on with me lately, Lord. Please give me the strength I need to carry on to be the mother You've called me to be. Meet our financial needs. And Lord, what do I do with Steven? Do Your will in my life and in my children's lives. Amen."

Elizabeth leaned her head against Chris's name. "I love you."

With a deep breath, she rose and hurried to the bookstore.

Walking up to the baseball field, Steven scanned the crowd, amazed at how many people were in attendance. He spotted Christopher right away, sitting with Linda. The gray-haired man next to her must be her husband. They'd never actually met, but if he remembered correctly, the man's name was Henry.

He turned behind the height of the bleachers and headed down the side. About halfway, Steven stepped up and caught Beka's attention. Was she waiting for him? She waved and pointed to the seat in front of her. He climbed several more steps. "You don't mind?"

"No, not at all. Of course, if you prefer to sit with the family—" She nodded to them.

"This spot's good." He sat and nodded toward Chris's family. "Is that Phillip sitting next to Linda and Henry?"

She leaned in. "Do you know Phillip?"

"I do." Steven glanced at him and their adopted daughter, Juwonya, who was now a teenager. Phillip held an infant child in his arms.

Beka pointed down the row on the other side. "Do you know Chris's other brother, Timothy, and his wife, Sarah? Their daughter is the one in pink."

Steven took it all in. What would it have been like if his sister and his wife and child would have lived? Would they have gotten together to watch his son's games? Deep down, he knew it was futile to even think about it or the past, but the "what if" was all he could think about lately.

He scanned the parking lot in hopes of spotting Elizabeth and distracting his thoughts. Steven caught Phillip's glance, then waited as Phillip headed up the bleachers toward him.

"Steven, how are you?" Phillip stuck out one hand while cradling the infant with his other. "It's been a long time."

Steven gripped his hand. "Who's this little one in your arms?"

"Our son, Jeremiah." He grinned and his face shone. "We brought him home yesterday."

"Well, congratulations to your growing family. God is good."

"All the time."

If Phillip noticed he'd avoided his question about how he was, he didn't let on. Steven pointed toward Phillip's daughter. "Juwonya has grown. How old is she now?"

Jeremiah answered with a small cry, but it didn't stop the pride in Phillip's eyes. "She's seventeen." He bounced the infant softly in his arms.

"She almost an adult."

"Please, don't remind me." Phillip chuckled. "I take it you've met Luke since you're here?"

Steven nodded. "He's a great kid. Actually, I had the privilege of meeting both the boys." Steven glanced over Phillip's shoulder and pointed to Christopher sucking on a lollipop. "He's a spitfire."

"You don't know the half of it. Well, I promised Samantha I'd get her a drink before the game. Besides, this one here is getting a little fussy. A walk will do him good. It's nice to see you again."

"Thank you, Phillip. It's great to see you as well." Steven's gaze followed him to the concession stand, then moved to scan the parking lot. *Where is she?*

When Elizabeth finally arrived at the end of the second inning and took a seat with the family, Steven breathed his relief. Linda touched her cheek, said a few words, and turned her attention to the game. But even with Elizabeth safe and sitting in front of him, the concern he felt lingered.

Beka leaned into his back. "Luke has been staring at you from the outfield."

"Has he?" Steven met his gaze and Luke spun around.

Beka continued. "He doesn't usually like men around his mom who aren't family, but it seems he's tolerating you."

Steven stifled his grin. He was sure Luke's call to the Miami-Dade police department had something to do with his tolerance, and embarrassment. "He's protective. I'm glad of that."

After the game, Steven headed down the bleachers straight for Luke's team and hung out by the fence. His gaze swept to Elizabeth. Her skin was pasty white, dark circles hung beneath her once vibrant eyes, and her shoulders hunched forward. When the huddle dispersed, he inched closer to ask if she was all right.

Christopher ran from the gate, almost passing Elizabeth by, when she caught him by his shirt. Christopher glanced around her and smiled up at him.

Luke pulled on his brother's arm, yanking

him straight.

Elizabeth placed a hand on Luke's shoulder and said something Steven couldn't hear. She took his bat, hat, and glove. He still couldn't tell what she was saying, but when Luke glanced at him, Steven took several steps in their direction.

Elizabeth hugged Luke. "I'm so proud of you. You did great."

"You think so? I did hit the ball good this time."

Christopher escaped from his mother's hold and ran to Steven in a flash.

Elizabeth didn't glance at Steven. "Christopher!"

Steven caught the little boy and held him in midair. Something was wrong with Elizabeth and he needed to know. Still carrying Christopher in his arms, Steven strolled over to her and Luke. "Great game, Luke." He placed Christopher on his feet.

"More, peas." Christopher bounced on the tips of his sneakers, almost falling a few times. "Up. Up."

"We need to go, sweetie."

"Peas. Peas." Christopher's fingers folded together as if he were praying.

"I don't mind. Really. I can take him to the car."

She nodded and glanced at him quickly. "Okay, Luke can show you where to go while I say good-bye to everyone." She hurried toward Linda. Christopher clawed at his arm.

"How about you ride on my shoulders?" Steven slung the light-as-a-feather boy onto his back, pretending he might drop him. Christopher's laughter squeezed his heart. Luke, on the other hand, didn't say a word through the parking lot.

When they arrived at the car, Christopher waved furiously at anyone who walked by. "Luke, how have you been since I almost landed in jail?" Steven held his gaze then.

"I...um...am sorry about that. Really I am. Since Dad—" He lowered his head.

His heart squeezed for the boy. He sensed Luke wanted to be the man like his dad was, but he was only a child. "I knew your dad, Luke. He was a good husband to your mom and a great dad, too, I bet."

Luke ran his shoe along the concrete. "You knew him? I've never seen you before."

"I had the privilege of seeing you after you were born. There was nothing but love in your dad's eyes when he held you against his chest and spoke about God's forgiveness and redemption. He loved you Luke, so very much. Don't ever forget that."

"Mommy." Christopher giggled in his arms. Steven and Luke both turned to Elizabeth, the intensity of her stare searing him to the spot where he stood.

"Time to get down, champ." Steven pulled at the three-year-old, but Christopher attached himself to back of his neck. He knew a few tricks of his own. With gentle fingers, Steven reached up with one hand to hold him and the other to tickle. Laughter bubbled out and the squirmy little boy let go.

"Okay, in the van." Elizabeth slid the door open. "We're meeting everyone for lunch so we need to hurry." After the boys got in, she slid it closed, and looked up at him. "You were there at the hospital? When?"

"Maybe we should talk about this another time. It's not something I want to rush through."

She hesitated. "Okay." Her voice trembled as did her hands.

Steven pulled the noisy driver's door wide, held it open, and waited for her to sit. "Elizabeth, are you all right? You seem—"

"Do you want to have lunch so we can talk?" She interrupted.

"That would be nice." He searched her eyes for a glimpse of what she wasn't saying. If only she'd let him in, just this one time. Taking his wallet out of his pocket, Steven slipped out a business card and handed it to her. "We'll talk more tomorrow, and set a time?"

"Sam's coming in around lunchtime. I'll call you around then if it's a good time for you."

"Anytime is good. I'll talk to you then." Steven waited for her to slide in and then closed the door. The engine came to life after the second try. As she drove away, his thoughts flashed back to Luke's birth.

How much should he tell her?

Chapter Eight

Arriving at Eric's office on Wednesday morning, Steven's steps lightened for the first time in months. He'd soon be providing for Elizabeth and her children. He stopped at the reception desk. "I'm here to see, Eric. Steven Moore is the name."

The receptionist rose to half his height. Her blonde hair was pulled into a tight bun. "Yes, sir. Right this way."

He followed her to the office where she knocked on the door. Eric's voice boomed. "Come in."

Steven entered his office and Eric held the telephone receiver to his mouth, waving for Steven to have a seat in the chair. The brown leather crumpled beneath him.

He hung up. "Sorry about that. So, you're here to draft a new will." He opened his drawer and pulled out several sheets of paper before closing it.

"Yes. Leaving everything to Elizabeth and the children."

"Are you sure you want to do this? Isn't there anyone else?"

"I have no one. No family. I'm alone in this life."

Elizabeth drove to work early anticipating the start of their annual Easter sale, leaving the children still in bed at Henry and Linda's. The bell rang over her head as she entered the bookstore. She left the *Closed* sign in place and then flipped on the lights. She set her bag on the counter and, once the lights shone bright, searched for the sale signs under the counter. Placing them by the register, she glanced at the special order list and the items she purchased for the store. Never did she think her children would be the recipients. Yesterday Steven surprised her by buying gifts for the boys, saying they were presents he wanted to give them when he left. Now the back room held unopened cases of baseball cards, two books filled with baseball facts, a train set, and two picture books with facts about trains. Steven had spent more money on baseball cards in this one purchase than she'd spend on two weeks' worth of gas. She'd tried to dissuade him but he'd insisted, saying he needed to do this.

She closed her eyes and rubbed her temples. The look in his eyes when he spoke, almost like he was pleading, broke the hardening of her heart toward him. She began to understand that the hardening of her heart had nothing to do with Steven, but with her.

She was in turmoil, even as she carried the

signage to the different shelves and book racks, adding ninety-nine-cent price points. She still loved Chris, but she wanted to see Steven again.

The bell rang over the door and Sam's smile radiated as she entered. Elizabeth forced a smile she didn't truly feel. "You're early."

"Since we're having a sale tomorrow, I thought I'd help with signage." Sam scanned the store. "But it looks like it's already been done."

Elizabeth walked to the coffee station and took out several filters from under the cabinet. "I put the sale signs out and I'm starting to work on our supply list." She pointed at the list by the register and her vision blurred. She blinked hard and her eyes cleared. She finished making the coffee and sat down for a minute while Sam looked over the list. "Sam, do you mind if I head home. I'm not feeling well and I think I need to rest in my own bed for a while."

Sam set the supply list down. "Of course. You do seem a bit pale. Are you all right?"

Elizabeth rose from the chair and walked to where her sister stood. "It's nothing rest won't cure. Thanks, sis."

"I'll add a few things and place an order later this afternoon."

Elizabeth grabbed her purse from beneath the counter. The action sent her heart racing. "I haven't paid the last bill so you'll need to pay it first." Sam said something but her voice was blocked out by the pounding in Elizabeth's ears.

Sam grabbed her arm and drew her attention.

"Are you sure you're all right? I'm starting to worry about you."

Elizabeth presented her sister with the most convincing smile she could muster. "I'm fine." She patted her hand. "I'll call you when I get home, to soothe your mind."

"Yes, you do that as soon as you walk through your door."

"I will." Elizabeth kissed her sister's cheek. "Talk to you in a few." She opened the door and the bell chimed, then chimed again as it shut.

Five days she'd had this dull pain at the sides of her temples, but now it flamed into an indescribable pain.

I'll feel better after I rest a while. She told herself that as she drove home, gripping the steering wheel. Her vision blurred once again. She blinked against the blurring but her eyes didn't clear.

Her chest tightened and she forced herself to focus through the blackness surrounding her on every side. *Lord, what's happening to me?*

A horn sounded and she pulled at the steering wheel. Tires squealed. Her neck whipped back and the sound of metal crunching echoed in her ears. Pain seared the side of her leg.

Steven read over his new will and peace settled over him. He was doing the right thing whether or not Elizabeth agreed. Love wasn't based on conditions, but an unconditional love that is not self-seeking, keeps no record of wrongs, is willing to protect, trusts, and always hopes—a love he'd carry to his grave.

Eric held out a pen. "You still aren't going to share this with Elizabeth?"

"No, it might cause problems and I don't want her to feel obligated to me in any way." He took the pen and scribbled his signature along the lines indicated and dated each one. "And you'll take care of the other things I've asked?"

"I'll work on them today. I'll call you when everything is ready for you to sign at the bank."

Steven handed the paperwork back to Eric. "Thank you. I appreciate your help. You've been a great friend and sounding board."

"Anytime. Now on to a less pleasant conversation."

Steven raised a brow. "And rewriting my will seems pleasant?"

"Point made." Eric smiled but it faded. "We both know how important prayer is in any circumstance."

Steven opened his mouth to speak, but on hearing the ring tone he set for Elizabeth, he held up a finger for Eric to hold that thought. He hadn't expected her call this early. Hopefully she wasn't cancelling their lunch. "Hi, Elizabeth."

"Steven...I'm on the side of the road. My head is pounding. I'm scared...I...I might have blacked out."

He jumped to his feet and headed out the

door. "Where are you?"

"I was going home. I'm not sure." Her groggy voice breathed into the receiver. "My leg…"

Her words trailed off and panic set in. "Elizabeth!" He ripped open the door to his car and sank into the seat. The engine roared to life. He threw it in drive and barreled down the street with a glance at his phone's screen. The call hadn't ended. She was still on.

"I'm close to your house. I'm heading in that direction." Holding his cell with his shoulder, he searched each road for her vehicle. "Please, Lord, she's not responding. Where is she? Guide me to her."

The streetlight turned red. He stopped and glanced around. "Elizabeth, talk to me." Nothing.

"Please say something."

Something urged him into a U-turn and he drove away from the house. "Hang on, Elizabeth. Hang on for your children. Hang on for me." *Don't leave me this way.*

Held up at another light, Steven glanced to the left, to the right, and caught a glimpse of a cluster of people standing around a van, Elizabeth's van. "I see you. I'm coming, Elizabeth. Hang on." He dropped his phone, checked the traffic in either direction and gunned it, tires squealing through the intersection. Her van rested against a light pole crushing the driver's side door.

Steven brought the car to a screeching halt, pushed the trunk button, and rushed to his medical bag. "Did someone call an ambulance?" he yelled as he ran to Elizabeth's vehicle.

"Yes," someone responded as Steven opened the passenger side door and slid into the seat. The door was indeed jammed into her side. Her arms seemed free.

"Steven?"

Her voice was weak, but the lovely sound twisted his heart. "I'm here, Elizabeth."

"I held on."

Tears sprang to his eyes. He wanted to collect her in his arms and hold her there for a lifetime. Instead, he ran his fingers over her sweaty brow and gently moved her hair. He found several small abrasions he assumed happened when the windshield shattered. He opened her closed eyelids and checked her pupils. His fingers felt for her pulse. Much too high. "Elizabeth, where do you hurt?" He yanked out his stethoscope from his bag.

"I'm scared, Steven." She began to cry. "Please don't leave me."

It took every ounce of his professional training to turn off his feelings for this woman and treat her like one of his patients. "Shhhh. I'm not going to leave you. But I need to know, are you hurt anywhere?"

"My leg. I think the door is against my leg. My head hurts. The pain in my neck makes me nauseous."

"I'm going to listen to your chest. Are you on any medications?"

"No," she whispered, catching her breath.

Her heart raced. "Does your chest hurt?"

"There's pressure. Tight pressure."

"Any family history of heart disease? Do you have high blood pressure? Are you diabetic? Have you ever had a seizure?"

"No."

"Did these symptoms start after the accident?"

"Days ago. Just worse. Except my leg."

Sirens sounded in the distance and grew closer by the minute. "The ambulance will be here soon."

Elizabeth opened her eyes and held out her palm. Steven wrapped his large hand around her smaller one. The distance he tried to put between them faltered. "I won't leave you."

She closed her eyes again. Tears ran down her face. He lightly trailed his finger across her cheek. *Not today, but soon.*

Elizabeth closed her eyes as she entered the ambulance on a gurney. Her neck was held in place with something called a C-collar. Ragged breaths passed through her lips. The doors slammed shut, two bangs pounded against the vehicle before they drove off. The siren blared as the ambulance swayed back and forth.

Nausea and panic rose. Her heart pounded in her ears and her body shook uncontrollably. "Steven?"

"Elizabeth, I'm Stacy, one of the EMTs. Dr.

Moore is following us in his vehicle. He said he would meet you at the hospital."

Tears rolled from the corners of her eyes.

Chapter Nine

Elizabeth slowly opened her eyes, then blinked. In a nearby chair, Steven sat with elbows planted on his knees, face in his palms. She whispered, "Hey."

He glanced up, dark eyes cutting through her, taking her in. "How are you feeling?"

"Sleepy. My head and leg hurt. Neck's sore."

"Do you feel like talking?"

She started to nod, but thought better of it when pain jabbed her head and neck. "The children?" She rubbed her fingers on the side of her head, the IV in her hand pulling with each pass. "I hate IVs."

"They're with Linda and Henry." Steven rose and placed her hand at her side, then took over where she'd rubbed. His fingers moved in slow, tender, circular motions. Her scalp tingled from his touch and she fought a wave of tears, closing her eyes. Guilt shook her from him being here, caring for her instead of Chris. Was it wrong she didn't want to be alone? Weary from the car crash, fighting the pain in her leg and head, she gave way to her tears.

Steven placed a tissue in her palm. She wiped

her eyes and gave in to the soothing motion of his fingers, the pressure subsiding a bit in her head. "What's wrong with me?"

"You have a deep cut where the car door smashed into your leg. They stitched the wound, glue was applied, and perhaps you can shower tomorrow."

"I don't remember." She pressed her fingers to her eyes. "Is that all? I felt blind while I was driving. My vision shrank to almost nothing. I think I was driving toward oncoming traffic. A horn. That's what caused me to swerve. I had the strangest feeling I was going to black out."

"I believe the doctor will ask you to monitor your blood pressure since it was too high. In the ambulance you were 198 over 110. You're at risk for a heart attack or stroke with numbers like yours. I'm waiting to hear the results from your MRI."

"I had an MRI? Okay. What will that tell?"

"A MRI will tell several things, but also if there's hemorrhaging in the brain." He leaned over her, his dark eyes probing her neck, face. Heat rose to her cheeks as she watched him.

His gaze slowly found hers. "I knew better. I saw a few of the symptoms. Exhaustion, pale skin, the pounding pulse in your neck. The times I saw you rub your temples. Headaches. You have them often. Diabetes can cause the same symptoms. The nurse will come in and check your A1C for your sugar levels during the last three months."

The intensity of his gaze grew. "I've been

afraid of stepping over some kind of boundary with you, Elizabeth, being too personal, asking too many questions, but when your health was a concern, I should have asked."

Elizabeth's head now pounded at his nearness. She wanted to close her eyes and will the pain to cease, but all she saw was the way Steven looked at her, as if he were engraving every inch of her neck, mouth, and face to memory. Her breath grew shallow. The monitor gave a loud beep and her eyes flew wide. He glanced up quickly toward the machine and took several steps away.

They both knew what he'd done, the reason he walked away and turned his back. He'd gotten too close and allowed her to see through him; the longing she denied him years ago hadn't faded. And yet, by his nearness, he witnessed the stirring of her heart, a yearning to be cared for and wanted. The monitor was proof of her reaction to him, and what he saw terrified her.

"I think they'll keep you for thirty-six hours, then reassess if you're able to go home, but I'll know more after the results. I'll see if the MRI has been read." Steven walked out of the room.

Elizabeth searched for the nurse's button and pushed it soundly. A nurse answered, "Can I help you?"

"Yes, can I get more pain medicine?"

"A nurse will be right in."

Elizabeth draped her arm over her face. She wanted it to all go away, the physical pain, the emotional turmoil of Chris leaving her behind and Steven being here, the guilt for loving one man and caring for another.

A nurse came in. "How are you feeling? Can you rate your pain between one and ten, ten being the highest?"

"Ten. Definitely ten."

"You've been prescribed Dilotin so this should help." The nurse inserted a needle into her IV and slowly injected, stopping every so often until the fluid pushed in her veins. Elizabeth inhaled a long breath as warmth seared through her body. Every muscle relaxed and the medicine did its job, sweeping away every fiber of pain and lingering thoughts as she closed her eyes.

Steven returned to the waiting room three hours later and sank into a chair. Elizabeth's family was visiting and it wasn't his place to intrude.

He thought back to the moment he stood over her bed. The monitor beeped, showing her pulse had risen because of him. What he'd seen in her eyes pained him, for there was no hope or future where they were concerned, but as he stepped away, he saw guilt. She wanted him there with her, while guilt ate at her because she still loved Chris.

He shouldn't have come. He was a selfish man for stepping back into Elizabeth's life when he'd walk out of it permanently within days. Steven shook his head at himself, running his fingers through his hair.

This was his fault, the turmoil he witnessed in her gaze. If only he'd never come to Miami none of this would have happened.

And yet, he was glad he was here today no matter how hard it was to see Elizabeth contorted in the crushed car, reminding him of his wife's death. He prayed for Elizabeth, and when worry took control, he prayed again. When she awoke, all he wanted to do was take her in his arms. No matter how hard he hid his love for her, she unveiled his deepest desire within seconds. Elizabeth understood him.

"Steven."

He looked up to find Samantha and Phillip heading toward him. Phillip held out his hand. "Thank you for calling us, for what you've done."

"I wish I could have done more."

Samantha sighed. "We were relieved to hear the MRI came back normal, but I can't believe she has diabetes. It doesn't run in our family. The doctor thinks it's the reason for her accident. He also said that since she had gestational diabetes she was at a higher risk."

"They have classes that discuss the ins and outs of diabetes, and healthy eating, that will be beneficial to her health. If she's able to control the diabetes with her diet, she won't need medication," Steven said, looking down the hall. What about her blood pressure? He hadn't heard anything more about it.

"Well, we should go," Phillip said, turning to Samantha. "I'd like to get Jeremiah home and for you to get some sleep. You'll be back in the morning and you're still exhausted from the trip."

"But someone needs to stay."

"I'm not going anywhere." Steven said.

Phillip placed a hand on the small of her back and leaned close to her ear. "I think your sister is in good hands while you're gone. Better. He's a doctor, remember."

"Fine. Fine. I can tell when I'm beat." Samantha smiled at Steven. "Now you take good care of her and I'll see you in the morning, *Doctor*."

"Yes, ma'am." Steven chuckled as they strolled toward the emergency exit. What would it be like to be a part of a family like the Roberts? A family who always seemed to accept others as if they were a part of the family regardless of who they were? It was obvious whom their lives centered around, even during heartache. They stood together, strong in the Lord.

Family. He looked down the hall leading to Elizabeth's room. "Lord, you've known the desires of my heart, to have a family again, children to bend a knee at the side of their beds in prayer, to tuck in bed at night. A wife I could love passionately and who will love me equally in return. I wanted a marriage with Elizabeth."

Steven took several steps down the hallway. "Lord, I guess your answer was no."

The door to her room was closed so he knocked before entering.

"Come in." Elizabeth said.

Closing the door behind him, Steven went to her bedside and stood an arm's length away. "How are you feeling? Can I get you something?"

She pointed at the table where a yellow pitcher of water and a foam cup with a straw stuck out. "Sam beat you to it."

"How are you feeling, then?"

"Still hurting, especially my neck. I've taken all the Dilotin I can for right now. They offered another pain medicine, but I'm trying to hold off."

"If you need the medicine, take it."

A nurse walked in with a rolling cart to check Elizabeth's vitals. "I'm Allie and I'll be your nurse until seven tomorrow morning." She wrote her name on the dry erase board hanging in the room. "Our number one concern right now is controlling your pain and then the second is bringing down your blood pressure." She set the marker down and walked to Elizabeth. "Any questions or concerns?"

Elizabeth took a deep breath. "I can't think of anything."

"If you do, let me know." Allie stuck the thermometer under Elizabeth's tongue. "98.6" She wrapped the blood pressure cuff around her arm. A few seconds later it beeped. "180 over 96. Still high. Have you been taking blood pressure medicine?"

"Never. I didn't know I had high blood pressure."

"Maybe they'll start you on something while you're here. Have you eaten?"

"Not yet."

"I'll check and see what you're able to eat. The kitchen is closed, but we have a few things I can get you."

Steven sat back in his chair as the nurse left the room. He looked to Elizabeth and found her watching him. She said nothing. "Phillip and Samantha came to see me in the waiting room before they left. I told them I'd be staying with you tonight, but then thought it might be best to ask you first. If you don't feel comfortable, I'll leave after you fall asleep. Your sister will be back in the morning."

"I didn't think you were coming back."

So this is what she was thinking. How could he not return? Steven couldn't take his eyes from her beautiful gaze, despite wrestling with the feelings, the words he'd hidden for so long. "While you were stuck in the car this afternoon, you asked me not to leave you and I meant what I said. I won't leave until it's time to return to Atlanta, unless you tell me to leave before."

Allie walked in with two sandwiches, a *Diet Coke*, and a *Sprite*. "The diet is for you and the *Sprite* is for him. I hope you both like turkey, it's all we have."

"Perfect." Steven said, taking the drinks and sandwiches and placing them on the bed tray.

Allie reached into the pocket of her scrubs and slipped out a glucose tester. "Have you ever used one of these?"

Elizabeth moved her head carefully side to side. "I haven't."

"Then let me show you." Allie went through the instructions on how to use the glucose tester, pricked Elizabeth's finger, and waited for the results. "220 and you haven't eaten anything since when?"

"About four hours ago."

"Okay." Allie looked at Steven. "Make sure your wife checks her glucose levels like I recommended. Instructions are still in the box, but if you need help, buzz me and I'll be glad to. Mrs. Roberts, it's important you have this down before you leave." She glanced around. "Need anything else, let me know."

The door closed behind Allie and neither Elizabeth nor he spoke. Allie assumed they were married, and it was farthest from the truth. Elizabeth would ask him to go now and he couldn't bear the thought of those being her last words to him. Steven stood and collected his keys from where they lay on the windowsill.

"Where are you going? I thought you said you wouldn't leave, only if I asked?"

"I don't want to make you uncomfortable, Elizabeth. I know this is hard on you. It would be easier if I left. I'm trying to save you from having to say the words."

"I admit, this is difficult. You being here at the hospital, in my life..."

"I'm sorry Chris isn't here."

"I don't want to hurt you, Steven. I did that once by not talking things through with you. I just left. I don't want that to happen to us again."

"We both made mistakes. We're both responsible for what happened between us."

"And I don't want to make any more mistakes. I need a friend but nothing more. If we can be that to each other, then I want you to stay. If it's too hard or if one day you wake up and find you can't be that friend, then please don't stay."

How could he leave her? How could he stay? Didn't she know what she did to him? He looked over, meeting her stormy gaze. The emotions swarming across her face, stabbed at him. She'd been through so much with the loss of Chris, the same reason she called him after her accident. Tears edged her long lashes. She needed him now.

"If I stay, no more mistakes, we need to be honest with each other about how we feel. You need to know where I stand, but once you hear what I have to say, if you want me to go, tell me right away. Don't keep me here out of concern for my feelings. We owe it to each other…as friends."

"Okay."

Steven sat down beside her in the chair he'd occupied earlier and took her hand in his. "I need this. I need to be able to hold your hand, like you held mine while you were trapped in the car. You needed the touch, the assurance you weren't alone. I need the same in return." He glanced down at her hand, and rubbed his thumb over her knuckles. "I'll know you're here for me."

"Steven, we can't go around holding hands. What will the children think— my family?"

"Never in front of people, and not all the time. Every now and then, when either one of us needs an assurance we're not alone."

She closed her eyes and laid her head back against the bed, her brows dipped. Perhaps it was wrong of him to ask. He started to pull his hand away, but Elizabeth's fingers tightened. "My head hurts is all. Stay."

"It's been some time since your last dose of medicine. Let me check at the nurses' station when you're allowed more."

"I'll make it a few more minutes. There's something else I need. I need to talk about Chris and not be afraid of how it affects you. He is and will always be a part of my life. My love hasn't died because he isn't here."

Steven covered her hand with his other and met her gaze. "Please don't *ever* be concerned about how I feel when it comes to Chris. I know how much you love him, Elizabeth, and it was obvious how much he loved you every time we were together." Her grip slackened within his hand. "Are you all right?"

"Tell me, when was the last time you saw Chris?"

He didn't foresee explaining his last conversation with Chris while she lay in a hospital bed with high blood pressure. He needed more time. "When Luke was born."

"Why did you come to the hospital?"

"To see Chris."

"But why?"

When Chris called him from Atlanta, he never said why. Steven drove through the night afraid of what he'd find at the hospital. It wasn't what he expected, Chris standing in the NIC Unit holding a five pound baby boy. Steven fought jealousy like never before, but when Chris held Luke out for him to hold, the need for repentance ate at him. Luke was a blessing for Chris and Elizabeth, a symbol of God's mercy and grace. And then, holding the child, an instant love enveloped his heart. It was then Chris began making his intentions known. Steven still remembered his reaction.

"Chris, please tell me you didn't bring me here to see if I still had feelings for Elizabeth?"

"You came when I called with no questions asked, and here you are, standing next to me. I think we both have our answer. Wouldn't you agree?"

Steven couldn't answer. Instead, he focused his attention on the newborn in his arms, features similar to Katherine, to Elizabeth.

"Elizabeth had mentioned at one time how you wanted a large family, and in the past she had asked about adopting children from Goma like her sister and my brother have been discussing. If I'm not mistaken, I believe adoption was a dream you and Elizabeth both shared at one time. If anything should happen to me overseas, take care of my family, Steven. Adopt my children as your own."

"You can't be serious."

"Very. If anything should ever happen to me, I need to know they're loved. There's no one else I'd give my

family to besides you." Chris ran a hand over Luke's bald head. "We are all adopted by Christ, therefore making us family. And as my brother, you're my kinsman-redeemer. She loved you once, she'll love you again."

Now, eleven years later, how could he possibly tell her what Chris had asked of him? "I came to the hospital to make sure you were all right. I've always cared about you, Elizabeth, just like today." He gently squeezed her hand, then released her. "Let me check on your medicine. We don't want your pain to get too high." He stood and placed his keys back on the windowsill.

Chapter Ten

One full day and Elizabeth already longed for home. She missed her boys, and when fleeting moments of sleep came, she dreamed of Chris and Katherine. Steven never asked about her restlessness but he must have sensed it because he began reading from the Bible he found in the one of the drawers. His voice soothed her and eventually she'd fallen back to sleep. The cycle repeated along with nurses checking her vitals. Now she lay waiting to fall asleep once again.

She looked over at Steven. The bathroom light he left on for her if she needed to get up shone enough to show him deep in thought. She waited for him to look at her, make conversation, but he never did. Finally, she spoke. "What are you thinking?"

He jerked slightly in his chair, then shifted to look at her. "The hospital."

"I guess they're missing you not being there." He remained quiet except for a small sigh. "Do you miss it? Are you looking forward to going back?"

"I wish I had more time. I wish I never had to leave." He forced a smile, then a softness lightened the lines around his mouth. "I've enjoyed getting to know your boys and seeing you again. This has been a great vacation. I wish I would have retired long ago."

"Would you stay in Atlanta if you retired?"

"Do you remember the little town I took you to? Monticello?"

"I do, and your house looking over the large pond, the view was breathtaking. I remember thinking I could see myself living in a place like that, quiet, seeing God's creation each morning firsthand." Although she never entered the house, she'd loved the wraparound deck. She closed her eyes, recalling the beauty and the reflection of the trees in the tranquil water. The smell of cedar still lingered in her memory.

"I'd live there."

"I would too." She said in a yawn. She turned over to her side, drawing the covers with her. "Pray for me, Steven. I miss my family. I miss Chris."

Steven covered her with another blanket. "Always."

She slowly exhaled, remembering a time Chris chased her and Luke along the beach in front of their condo. He was so handsome—tanned body, blond hair a mess—and when he smiled, her world grew brighter. If she could, she'd run to him. Hold him so tight and never let him go.

Tears slipped down the sides of her face. She sniffled and wiped the blanket against her eyes. "Shh." Steven whispered and tucked a piece of hair behind her ear. "It's all right."

"Will it ever be all right?"

When Elizabeth awoke the next morning, small, featherlike kisses caressed her cheek. She opened her grainy eyes and blinked twice at the little face. Something jabbed her in the stomach. "Oh, Christopher." She snuggled him to her chest. "Mommy misses you." She glanced at Steven and smiled her thank you.

"Miss Mommy." Christopher threw his arms around her neck and planted a sloppy kiss on the corner of her mouth. She winced at the pain in her head, but her heart swelled with love for her baby boy. She fought him for one final hug before releasing her hold. "Is that all I get?" Christopher sat on the edge of the bed, feet dangling off, arms up in the air. "Up Sebeen. Up!"

Elizabeth looked up at Steven. "Sebeen?"

"I think it's short for Steven." He lifted Christopher in his arms and her little boy leaned over and waved at her.

She waved back. "How did you manage to get him here?"

"I have my ways."

"I'm sure all you had to do was blink those dark eyes at Linda and she'd cave right in."

Steven chuckled. "Somehow I don't think that would've worked on Linda. Although I'll remember that the next time I want a woman to fall for my charms." He winked at her, lifting Christopher to his shoulders. "I think Christopher and I are going to go for a walk. What do you say, buddy? Ready for a ride?"

"Bye. Bye. Mommy." Christopher waved, then flattened his hands on Steven's forehead, making a smack noise. Steven chuckled again as he left the room with her little boy on his shoulders.

Christopher is a whirlwind. Elizabeth leaned back against the bed and exhaled a deep breath. She looked at the clock on the wall. Almost seven-thirty. Another day in this place, would she survive it without going crazy?

Allie came into the room. "I'm heading out, but I wanted you to test your sugar one last time before I order your breakfast." Allie handed her the tester and Elizabeth did everything the nurse had showed her. She'd have to thank Steven for the additional coaching. The machine beeped when she finished and Allie began writing.

"Is 130 good?"

"It's right where it needs to be. Do you need anything before I leave?"

"Not really. Do you know when the doctor might come in?"

"Dr. Avert is making his rounds now. He should be here soon."

"Thank you, Allie."

"My pleasure. You take care of yourself."

After Elizabeth washed up and returned to the bed, there was a knock. A slim man with greying hair came into the room.

"Mrs. Roberts, I'm Dr. Avert. I've been over your chart and it seems you have diabetes and high blood pressure, which could have caused your blurred vision and the blackout feeling you encountered during your accident. I'd like to continue to monitor your sugar levels before I release you later this evening. You'll need to make an appointment with a nutritionist to help you better understand diabetes. If you can control your sugar levels by eating, you won't need medicine at this time. On another note, how do your head, neck, and leg feel?"

"Better."

"Good. I'm prescribing you something for your high blood pressure because even though you are still young, you're at risk for a stroke or heart attack. You'll take one pill a day starting today. You'll also need to make an appointment with your family doctor. Any questions?"

"I'm not sure. It's a lot to take in."

"Well, I'll be around if you have any more questions."

"Thank you."

The doctor left the room, passing Steven and Christopher coming in. She waited for the door to close. "I didn't know you were standing there."

"I wanted to hear what he had to say and I figured we wouldn't make too much noise. Isn't that right, Christopher?" Steven set him down on his feet. Christopher had smeared chocolate all over his hands, face, and shirt, on the back of Steven's shirt, and who knows where else.

Elizabeth smiled up at Steven. "Both of you are a mess."

"I figured. Let me clean us up." He took Christopher's chocolate hand and walked him to the bathroom.

She couldn't help but watch them together, hand in hand, entering the bathroom. Steven always loved children and desired a large family. She hurt for him thinking about the loss of his only child in a car accident. He lost not only his son, but his wife as well. She understood that part of his pain, although she still had her children. How much harder it was for him. He no longer had a family—the only family he'd ever known. He'd never liked being alone, he told her more than once when they dated. *Orphaned.* To him it was a cruel word and one day he wanted to adopt as many children as she would allow. But they'd never married.

Christopher came running to the side of the bed and struggled to climb up but Steven lifted him next to her. "You stay with your mommy while I find something for you to watch." Steven flipped through the channels and stopped on a cartoon for younger children. Christopher nestled back against the pillow, his head against her chest. Steven covered them both with a blanket and returned to the chair he'd been sitting in since yesterday.

"Steven, do you still dream of adopting?"

He turned his attention to the television. "It was only a dream."

"Why didn't you? It's not too late."

"Because the dream included someone who had the same dream. She's the one who taught me to dream, how to believe in myself and to never give up. But that dream no longer exists."

Oh, Steven, I'm so sorry for hurting you. I was afraid.

Steven rested his hand, palm up on the bed. His hand, warm and inviting like the man himself, waited for her. She slipped hers within his and he intertwined their fingers. Christopher leaned over her and plopped his hand on top of theirs and refocused on the cartoon. Steven grinned and turned his attention to the television.

Elizabeth's heart galloped at the sight of their hands together. The picture of a family—without Chris.

In the distance a ringing sound cut through Elizabeth's dream. It took her a moment to recall she was at the hospital, not dancing in a rainstorm with Gene Kelly. Or was it Gene Kelly? She wasn't sure. She must have fallen asleep during the movie at some point.

"Hey Mike," Steven said softly. "She's asleep and doing better. She'll go home tomorrow."

After a long pause, Steven sighed, "I know."

Elizabeth blinked her eyes open. Steven sat hunched over in his chair, palm on his head. "Two or three more days."

Steven began to rise from his chair and Elizabeth slammed her eyes shut, not wanting to be discovered listening in on his conversation. "Hold on." His voice was soft but firm.

Elizabeth snuck her eyes open slightly. The door was partially cracked and light shone into the room. Steven voice drifted to her from the hallway. Something in his tone made her uneasy. She slid out of bed and listened at the door, keeping herself hidden.

"Mike, I said I'll call tomorrow. Yes, I'm tired. Please, it's not a good time to talk right now." Once again there was a long pause and she glanced around the door. Steven's body slumped against the wall facing the opposite direction. He nodded a few times as if Mike could see the action over the phone.

"I'll call you after I take her home. No, I'm not sure. All right. Bye."

Elizabeth scurried back to the bed and flipped the blanket over her by the time light from the hall flooded the room. She raised the bed as if she was getting up for the first time and swung her feet over the edge. Steven came to her immediately.

"Do you need something?"

"Yes. For you to turn around."

Understanding dawned and the worry lines above his brows vanished when he smiled. "I think I'll go for a walk then to give you a few moments to yourself."

Elizabeth watched as he left the room and shut the door behind him. She wasted no time taking care of her needs and climbed back into bed. What were Mike and Steven discussing in the hall?

Chapter Eleven

Steven's body rebelled as he stood from his makeshift bed and righted the cushions, returning it to its original form of a chair. He sat, rested his head against the back, and closed his eyes once again. The adrenaline had worn off from Elizabeth's accident. His limbs felt as if he'd swam the forty-eight miles of the Panama Canal—twice in one day. Where would the strength come to help Elizabeth? He had to find it somewhere. Mike was right. It was time for him to head home.

Elizabeth stirred and slowly turned her head toward him. "Hi." Her pasty white complexion now held a rose hue that was quite becoming—and healthy.

"You're ready to go home, aren't you?"

She smiled. "Still reading my thoughts, I see." In a move that surprised him, she held out her hand, turning her palm upward.

A desire to hold her greeted him on contact and he leaned close to the bed, pressing her knuckles against his forehead. His eyes slid closed as she rubbed her thumb along the side of his hand.

"Steven, if you're tired, sleep."

"There'll be plenty of time for me to sleep later." He mumbled. "I only have a short time left."

"If you need to return to Atlanta, I understand. It sounded like Mike needed you."

Steven slowly sat up and focused his attention on their hands. How he wanted a life with this woman. At least God had given him this time, his dreams wrapped up into this moment. How he never wanted it to end. She started to pull her hand away, but Steven squeezed her palm. "Let me hold you a moment longer." His throat clogged with emotion.

Elizabeth ran her other hand softly over his knuckles. "When will you be leaving?"

"In a day or two."

"I'm not sure when you'll be back in town, but...will you let me know?" She shrugged. "Maybe the four of us can go to the park or something. Have a picnic."

"I'd like that more than you'll ever know." He released her hand and leaned back into the chair. "I think I'll take you up on your offer to rest a bit." He closed his eyes and turned his head away from her, hiding the emotion that surely showed on his face.

There was finally hope for them, a future, and for a moment, he saw the two of them hand in hand at the pond by his home, watching the boys fish along the bank. They were happy.

Steven squeezed his eyes tight to stop the tears. It was too late.

Elizabeth ignored the television and its barely audible sound. Nothing captured her attention but Steven. Nothing caused him to stir, not the nurses when they came in for her vitals, not the many doors they closed behind them, not the doctor who came to release her. The pullout bed must have been terribly uncomfortable for him to be so tired.

Elizabeth changed out of her hospital gown and gathered her belongings. She kneeled next to Steven, concern nestling within her heart. "Steven," she whispered, touching his shoulder. A deep moan rumbled in his throat as he turned his face toward her. She couldn't help but finger the few short strands of hair that stood on end. His eyes opened and she smiled, letting her hand fall to her side. "I've been discharged. You don't mind taking me to Sam's, do you?"

"No."

She rose and sat on the edge of the bed, watching him. "Do you feel a little more rested?"

He ran his fingers through his hair and took another long breath. "I guess I was more tired than I thought." He blinked and met her gaze. "How are you feeling?"

"Better. My leg is bruised, but it's healing. Now I only need to remember to take my blood pressure medicine and check my sugar four times a day." She was about to ask how he was feeling when he rose from the chair and collected his keys from the windowsill.

"I'll pull the car around and meet you out front." He grabbed her things from the floor and headed out the door without a backward glance.

She couldn't shake the feeling something was wrong between her and Steven. Had she said or done something to offend him? Hadn't they agreed to speak honestly with one another? Perhaps it was up to her to mention her confused feelings where he was concerned, but she did want to see him again.

A few minutes later a nurse pushed a wheelchair through the door. "A little birdy told me someone is ready to leave."

"I wouldn't exactly call him a little bird." Elizabeth smiled at the nurse.

"No, your husband is more like a lovebird if you ask me."

Steven pulled the car around to the front of the hospital and parked. He looked toward the front doors and, not seeing Elizabeth, slid his phone from his pocket and began texting Mike.

Can't drive home. Made plans to fly out tomorrow night.

Are you all right? Mike texted back.

The car door opened unexpectedly and he quickly stuffed his phone back into his pocket. He started to get out but Elizabeth was already sliding into the seat. She thanked the nurse and closed the door, then looked at him. "Thank you, Steven. Thank you for everything."

His heart warmed at her words and the way she looked at him now made him want to be the man he used to be, strong, in control, a man who would be there for her for years to come. As he drove out of the parking lot, he was determined that she would remember him this way. She didn't need to know that since he walked back into her life he was pretending to be that man. By tomorrow night she'd never know otherwise.

"Steven, is everything all right between us?"

Instinctively, he held out his hand and wished he hadn't felt her touch against his fingers, the yearning to never let go. Last night he told himself to keep a distance, and repeated it several times in hope that his heart would listen. Obviously it hadn't. If only his heart could win another battle altogether. "I'm leaving tomorrow night."

"Oh." He heard the disappointment in her voice. "Will you at least have dinner with us before you leave, even if it's only for an hour? I know the kids would love to see you again." She nudged his arm with her elbow. "I'd like to show you I can cook now, maybe not as well as you, but a much-needed improvement since our college days. Besides, you need to give the kids the presents you bought them."

The turquoise in her eyes sparkled and he tore his gaze away. "I'd be happy to come."

Mike asked if he was all right. He used to be a man that looked straight into the eyes of his future. A future of love and a life filled with happiness. No, he was not all right.

Death had caught up with him first.

Elizabeth drew the curtains back and watched as Steven slowly pulled out of her sister's driveway and drove out of sight. She stared after him longer than she should have, but a nagging feeling nestled in her heart. She couldn't shake the sense that something was wrong.

She turned to find Sam regarding her. Her mouth opened but thankfully Luke and Christopher came into the dining room, disrupting questions Elizabeth didn't want to answer, feelings she didn't want to explore.

Both boys chattered while she hugged Luke tightly against her chest, then lifted Christopher off his feet and wrapped him in her arms. "I've missed you both." She met her sister's gaze. "Thank you for caring for them."

"You know I'm always here for you, regardless."

Elizabeth nodded and gave her sister a smile. "I know." She looked at the boys. "It smells great. Do you know what Uncle Phillip cooked for dinner? Your mommy is tired of hospital food."

Christopher wiggled his legs vigorously to get down. "Me hungry too!"

Sam giggled and followed them, sneaking around the corner.

"It smells like fried chicken," Luke said.

Elizabeth set Christopher on his feet as they stepped into the kitchen. Phillip smiled up at her from the stove. "You're looking much better than the last time I saw you." He looked past her. "Where's Steven?"

"Said he had to go. Things to do. He's leaving tomorrow."

Something passed over his eyes. "Well, with Juwonya at a friend's and our little man still napping, let's dig into this feast." Phillip carried a platter of pan-fried fish while she snatched the bowl of salad from the counter. Several sides already waited on the table. While Phillip said grace, Elizabeth became lost in her own thankfulness, for the Lord, His protection, for Steven once again being there for her.

After dinner Elizabeth found a quiet spot outside on the porch swing and looked up at the stars, her thoughts not far from Steven and Chris. She took a breath as she continued to gaze at God's creation. The stars seemed to wink at her from on high as if they were privy to a secret they alone knew. She wished for her future to be clearer, but what would she have done if she had known Chris's plane was to crash and she'd lose him forever? It was pointless to think of such things because she'd only grieve more. Life was difficult enough without the "what if's" and "what was." She couldn't change the past no matter how much she wished Chris could hold her again, or how much she longed to hear his laughter playing with Luke. He wasn't coming back. She hung her head, swallowing against the tears.

"Are you all right?" Phillip came and sat beside her.

She swiped at a runaway tear. "I didn't hear the door open."

"Lost in thought?"

She nodded. "Yeah...thinking about Chris."

"I miss my brother too. The sound of his laughter. His teasing. And let's not forget his competitiveness at mini-golf."

Elizabeth gave a little chuckle. "Or bowling, running—"

"Or of you." He turned to her. It was too dark to see his expression clearly, but she understood his meaning. "There was a time Chris was jealous of Steven because of what you both had shared in the past."

"I know, but why are you mentioning this now?"

"Because there's something you don't know. Chris asked Steven to come to the hospital when Luke was born."

She turned on the bench and faced him. "Why would he do that? And why didn't he tell me?"

"Chris asked Steven to take care of you and Luke if anything should happen to him on the mission field."

Elizabeth jumped up from the bench and stood on the edge of the porch, staring into the distance, her stomach twisting in knots. She started to speak but a lump lodged in her throat.

Phillip came alongside her. "Chris respected

Steven and knew he was an honorable man, but most importantly, that he loved you."

She could no longer stop the tears from streaming down her face and no longer did she care. She had held them back much too long and her heart was ripping in two. "Did Chris know?" Her words came out breathless. "Did he know he was going to die?"

"We all die, Elizabeth. No one knows the time or place, but I know Chris wanted you to be happy. He wanted you to be cared for and loved."

"Why are you telling me this now?"

"Because Steven is here and it's obvious his feelings for you haven't changed. I've only questioned why he's waited so long. It's been almost four years since Chris's death."

She wiped away her tears with her sleeve as strong arms wrapped around her shoulders. She sank against him. "I miss Chris so much."

"As do I...but I have to keep living. Chris would want you to do the same."

"Sometimes it hurts too much."

"God's given you the strength so far, you can trust Him wholeheartedly. He's not going to fail you now."

"I'm scared of the unknown. Pray with me, Phillip."

He held her close. "Dear Lord, please be with Elizabeth. She misses Chris and her heart still grieves for him. Heal the pain from losing her husband, and in the process, open her heart to love again. I know she cares greatly for Steven. Guide and direct her, giving her peace for her future and the future of her children. Your word says You will never leave or forsake us. Thank You for walking beside us in happy times and carrying us when we can't walk. We rest in Your grace and mercy. We rest in Your love for us. Amen." He gave her another hug before releasing her, then wiped his palm across one of his cheeks.

"I didn't mean to bring tears to your eyes."

He looked up at the sky. "Believe it or not, these are tears of joy. My brother is up in heaven happier than he'd ever been on earth, and one day I look forward to seeing him again. But right now, I'm so thankful God's allowing me to be here with Samantha and our children." He looked back at her. "Don't be frightened of the unknown. Sometimes we just have to step out in faith and that's when God does the impossible." Phillip left her and entered the house.

Faith. It took faith for Phillip to continue to be a missionary in Goma after his brother died. It took faith for him and her sister to fight to adopt two children from the same war-torn country by believing they would be parents.

Elizabeth had faith or she never would have survived the pain of Chris's death. She had faith God was with her and helped her to care and provide for her children. Yes, she had faith, but did she have enough faith to survive another major storm in her life?

Steven lay on the hotel bed tired, crushed under the weight of knowing he'd never see Elizabeth after tomorrow. Even after everything they'd been through, deep within him there had always been a seed of hope, waiting to be nourished and cared for, but no longer. He had to let her go.

"Steven." Mike called to him from the other end of his phone.

He turned his ear to his friend's voice and studied the dime-a-dozen picture on the wall. Pink and red tulips…spring. What if he'd never see the season again? Tears flooded his eyes. "I have to let her go," he whispered.

"Steven, you can't give up. Are you listening to me?"

The more he thought of leaving Elizabeth, the more his heart grew faint. He ran his hand across his face, wiping his tears. "I hear you," he finally said. "I'm too weak to battle."

"Talk to me, man. Are you at the hotel?"

"I am."

"Did you see your attorney like you planned?"

"I did. I've left everything to Elizabeth. Opened a $100,000 college fund for each of the boys. Her home was months away from being foreclosed. I paid it off. I had Eric take care of the details."

"Good. Now all you have to do is not give up, not on Elizabeth, or your health."

"I'm dying, Mike. What am I supposed to do? Ask her to marry me? I have nothing to offer her but pain and she's already had enough to last a life time."

"Don't you think that's her call to make? At least you should tell her what's going on."

They'd already talked about this and he wasn't changing his mind. The less Elizabeth knew the better. She deserved happiness, a life, the one he always thought he could give her. Now he knew it was a life that didn't include him. "I'm tired."

"All right." His friend gave a deep breath. "Get some rest. See you at the airport."

Steven ended the call and the weight of his body seemed to press him farther into the mattress. His breathing became shallow, suffocating. Maybe this was how death came.

Chapter Twelve

The next morning Elizabeth readied the boys for Steven's visit. He had called and asked if he could come early, and with the mere thought of him leaving for Atlanta, she didn't hesitate to agree. He mentioned he had a few errands to run before stopping by the bookstore to pick up his presents for the boys, so Elizabeth called Sam to let her know he'd be coming.

Now she stood in front of a full-length mirror, gently fingering the long curls in her hair, embarrassed she'd gone to such great lengths on her appearance for Steven's visit. She even applied makeup. Should she take it off?

As she started for the bathroom counter, the doorbell rang. Her stomach fluttered as she ran her hand down her jeans hoping she looked okay. Well, more than okay. If truth be told, she wanted Steven to look forward to seeing her again after today. She wanted more time with him to figure out these feelings that seemed to bombard her now that he'd dropped back into her life.

The doorbell rang again and Luke yelled for

her. She took a deep breath and made her way down the stairs, reminding herself to take it slow. She didn't want to fall on her face in front of Steven, though she'd done so before.

Nearing the last step, she glanced up and found Steven's dark gaze following her. Her stomach did a flip and she felt instantly shy. He came to her, taking her elbow like some kind of Prince Charming, assisting her off the last step.

"I guess you made it." *Of course he made it. He's standing right here holding you.* His smile was bright as it lingered on her face.

"Sebeen!" Christopher shouted from the playroom door. His bare feet slapped against the hardwood floors as he ran full speed to Steven.

Steven released her and immediately snatched her son into his arms. "It seems your mommy isn't the only one who's happy to see me." He regarded her. "You look beautiful." His whispered words lingered, as did his gaze.

"I want up." Christopher pointed above Steven's head.

Steven chuckled. "I think I've created a monster." He slid the little boy above his shoulder and walked him across the living room.

Elizabeth scanned the room for Luke and found him standing close to the front door, taking in the scene before him. What did he see? She wondered as she neared. "Why are you standing by the door? Come on." She held out her hand but he didn't take it. Instead, he walked past her and sat on the couch, arms folded across his chest.

Steven plopped Christopher on the couch next to his brother and announced he had surprises for them in the car but they had to wait there while he brought them inside. Steven collected her hand and walked her outside to his car. "I see that worried look on your face." He unlocked his car and clicked a button for his trunk to lift. Steven faced her. "Luke's a good boy. He's still unsure of me but he only wants to protect his family. Don't say anything. I'll be gone after today so it won't matter." He began digging in his trunk, handing her a few light bags.

She wanted him to stop handing her things and talk about this. It did matter. Steven mattered, and surely it would come up again the next time he visited. "I care about you, Steven. It matters to me."

With both their hands full now, Steven nodded. "I know." He clicked a button on his key ring, closing the trunk. "But for me, for today, let's not mention it. Let's enjoy our day together?"

Steven's eyes pleaded for her to agree. He had come to spend time with them and she hoped they'd have a good time together. No, she didn't want to be the cause of ruining their day. "All right." She followed him into the house. Once through the door, she caught Christopher running back to the couch as fast as his legs would take him. Knowing he'd been caught, he dove to the couch and bounced off the stack of flowered cushions like a ball and landed bottom first on the floor. The look of shock on his little face forced Elizabeth to hide her chuckle. Luke on the other hand laughed and Christopher's lips protruded into a frown.

Steven set his bags down and stood Christopher to his feet and pretended to brush him off. "Did you fall down? All you have to do is stand up again and brush yourself off. There. All better."

Christopher smiled up at him, taking his hand. "Better. Toys?"

Elizabeth bit her bottom lip to keep from laughing. Her son had a one-track mind. To him, this was like Christmas.

Steven shuffled his hair. "You sit over there next to your mommy, and Luke, how about you sit across from him next to me. We need enough space between you."

Once they were sitting, Steven handed them their bigger gifts while Elizabeth handed them their bags of books. She slipped her phone from her pocket and snapped a picture as Christopher yanked out the train set and his eyes widened.

"No way!" Luke yelled, catching her attention. He looked at Steven with awe. He held up the box full of baseball trading cards. "This is heavy."

Steven's eyes were bright, his smile held her there motionless. She'd missed seeing this side of him since he arrived, where joy was found not only in his smile, but in his eyes as well. She could read this Steven, she knew this Steven, the one who always did everything for others and never asked for anything in return.

Elizabeth held up her phone and focused the

camera. Shot after shot, she watched the way Steven interacted with Luke, the happiness in their features…the way Luke held on to his every word. Her heart stirred with emotion. Chris wasn't coming home after four years, no matter how many times she wished it.

Christopher climbed into Steven's lap and Elizabeth continued to watch them, desiring to be in their circle, sitting close, laughing, and sharing this intimate moment. She'd been praying for God's peace concerning Steven ever since her talk with Phillip. His words were still heavy in her mind. But this was what she wanted—prayed for. Peace had indeed found her and settled around her shoulders like a cloak. *Lord, but I don't know if my heart is ready. Help me to look to You for my future. Show me the way.*

Two hours later, Elizabeth pulled on Christopher's swimming vest and patted him on the bottom. "All set." He briefly looked to her before charging full speed through the bedroom door. She giggled and her stomach rumbled. She hadn't eaten breakfast, although she made sure the boys had before Steven arrived or Christopher wouldn't have eaten either. Now she headed into the kitchen and grabbed a pack of peanut butter crackers from the snack basket on the counter. She'd have to learn to eat at regular intervals if she planned on living without medication for her diabetes. Maybe after Steven left for Atlanta she'd put herself on a routine.

Elizabeth stepped into the screened patio and a smile lifted the corners of her mouth when she saw

Steven cleaning her grill. Since he needed to leave for the airport at five, they planned to have an early dinner and he insisted on helping. Most everything was ready but the grill. She glanced at the kids swimming in the pool, then back at Steven, who turned to her as she approached.

"Hungry?" He closed the lid to the grill. "I could eat at any time."

"The kids wanted to swim." She opened the wrapper and held out the pack to him. "Want one?" She stuffed a cracker in her mouth.

"I'm fine. But I was thinking about a swim." He nodded toward the pool. "How about it? Want to go?"

Was he crazy? She wasn't getting into a bathing suit in front of him. Elizabeth began to decline his invitation when pieces of cracker caught in her throat and she began to cough. Steven went into the house and came back with a bottle of water. "Thank you." Her voice broke and she took to coughing again. Steven ran his palm along her back in circles. A moment passed before she was able to take a sip of water and swallow down the remnant of food.

"Mom, you okay?" Luke hung on the side of the pool.

She waved her hand in the air, taking another sip of water. "I'm fine. That's why I tell you boys to never talk with food in your mouth." Luke quickly dove under the water and continued to search for his sinking water toys as if she planned to give a lecture. She looked to Steven. "Maybe I should take my own advice."

"Maybe." His hand stilled on her lower back. She knew he was leaning toward her but didn't know how close until she looked up into his gaze. "Swim with me."

She glanced at Christopher splashing Luke as he swam by the steps, pretending to be a shark. Heat warmed her face and she wished she were standing on those steps splashing water against her cheeks. "I can't."

It was the only explanation she could give him. After Christopher's birth, all that mattered was her children's happiness, putting food on the table, and keeping their home. Her appearance mattered little. With the way Steven looked at her now, with anticipation in his eyes, she wished insecurities didn't hound her.

But they did. Had, since the day Chris stepped outside the bounds of his vows. Right into the arms of another woman. Down deep there was still a part of her that couldn't shake the feeling she wasn't attractive, no matter how many times Chris told her she was beautiful or showed affection. Now twenty pounds heavier... "I'm sorry, Steven. I can't," she whispered, fighting back the tears, insecurities growing by the minute.

Steven moved his palm from her back and slipped his hand into hers. She leaned into his chest as she'd done many times in the past. He made no attempt to hold or caress her and she took strength in him. His chin rested on the top of her head. "You're beautiful—inside and out. Nothing can change that."

How did he know what she was thinking? How was it he read her like a book and still could after all these years? "Three kids can."

"Yes, children can change you. They give you more blessings and love within a lifetime than you ever dreamed possible." Steven motioned toward the pool. "I have my swim trunks in the car if you don't mind me jumping into the water with the boys?"

"Not at all." She walked to the steps, rolled the bottom of her jeans to look like Capri pants and sat at the water's edge.

"Are you getting in with us?" Luke asked, swimming over to her.

She ran her fingers through the water. "I'm not, but Steven's getting his swimming suit out of his car."

Christopher came to the top step and grabbed her pant leg with his wet hands to stand. "Sebeen in otter?" He smacked his palms on top of the water several times, splashing her hair and cheeks.

She turned her face but was too late. Drops of water ran through her hair, along her scalp, and onto the front of her soaked shirt. "Yes, sweetheart. Steven is." She might as well have gotten in. She should get in. Steven was right of course. Her children were a blessing and she loved them with her life...but not enough to push her pride aside and make lasting memories? Wasn't Chris the one who taught her life on this earth was short and she needed to grab hold and live each day God gave her to the fullest?

Steven reappeared with a towel in hand. "Hope you don't mind I took a towel from the bathroom closet?"

Hopeful it wasn't one of the towels with the tattered edges that should have been used as a rag ages ago. "Of course not." She watched as Steven set his towel across a chair and jumped into the deep water. Was Steven a part of living each day that God had given her? Phillip's words returned to her. It seemed Chris had thought so.

With a deep breath she stood. "I'll be right back," she announced. "Christopher, you stay by the steps." He turned to her and nodded. Steven swam toward him.

She entered her bedroom and shut the door behind her. Pulling out her swimsuit, Elizabeth took another deep breath and stuffed her pride where her swimsuit sat since last year and dressed.

A few minutes later she stood at the pool steps, Steven's hand held out for her, water dripping from his well-defined chest. "Like I said…beautiful."

She blushed as he guided her in, his hands drawing her and Christopher near.

The next two hours seemed like a blur—Steven tossing Luke into the water, playing hide and seek in the shallow end, laughter filling the air, and the feeling of family touched her deeply as Steven prayed over their meal.

Later, while she and Steven loaded the dishwasher, he became quiet.

Elizabeth slid the last plate into the bottom

rack. "I told you I don't mind doing these later tonight." She closed the dishwasher door, washed her hands, then met Steven's downturned gaze.

He seemed to lean heavily on the counter. "I had a wonderful time today."

She looked to make sure the kids wouldn't walk in on them, then cupped his hand. "We did have a wonderful time." She smiled. "Thank you for coming."

He moaned as he stood. He looked down at their joined hands. "I have to leave now. I called a taxi and they should be here. After I say good-bye to the boys, will you walk me out?"

"Of course I will." Steven released her hand and walked a bit slower into the living room where the boys were playing. "Steven has to go back to Atlanta so come say good-bye."

Christopher ran to him and Steven sat on the couch, taking him into his arms. "Thank you, little man, for the hugs." He smiled but it didn't reach his eyes. "You have fun with your train and make sure your brother plays with you." Steven looked to Luke. "He'll never be too old to play with trains."

Luke's gaze dropped to the floor as he came to Steven. "I guess not."

Steven set Christopher on his feet and held out his hand to Luke. "It's been wonderful to spend time with you, Luke. You're a great ball player, brother, son…and man of the house."

Luke took Steven's hand in his own and tears welled in Elizabeth's eyes. She turned away from them and walked to the foyer to pull herself together. What was wrong with her? This was Steven. He'd be back. Her kids would see him again. She'd see him again.

"I think I have everything," Steven said behind her.

She opened the front door to find a taxi waiting at the curb. *Taxi?* She glanced at his car in the driveway. "Steven, what are you going to do with your car?"

Steven avoided eye contact and took her hand. Together they strolled to his beamer. He didn't say a word as he pulled his suitcase from the trunk or as he slammed it closed, or after he recaptured her hands and looked into her eyes. What she saw there confused her.

Love. Fear. Other emotions she couldn't name seemed to mingle together in his clouded eyes. She felt them in waves, washing over her, heavy. "Steven?"

He turned her palm over and traced his finger along the lines of her hands, seeming lost in thought, then pressed a key in the center. "This is for you."

Her hand tingled from his touch and her stomach filled with butterflies. "I can't take this."

Steven closed her fingers around the key. "And I can't take it with me where I'm going. The airport has strict rules about carry-on luggage." He cupped her fist. "Please, Elizabeth. You need a vehicle and I have to know you'll be safe while I'm gone."

She took a step closer. He smelled of chlorine

and barbequed chicken. It made her smile thinking of the afternoon they spent together. She was already looking forward to his return. "How about I take care of it for you until you come back?"

The taxi driver beeped his horn and Elizabeth sensed a struggle within Steven as he glanced to the taxi, then back to her. "I have to go," he finally said, lifting her chin with his finger. "I never planned on telling you like this. I imagined it differently."

"You can tell me anything," she said, the seriousness in his voice catching her by surprise.

He started to speak, instead brought his mouth to hers and kissed her so gently, so reverently, tears filled her eyes. "You must know..." he whispered, wiping the tear from her cheek. "I've needed to tell you for so long. I love you."

The taxi's horn sounded again and she clung to his wrist, not wanting him to go. Not now. Not like this. "Hurry back."

Steven climbed into the taxi and a minute later he was gone, her heart with him.

Chapter Thirteen

Steven concentrated on walking as he entered the plane and headed for first class. His body was giving way to exhaustion. A flight attendant must have noticed for she came to him quickly and took his bag, directing him to his seat where he fell back into the cushion.

The attendant placed his bag in the overhead compartment and then leaned down to him, meeting his gaze. She smiled, but there was concern in her features as she tucked her auburn hair behind one ear. "Are you all right, sir?"

Steven blinked at the young woman and the care in her voice. "Yes, I've been swimming for the last couple of hours and doing more than I'm used to. I think it took more out of me than I expected." Not to mention he'd been at the hospital for a couple of days because the woman he loved was in a serious car accident and now he was leaving her. Exhaustion didn't begin to describe what he was feeling.

"Good. I mean, that's not good." She blushed crimson. "What I mean to say is I'm glad you're not intoxicated. Not that you would be…"

Steven didn't know someone could blush such a deep red. He put on his best Dr. Moore smile, the same one he learned after he was told he had cancer. The same one he showed to his patients and their families when he struggled to get through the day. "No offense taken."

The stewardess returned his smile. "Thank you. Well…if you need anything, please let me know." Her eyelashes fluttered and just when her cheeks were returning to their natural hue, she blushed again and rushed out of sight.

He leaned his head back against the seat and closed his eyes, his mind searching for a memory of Elizabeth but unable to settle on one. He wanted to remember them all. Then he thought of her sweet lips and their gentle kiss. He pushed all other thoughts aside and lingered there for a time, the scent of sunshine in her hair, the softness of her skin, the look in her turquoise eyes when she spoke.

He hadn't noticed then, being so captivated by the moment, but he recalled now the pressure she placed on his wrist, gripping him tightly. His whispered words of love.

Hurry back. Her words repeated in his mind and deep pain stabbed his chest. He let Elizabeth believe he was returning—to her. Oh, how he wished it to be true, but wishes didn't come true. Elizabeth had never become his wife and he still had cancer.

His head fell into his hands. *Lord, please help Elizabeth to forgive me. I'm going to hurt her and I've never meant to. I shouldn't have gone to see her, but I had to, one final time.*

I'm such a fool.

Elizabeth tucked Christopher in bed, his eyes heavy with sleep, yet a smile teased his mouth as he said good night. "Good night," she whispered, then kissed his forehead before turning off the light. She headed down the hall to Luke's room where his light still shone.

"Hey," she said at the open door. "May I come in?"

Luke looked at her from his bed, hands behind his head. "Sure."

She strolled to his mattress and sat on the edge. He glared at the ceiling. "Something on your mind?"

"I guess."

Elizabeth wanted to make a few guesses but thought better of it. So she waited, hoping he'd share his thoughts. Several minutes passed and she wasn't sure if she should still wait in silence or say good night and head back to her room. When she was about to rise from her spot, Luke shifted in his bed, plopped on his side, and rested his head in his hand. "You like him, don't you?"

There was no need to ask whom he was referring to. Steven must have been on his mind since he left for the airport as well. "I do. Steven and I have been friends for a long time."

Luke began to fidget and sat up in bed. "I

mean more than friends. Like boyfriend and girlfriend."

She smiled to herself thinking of his use of the term boyfriend and girlfriend. "Is that how we seem?"

He nodded. "Yeah, I saw you holding hands."

Elizabeth inhaled a long, quiet breath, wondering how to proceed. She wanted Luke to like Steven and she felt he did. What if he didn't? Would he tell her? "Do you like Steven?" she finally asked.

"If I do, does it mean I love Dad any less?"

She took his hands into hers. "It doesn't mean that at all, sweetheart. It only means your heart is big enough to love your dad and love Steven at the same time."

"I didn't say I loved him." He cocked his head and met her eyes. "Do you?"

She was taken back. "You're asking some tough questions and I don't know how I feel about Steven. I do know I care for him deeply and I'm looking forward to having him come back. I can also tell you that I will miss him while he's gone." Luke leaned against her shoulder and she planted a kiss on his forehead. "If I'm honest, I'm scared to love Steven because I still love your dad. I miss him."

"But isn't your heart big enough too, to love them both?"

She ran her finger over his comforter featuring the Florida Gators, Chris and Luke's favorite college football team. "I guess it is, now that you mention it. I like the Florida Gators as much as I like the Georgia

Bulldogs and the Alabama Crimson Tide."

He smiled up at her. "You know Dad would say you really aren't a true fan."

She elbowed him in the side and he giggled. The sound was like music to her ears. "Don't remind me." She stood from the bed. "Are you going to sleep now?"

"Yeah, after I play an air mission on my phone." He yanked his phone from his nightstand and she heard it come on. "That's a really nice car outside."

She leaned down and kissed his cheek. "It is nice. Steven's a lot like your dad and Uncle Phillip, thinking of others before themselves, like Christ showed us to live."

His brows furrowed. "Is Steven a missionary too?"

"He's a doctor. He works at a hospital in Atlanta, Georgia helping babies that are born early."

"Like Christopher?"

"Like Christopher. Your little brother is a blessing just like you."

Luke smiled up at her. "Love you, Mom."

"I love you, too." But before she could say good night, he had already started his air mission on his phone. She watched him for a moment longer. Her little boy was growing up much too fast.

Elizabeth made her way downstairs to check the doors throughout the house to make sure they were locked. She glanced at the clock on the stove when she passed. Eight o'clock and her boys were in bed. She fixed herself a glass of water, thinking about Steven and how wonderful he was with her children. She could still envision his strong form coming out of the water with her sons hanging on his arms to keep him from leaving the pool. Her heart fluttered.

She glanced at the clock again when a vibrating sound caught her attention. Something seemed to rattle then stopped. After a moment it started again. The closer she came to the noise, the more it sounded like her cell phone, but how could it when she'd placed it on her night stand earlier?

The phone stilled but started ringing again and this time she caught a glimpse of it on the kitchen bar. It was tucked next to the wall, lying on a cloth napkin. She picked up the phone and looked at the screen.

Mike 4 missed calls 4 messages

Steven's phone. He left it here.

She answered quickly, but before she spoke, Mike said, "Where are you? Are you all right?"

Elizabeth's mind reeled. Why was Mike so panicked? It wasn't like him, not the cool, think-before-you-speak Mike.

"Never mind. I see you. All I kept thinking about was you passed out somewhere and there you are sitting on a bench. I'll stay on the phone until I reach you. You've got your head down. Are you all right?" Mike went silent.

Why would Steven be passed out somewhere when he didn't drink or do drugs? She had to know. "Mike, what's going on with Steven?"

"Elizabeth?" Mike whispered her name through the phone.

"I couldn't tell her, Mike. I just couldn't." Steven's voice sounded desperate and she wanted to reach out to him. See him. "No matter how many times I tried to tell her that I—"

Elizabeth's heart stopped. She looked at Steven's phone and it said the call had ended. Mike had hung up on her?

In disbelief, she immediately called back, but it went straight to voice mail. She hung up and began to pace. What was Steven going to say? What couldn't he tell her? Why did pain and desperation radiate through her at his words?

She allowed Steven to walk back into her life after all this time and what did she know of his life now? Fear clutched, tore at her. No, Lord, he can't be married. Please, Lord, no. She couldn't love a married man.

Did she love him? She pushed the question aside. She didn't want to think about anything else. All she wanted were answers to what Mike and Steven were hiding and she had no way of contacting Steven.

The hospital. She'd leave a message for him to call.

She moved the bar stool and sat, searching for the hospital's number. She dialed, her heart racing out of her chest.

The operator answered. "Atlanta's Children's Hospital. How may I help you?"

"Yes, I need to leave a message with Dr. Steven Moore. He was my daughter's doctor and I have a question for him."

"Hold please while I transfer you to that extension."

Years ago Steven was Katherine's doctor. It might be misleading, but nothing she said was a lie. Mike and Steven weren't telling her something and she planned on finding out what they were hiding. Her kids were falling in love with Steven and their hearts were at stake. Right now she felt like a fool for allowing her own heart to desire his time and affections.

"This is Dr. Lewis. I believe you're waiting to speak with Dr. Moore?"

"I am."

"Dr. Moore is no longer with us, but if I might be of some assistance."

He was no longer at the hospital? "Um…no thank you." She hung up quickly, stunned. Was Steven moving away? Was this what he was trying to tell her?

Chapter Fourteen

Elizabeth spent most of the night on her knees in prayer trying to ward off each fear that rose to mind. Steven being married. Steven moving away. Steven saying good-bye for good. Now, as daylight broke, she loaded Christopher and Luke into the car and headed toward Sam and Phillip's house. She couldn't stay here and wait for Mike to return one of her many messages that might never come. She had to go see Steven for herself.

Sam was coming out the front door when she pulled up. Her sister opened the passenger's back door. "Hey there, you guys!" She unbuckled Christopher from his car seat and set him on his feet. "Phillip's in the kitchen making breakfast. Why don't you boys go in and get something to eat." Christopher ran off, but Luke glanced to Elizabeth as he got out of the car with his duffle bag over his shoulder.

Elizabeth tried her hardest to give Luke a reassuring smile. "I won't leave without saying good-bye." She watched him turn and walk into the house.

"Nice car," her sister said, looking at the interior as if she was purchasing it herself. "He just gave it to you?"

Elizabeth leaned into the driver's seat, grabbed what she was hunting for and then straightened, holding out a pre-paid credit card. "I also found this last night in the car's cup holder when I was looking for some type of clue to what is going on. I called. There's a thousand dollars on it. No note. Nothing. Only my name on the back of the card in black marker."

"Really?" Her sister turned it over. "What do you think it means?"

"Steven's trying to take care of her." Phillip said over her sister's shoulder. Sam spun and smacked his chest. He chuckled and wrapped an arm around her waist. "Didn't mean to scare you, but I thought it needed to be said."

Sam leaned into his chest and looked up at him. "How would you know what Steven would do?"

Phillip reached into his pocket with his free hand and withdrew an envelope. "Eric asked if I'd meet him at his office before our golf game yesterday because he had a client first thing. When I got there, Steven was there. Neither Eric nor Steven went into any details, but they gave me this envelope to give to you, Elizabeth." He held it out for her.

Steven said he had a few errands to run before he came over yesterday. Eric must have been one of them. Elizabeth ran her fingernail along the edge of the envelope, tearing the paper. She slipped out a bank receipt and gasped.

Sam came to her. "What is it? What does it say?"

Elizabeth handed her sister the receipt, hand shaking. "It shows the mortgage on my house has been paid in full—in cash, signed and dated yesterday." Her body wanted to crumble to the ground so she backed up against Steven's car. Tears filled her eyes and she swallowed against the knot in her throat. "I'm not going to lose my house now. No one can take my children's home from them."

Sam looked to her wide-eyed. "You were going to lose your home? Why didn't you say something? We could have helped you."

Elizabeth whisked the tears away, but it was useless. "I wanted to several times, but I just couldn't. I had to believe God was going to continue to provide for us whether Chris was here or not. That He loved me and the children and that the verses not to worry about what you'll wear, the food you eat, or not to be anxious about anything, but to give your prayers to the Lord, meant something."

Phillip grinned. "It seems God answered your prayers in abundance, but remember we are always here for you. Always."

Later that night, Elizabeth neared Macon, Georgia. With forty-five minutes before she'd be in Monticello, she decided to stop to freshen up, perhaps eat a bite though she wasn't hungry. She didn't know what to expect when she arrived at Steven's place, but she didn't want to forget she needed to eat and turn her visit into shambles. Her mind had spun for hours with questions she couldn't answer, and after her third time leaving a message with Mike to call her, she exited the interstate with a loud groan.

At the stoplight her phone rang and she glanced at the screen. *Mike.*

She scrambled for her phone. "Mike," she answered, her mind no longer on driving. "Let me pull over." She hurried the car into a shopping mall parking lot. The questions she thought of on the way now blended together, and she couldn't think straight. "What's going on?"

There was a long pause and Elizabeth couldn't stand the silence. "Mike. Please. Talk to me."

"Are you on the side of the road?"

"If you must know, I'm at some parking lot in Macon." She glanced around noticing for the first time that she had parked next to a fast food restaurant.

"Macon? Macon, Georgia?"

How could one question, embarrass, and frustrate her within the same breath? Embarrassed she was chasing Steven like some pre-teen with a boy crush, and frustrated that all of this could have been avoided if Mike would have called her hours ago. "Yes."

"Where are you in Macon?"

"I'm not sure. I'm by the interstate. Second exit in Macon."

"I'm only thirty minutes out. I'm coming to

see you. Get back on the interstate and exit the next exit. When you turn off, make a right. There's an Italian restaurant to your left. Grab something to eat and don't worry about waiting for me."

"Mike, Steven isn't—"

"I'll explain when I see you."

"Please, Mike. I deserve to know the truth. Does he have…?"

"How did you know?"

Elizabeth gasped, gripping the phone against her cheek. "Why didn't he tell me from the start? He's been with me day in and day out. How could he not have told me?"

"I told him to tell you…but he didn't want you to know—"

"He didn't want me to know!"

"To cause you more pain. He doesn't know how much time he has…the cancer…. It's bad, Elizabeth."

The anger she felt a moment ago evaporated within an instant. In its place, pain, —sheer, unrelenting, tortuous pain—shocked her to silence. *Steven? Sick? Was he dying?*

Her body trembled as the wake of his words rushed over her heart. "No. Not Steven, too. Please, Lord. No." She looked out the window but saw nothing. She felt blindsided, alone, and the pain she endured with Chris's death came back twofold.

Mike made some type of noise into the phone but it took her a few moments to realize she had been crying and he was calling her name. "Elizabeth."

"I didn't know. I thought…I thought he might have been married." She breathed into the phone, recalling the times Steven seemed tired when he didn't know she was watching, or his need to hold her hand, not to feel alone.

He was trying to be strong for her. He was trying to do this alone.

"I'm so sorry, Elizabeth. I thought you figured it out. Please forgive me. I never meant…"

"I can't talk right now, Mike. I'll see you at the restaurant, but I can't go in. Find me. I'm in Steven's car." Elizabeth ended the call. The phone slipped from her palm onto the floor. She covered her mouth with her palm and cried. How much more pain and death could she take? How many storms did she have to live through in a lifetime? She didn't know, but she knew she couldn't let Steven face his future alone, no matter what it cost her.

Elizabeth had wished she'd known the future and Chris's death. To stop him from going, to hold him tighter that last night, to say all the things a wife should say to her husband.

But no longer would she let time slip through her fingers. Steven loved her, she was sure, and though she wasn't certain about the depth of her love for him, they had time. She wiped her tears and straightened her shoulders. Whether it was days, weeks, months or years, she wanted every moment with him, and as she drove to the restaurant, the desire to love Steven grew.

Moments after she arrived, Mike knocked on

the car window. Memories of their college friendship rushed her at the sight of him, and the years between them vanished. He helped her out of the car and she fell into his arms.

"Oh, Mike. I wish I would have known," she mumbled. Mike said nothing but continued to hold her close. "I love him."

"It does my heart good to hear you say that. He needs you, now more than ever."

She pulled away, meeting his gentle gaze. "What else has happened? Could anything be worse?"

"A few months ago a friend of ours suggested Moffitt Cancer Center in Tampa but he refused, says he's not doing treatments."

"What type of cancer does he have?"

"Melanoma. He's had two surgeries to cut it out of the back of his neck, but it keeps returning. It was in the lymph nodes. He has stage 4 cancer. I'm afraid he's given up."

Elizabeth looked to the passing cars along the front of the restaurant, wishing Steven were with her now so she could tell him to fight. "He can't. I won't let him."

"I've prayed he'd fight, and when I realized he wasn't going to, I prayed for the two of you to reconnect, but it's done little for his will to survive. You and the Lord are the only ones who have the power to change his mind, to make him want to live again. If he knows you know, and you go to him, it has to make a difference."

Steven opened the double doors to his patio deck and strolled outside, inhaling a deep breath. He could live out here with the peace and calm surrounding him. It relieved his mind for a time each night when he was home from the hospital and tonight was no different.

He gazed upon the water, thinking about Elizabeth and the last time they were together. The softness of her skin, the easiness when they were together, the tenderness in their kiss, the way she filled his heart. It seemed so long ago. Time, distance, and death stood between them.

Tiny shards of pain stabbed his heart, or maybe it was his soul.

Lord, take me quickly.

A car sounded in the distance, coming over the dam. Steven turned and squinted to see through the trees but saw neither the vehicle nor the driver coming toward the house.

Chapter Fifteen

Elizabeth stopped the car at the beginning of the drive and glanced down the rocky path that veered to the left through the woods. She had followed Mike's directions leading her to Steven. Now with anticipation in her heart and prayer on her lips, she voiced her thoughts to the Lord. "Give me strength for whatever comes my way, courage to share my heart, and faith to travel wherever You lead."

As she made the left turn and drove over the dam, she was certain Steven knew she was here. She gripped the steering wheel and her nails dug into her palms as she rounded the last bend in the driveway. Steven came from the house, and a mixture of surprise and fear registered on his perfectly chiseled features. When he helped her out of the car, a hint of dark circles hung beneath his eyes.

Steven stared at her, holding her at arm's length. The warmth of his hands felt so right against her skin. "Is everything okay? Are the boys all right?" He breathed, eyes searching hers, waiting for her to answer.

How could she answer? *You left me and didn't tell me the truth. No, Steven, everything isn't all right.* But she didn't miss how his first concern was for the boys. *Had he begun to love them in such a short time?* "Yes, the boys are fine. Actually, Christopher sent his love. And Luke...he wanted to come. To see you."

Steven's body seemed to relax at the news and his palms slid from her arms, but his eyes pierced her, almost begging for answers to a question he had yet to ask. Was he afraid to question her in case she knew his secret?

To relieve the tension growing between them, she slid his phone from her pocket and held it up. What other reason could she give him for driving all this way? Of course she could have mailed it. "I thought you might need it." She shrugged, hoping her answer was good enough. He hadn't yet invited her inside and she wasn't leaving.

Steven's gaze slid to her outstretched hand. "You shouldn't have come all this way." He took his phone and placed it in his pocket. He looked down at the ground. "I'm glad you came. There are some things I should have said before I left."

This was it. The moment he'd tell her the truth of his illness, but what he didn't know is it wouldn't frighten her away. She would never run away from him again.

Elizabeth took a step and ran her fingers over his hands, caring hands that had helped so many. Hands she now wanted to intertwine her fingers through and hold close for whatever time God allowed.

"I can't see you any longer." He slipped his hands away. "There's no future for us."

Steven's words pierced her heart. She hadn't thought she could ever feel this way again—love again, endure rejection—but she was wrong. She closed her eyes.

"I'm sorry, Elizabeth. I shouldn't have stopped by to see you. I was wrong."

She kept her eyes closed, afraid of the emotions hiding beneath the surface. "Was it wrong?"

He was closer now, she sensed it, sensed him. "The desire to be near you..."

Although he hadn't touched her, the warmth from his presence surrounded her with comfort and peace. "God led me to you," she whispered, fighting back the urge to explain why she came. She opened her eyes, gazing into his. "Why did you come to me? What is your heart saying?"

"The Bible says my heart is fickle."

She took hold of one of his hands and intertwined their fingers. "Tell me, Steven." She lifted his hand to her lips and gently kissed his knuckles. "What is your heart telling you?"

"It doesn't matter."

"That's where you're wrong."

Steven forced himself to look away. Could the woman standing before him stab his heart any deeper? He could barely breathe. Heaven help him, he didn't know how to stop loving her. "I'm letting you go."

He turned and walked a few steps from her, needing the distance himself before he acted out what his heart wanted. He knew what must be done. "It was always a dream of mine, one I held so close, that we could love each other—but there was never really any *us*."

"How can you say that?" Elizabeth touched his shoulder, hurt evident in her voice. "I don't know what you've been telling yourself all these years, but down deep you know the truth. I gave you all that I was, my heart, body, and soul—and it was wrong then and frightened me. Things are different now. We're different. I'm not afraid."

"I'm sorry, Elizabeth." Her hand slipped from his shoulder and he hated himself for it. "I'll call the hotel in town for you to stay at tonight, but I think it's best if we don't see each other again."

He wanted to turn back, beg her to forgive him. Instead he walked away, self-inflicted wounds to the heart torturing him with each step. How he made it to the house he'd never know, but when he reached the back deck, Elizabeth was still at his side.

"I'm not leaving. We need to talk this out. We can work this through. I love you, Steven. I want to be here for you."

I love you, Steven. Oh, how he had waited, longed to hear those words. But another seven little words replayed in his mind as well.

I want to be here for you. His heart sunk straight to his gut as he turned and witnessed Elizabeth's calm demeanor, the gentleness in her eyes. Anger rose within him and his muscles grew taut. She knew of his cancer. "How did you find out?" he asked through clenched teeth.

Her eyes widened. She looked to the ground.

"Elizabeth, how did you find out? Who told you?"

She reached for him but he avoided her touch. "It doesn't matter."

"Who?"

"Don't you understand? It doesn't matter to me. I want to be with you. To care for you for the rest—"

"If I wanted someone to care for me I'd call *hospice.* I don't need your pity. I don't want you here." Steven stormed into the house and grabbed his keys from the kitchen bar. He turned to find Elizabeth standing in his way, but pushed past her. "I'm leaving. I know it was Mike."

Elizabeth grabbed his arm. "Please. Listen. Mike didn't mean to tell me. After you left your phone at the house, I called Mike several times. He never answered. I prayed, Steven. I felt like there was something wrong. God led me here. It was when I was in Macon that Mike returned my call. He already thought I knew because I was on my way to see you. But the reason I came was to tell you that I loved you."

Steven couldn't think, not with her eyes

pleading for understanding, for him to believe her, but could he? Mike continually pushed him toward Elizabeth. Perhaps Mike told Elizabeth the truth knowing she'd come, but Steven didn't want her only out of pity. No, Mike's deception was too great.

Steven stormed out of the house, down the deck steps, and toward his car without looking back. He had to see Mike. Nothing was going to stop him.

More than an hour had passed when Steven finally drove into the hospital parking garage and claimed his old parking spot. The aroma of ammonia hit him square in the face, filling his lungs, as he entered the hospital. A nurse smiled at him while he passed down the corridor toward radiology. He forced a smile in return, catching a glimpse of Mike to his left, speaking with a technician he remembered.

Steven stuffed his keys into his pocket and walked straight toward Mike, who eyed him suspiciously as he neared. He didn't wait for the conversation to finish. "I need to talk with you."

Mike handed the technician several files. "I'll catch up with you." The young man nodded and left. "I can already tell we need to take this somewhere private."

Steven said nothing but followed Mike as he led them down an all too familiar hall. Steven's gaze swept his empty office as they entered. Humidity and stagnant air had taken his place.

"No one uses it." Mike closed the door behind them, the sound echoing through the empty room. "I take it your visit has to do with Elizabeth."

"How could you tell her? Betraying me?" He moved past Mike and spun around, pointing his finger. "This is my life, Mike! Mine alone and I don't need you or anyone interfering!"

"Steven, you have to believe me. It was an accident. She called me, leaving messages, wanting to know what was going on, that she felt something was wrong. When I finally called her back she was in Macon. I thought she already found out."

"At least you two have your stories straight."

Mike took a step forward. "Now you listen to me. Yes, I wanted you to tell Elizabeth the truth. Yes, I think you both belong together. But I would never… I mean never, betray your trust."

Steven shook his head. "I want to believe you, but I don't. You pushed me hard toward Elizabeth and I know why, to fight this cancer, but it's too late. Why can't you understand?"

"I hope you're listening to what I'm saying because you're about to throw away something special if you don't get your pride out of the way. She loves you, Steven, and if you don't go after her, you never deserved her to start with."

Mike reached into his pocket and took out his phone, tossing it to him. Steven caught it and looked at Mike. "Listen to the messages. Check the dates and times yourself. Leave it at the nurse's station when you're done." The door slammed back against the wall as Mike stormed out.

Steven found the messages Elizabeth had left and began listening.

Misery left Steven raw and exhausted. He'd been wrong. Elizabeth had come to him of her own accord. Did that mean she truly loved him as she said she had? He recalled her pleading eyes.

He rested his head against the driver's seat. What a fool he'd been. What would he say to her if he had a chance to make things right? What did it matter, she'd be long gone when he returned. He didn't blame her. He basically threw her out of his home.

He ran his fingers through his hair. The pain his words caused her and his callous behavior were palpable. How could she ever forgive him?

"Lord, what do I do? How do I make it up to her? Show me."

Rain began to fall and when he returned, Elizabeth was gone.

Elizabeth slammed the car door, heart pounding as hard as the rain against her weary body. There was nothing she could do but walk back to Steven's, and if he was there, ask for a ride to the motel. She couldn't find it, and for as many times as she had driven around town, she should've been aware that the turn-off she attempted was nothing more than sludge. She kicked the back tire stuck in the mud.

With a deep breath she looped her arm through her bag and rested it on her shoulder. She double-checked her phone for the slightest signal. Nothing.

Darkness sprawled out like a canvas as far as the eye could see. She trudged her way through the rain, miles through town, and by the time she climbed the steep hill to the house, Steven's car was parked out front. Her stomach did a flop when she noticed a light on inside. She wasn't ready for the confrontation that was about to take place. Tomorrow, she'd tackle it head-on, but not tonight. She was hungry, tired, soaked through, and missing her boys so much she ached. No, she wasn't ready for this, but what choice did she have?

With barely enough energy, she lifted one foot after another up the steps to the front of the house and rang the doorbell. Rain that had finally stopped ten minutes ago dripped from her hair, and she shivered in the cold, her clothes clinging to her body.

Steven pulled the door open. The look on his face, aside from the surprise, made her want to crawl under a rock. "Hi." She wiped her cheek with the back of her hand, noticing his wet hair and the towel slung over his bare shoulder. "Car got stuck in the mud. I couldn't find the motel. I hate to bother you, but…"

He ushered her inside, taking the bag from her arm, then closed the door behind them. He hurried toward the kitchen. "You're soaked. You need to get out of those clothes." He set her purse on the kitchen bar.

"I'll be fine once I get to the motel." Steven

walked by her then down the hallway, but she stayed standing in the living room. "If you don't want to take me, I can call a taxi instead from your landline. It seems my phone is useless here. No bars."

Steven returned with a set of towels and other essentials for a shower. "There are no taxis here. Everyone helps everyone." He held the supplies out. When she didn't take them, he tucked a wet strand of hair behind her ear. The warmth of his touch drew a shiver up her spine. "Please stay."

"You didn't want me here, remember?" Her tone held more resentment than she intended. She wasn't angry, just hurt and now confused. He'd told her he didn't need or want her, so what changed?

Steven looked at her, thoughtful. "I was wrong. I'm sorry. And I forgot to call the motel."

She took the towels and gave him a small smile. "I'll take the upstairs. Do you have a shirt I can borrow?"

His gaze roamed her wet clothes. "I'll leave a few things at the bedroom door. Tomorrow we'll worry about the car, but I'd like to get your things tonight. Do you know where the car is?"

"Not really. I had to walk through town to get here but I stayed on the same road."

"I'll go check it out. Hopefully I won't be long so we can talk. There're some things I need to say before you return home tomorrow."

Elizabeth nodded, although she felt anything but agreeable. He said he was sorry, she reminded herself, but why didn't she feel any better? Steven closed the door as he left and the sound echoed through her heart. He still planned to send her away.

"I don't want to go," she whispered to the empty house. Tears threatened while the reality of his words hit her hard. She'd never see him again. "Lord, what do I do?"

Chapter Sixteen

Steven awoke in the middle of the night, his heart heavy, restless. He lay in his bed and looked up at the darkened ceiling. If only he'd been able to speak with Elizabeth before she'd fallen asleep, perhaps the dread that came over him wouldn't be plaguing his heart now.

He had to do what was right for her. Being with him would be like a death sentence, waiting for the day to come. No, he wouldn't hurt her any more than he already had. There was no future for them.

He closed his eyes, recalling how he stood over her bed last night and watched the woman he loved sleep. How her chest rose and fell. How her lips parted slightly as she breathed. How he prayed for her to find love again and have the baby girl he always wanted her to have. And how he prayed for himself, to find peace in the time he had left in this life.

"Lord, please show me your peace."

Steven felt something move at the end of the bed. He startled and sat up quickly. Was he seeing things? Elizabeth lay at his feet. Steven pushed back the hair from her face. "My Lizzy," he whispered the name he claimed for her so long ago. So beautiful.

He ran a finger down her cheek. When she didn't answer, he drank in the sight of her in his old baseball shirt as the moonlight caressed her face. Her long hair sprawled out every which way. He couldn't help but gently run his fingers through her silky hair. The longing for her he held so tight all these years began to unravel and there was nothing he could do to stop the flood of emotions that washed over him. Chris's words at the hospital came to mind.

"We are all adopted by Christ, therefore making us family. And as my brother, you're my kinsman-redeemer. She loved you once, she'll love you again."

She loved him again. She said so herself. How had Chris known?

Elizabeth's eyes slowly opened. A sleepy smile kept him in place as he looked at the woman at the foot of his bed. "Steven." Her eyes brightened as she sat up. "I had to come to you. I'd been praying and felt as if the Lord was telling me that I was your Ruth. Ruth went to Boaz and laid at his feet, giving herself to him. Cover me with your garment, blanket, or whatever, but love me. Be my kinsman-redeemer. Please. Don't send me away. Marry me instead."

A chill ran through Steven and tears formed in his eyes. *How had she known? God, is this you? Lord, who am I that you would think of me.* He lifted the blanket from the bed and as he draped it over Elizabeth's shoulders, peace settled over him. Tears rolled down Elizabeth's cheeks and he began kissing them. "Marry me today," he whispered, kissing another. "I don't want to wait another minute, hour without you as my wife."

Not waiting for a response, Steven pulled her close and kissed her with all the love he held inside. Elizabeth deepened the kiss and Steven felt lost, no longer in the past, but the present, and in his glorious future. He wanted to live in the arms of this woman, tasting her lips and feeling her near. *Lord, help me to live,* his heart cried.

Before passion swept them away, Steven held her at arm's length, thankful she was still wrapped in the blanket he covered her with. He inhaled a labored breath. "I won't let us make the same mistake twice." She rested her cheek against his face and he savored their closeness. "I think it's time for us to get off the bed."

Elizabeth blushed. "I don't remember reading where Ruth kissed Boaz. Maybe it was a good thing." She touched her lips with her fingers and gave him a mischievous look.

Steven helped her to her feet and took the blanket from her, laying it across their soon-to-be marriage bed. He wrapped his arms around her waist and kissed her softly. "What a shame."

She chuckled, intertwining their fingers. She glanced toward his clock. Four in the morning. "By any chance, are you hungry? I went to sleep without eating and now that I'm awake..."

"I'm not sure what I have, but we'll find something," he assured, walking her into the kitchen then opening the refrigerator door. A box of buttermilk pancake mix and a package of hot sausage rested on a shelf next to a see-through container of orange juice. "Mike brought a few things." He held up the pancake mix. "Interested?"

"I'll help cook." Elizabeth swiveled to a cabinet and yanked the door open. "There's nothing in here." She tugged on the next handle to reveal yet another empty shelf.

Steven shrugged. "There's only me so I live simply—until now." He drew her to his chest and caressed her lips with his own, relishing how she felt in his arms, how the air between them mingled as one.

Breathless. That's what she was in his arms, with his loving touch. How could she have walked away from him all those years ago? Unbidden tears sprang to her eyes. With a sad smile, she patted Steven's chest and moved from his embrace, looking for a bowl. Finding one in the next cabinet, she set it on the counter. Steven came to her, lifting her chin with his finger.

He searched her eyes. "What is it? What's bothering you?"

"I was thinking about the past."

"Chris?"

She shook her head slightly. "Us."

A loving smile crossed his face. "It doesn't matter anymore. God is a God of restoration. He's restored us. But He also brought two wonderful boys into my life, and though I will never be able to take Chris's place, I will love them as my own. I already do."

Elizabeth cupped his cheek and looked into his red-rimmed eyes. "You'll be a wonderful father."

Steven covered her hand with his and pressed his cheek against her palm. "I want them here, with us. Today. I want them to be at our wedding."

Her heart swelled at the love in his eyes, but how could she get the children here? "I need to call Phillip. Perhaps he could meet us halfway."

"You call. I'll pat out the sausage."

She turned to go, but paused a moment, glancing at her soon-to-be-husband. He took a pan from the cabinet and set it on the stove. He wore a dark gray shirt and long navy shorts and her eyes were drawn to his well-defined body. To the eye, he was a picture of perfect health, yet she knew the truth. He was sick, and he'd chosen to walk this path alone. Her heart ached at what she'd almost missed. What she'd almost let slip from her grasp. From this moment on, Steven would never be alone.

Elizabeth hurried to the room where she stayed and lifted her phone from the dresser, hoping the connection was good. She returned to the kitchen where the aroma of sausage and the light hum of a fan filled the space. Steven stood over the stove, spatula in one hand, humming. "Happy?"

He turned to her. His dark eyes smiled, crinkling at the corners. His face shone bright, more striking than she could ever remember. "Very."

Her heart skipped. "Good."

She pulled her gaze away and frowned down at her phone. No service.

He pointed his spatula toward the deck. "It's better there."

The moon shone on the outside deck. She took a breath and pressed a hand to her chest, her heart racing. This was really happening. She was marrying Steven. Her first love. What would Phillip say? How would her sister react, learning she'd be moving to the small town of Monticello, Georgia? What would Luke say? She dialed Sam. Phillip answered.

"Phillip, is Sam all right?"

"Fine. She's still asleep."

"Oh." For the first time, Elizabeth looked up at the sky. It was still early. Phillip did like to rise before dawn. Maybe it was for the best to speak with him first.

"I can wake her."

"No. No. I wanted to speak with the both of you, but it's all right. It's about Steven and me."

"When are you getting married?"

She giggled. "You're mighty sure of yourself."

"As I said before, God has a plan, and I think you both know what that plan is now."

"We do, but it's still hard to believe that after all this time we're going to be married. I still can't wrap my head around it." She paused, sitting down on a wooden bench. "I'm nervous, Phillip. Can I be a good wife to him? As I'm talking with you, doubts are starting to creep in, old fears…"

"When are you getting married?"

"Today, if you can meet us halfway to bring the kids. Steven wants them there when we say our vows."

"He's a good man, Elizabeth. He'll be a wonderful husband to you and father for the boys. And as much as I believe this to be true, I know without a doubt you will fill Steven's heart and life in a way only you can."

Elizabeth inhaled a long breath, taking in her brother-in-law's words. She closed her eyes, fighting back her tears. She was opening a new chapter in her life but could she let go of the old?

"Can you give me the address where we can meet up? Let Steven know we'll bring the children to you. You can't get married without us. Your sister would kill me."

Elizabeth pictured Phillip smiling. She swallowed the lump in her throat and wiped a fallen tear. "Thank you... Let me go inside and find out the address." She re-entered the house and Steven met her gaze as he was setting two plates at the breakfast bar. His smile faded. She held the phone out so Steven would know she was still on the phone, then placed it back to her ear. "Phillip wants to know where we should meet. They want to come to the wedding too."

Steven nodded, rattling off an address that she repeated. "Elizabeth, tell them we can meet here and they can stay as long as they'd like. There's plenty of room. There's even a mother-in-law suite on the other end of the house. Two bedrooms, two baths, and a full size kitchen."

She relayed the message, adding her own. "I know this might come as a shock to Luke."

"Now don't you worry. I'll talk with him," Phillip said, reassuring her. "Do you need anything from the house? We'll stop by and let the children grab a few things."

"Nothing that I can think of right now."

"It's almost six. We'll head to Henry and Linda's so our kids can stay with them before we head to the house. I'll call you once we're on the road to give you a better idea when we'll arrive."

"Thank you, Phillip. Talk with you soon." The call ended and she set her phone on the kitchen counter while Steven placed several pancakes on each plate. She slid behind him and grabbed the dish of sausage resting on the stove. "I didn't realize I took so long. Thank you for cooking."

Steven collected her hand when he sat and intertwined their fingers, meeting her gaze. "I'm glad they're coming. I know how much it will mean having them here."

She nodded, glancing down at her food, thankful for the man next to her as he said the blessing over their meal. She didn't want to hurt Steven even though she was aware of his glances as she ate. She couldn't bring herself to voice her thoughts: her insecurities about being his wife, his illness, and how she feared Luke's reaction to their marriage. The feelings weighed so heavily within her heart that she continued to eat in silence.

"Elizabeth," Steven finally said. "If you have doubts..."

She pushed her plate aside and took Steven's hand, much like he had held hers after her car accident. She rubbed her thumb over his hand. They both needed assurances—that honesty and communication would reign and that they would be together from this day forward. "I have no doubts about marrying you, Steven. But there are other things... I've been sitting here..."

"Letting your thoughts fester?"

She glanced down at their hands. "Yes. I can't stop thinking about Luke and how he'll take the news of our marriage. I've been thinking about the Roberts, especially Linda, Henry, and Phillip. How important they are to me, to the boys." She looked into Steven's dark eyes and saw the compassion radiating from his gaze, giving her strength to press forward. "I love them, Steven. I need them in our lives. They were my strength; my rock these last few years."

"I'd never take your family away or try to build a wall between you. I know how important family is and I'm thankful to soon be a part of yours, including the Roberts. As to Luke, it's my prayer he accepts me into his life, but we'll know soon enough how he'll feel."

Elizabeth recalled how her son acted when Steven left to catch his flight. "Luke was asking questions about us. Even though he hadn't said so, I had a feeling he didn't want you to go when you left."

"What type of questions?"

She tucked a strand of hair behind her ear and smiled. "He saw us holding hands and asked if we were boyfriend and girlfriend."

Steven grinned and leaned forward. "And what did you say?"

At his nearness, she also leaned in, his lips only inches away.

"Tell me," he whispered, his gaze dropping to her mouth.

She struggled to find her voice. "That I was looking forward to your next visit…that I cared for you deeply."

Steven pushed the rebel hair from her eyes, his thumb grazing her cheek. "I love you." His fingers ran through her hair.

Her eyes slid closed and she sighed, feeling the warmth of his breath, the touch of his mouth against hers. She savored the moment, the kisses, and the promise of what was yet to come. She only hoped she'd be able to make Steven happy.

Chapter Seventeen

Try as she might, Elizabeth couldn't conjure up her boys or make the miles and hours between them tick away any quicker. Steven must have noticed her restlessness because he suggested a drive. Immediately she agreed, although now she wished she knew where he was taking her. After two hours sitting in the car, seat belt tightly fastened, she felt like a caged animal.

Steven squeezed her hand. "We're almost there."

"Where did you say we were going?"

He glanced at her, a mischievous smile playing at the corners of his mouth. "I didn't say." He turned off the highway, leaving behind the downtown Atlanta traffic.

"Keeping secrets, Mr. Moore? I must say it's not a good way to start a marriage." They turned down another road and drove past the entrance to the hospital where he once worked.

"Just this once." Steven pulled the car into the hospital garage, punched in a code, waited for the gate arm to lift, then drove in. "We're picking up someone."

She straightened in her seat and scanned the garage. Her gaze found Nicole, then noticed her round middle. Elizabeth smiled. "I didn't know she was pregnant at the wedding. She's finally going to have a baby after all these years." She immediately thought of Sam and how desperately she wanted to give Phillip a child, but it was God who gave them children to love through adoption. "How far along is Nicole?"

"Five months. John tells me she's ready, they're both ready to hold this baby." Steven drove around the bend and waited in the patient pickup line where Nicole stood, arm resting on her stomach.

Instinctively, Elizabeth palmed her middle. She loved babies, children, and a twinge of regret fluttered through her heart. She took a long breath and her hand slipped to the seat. Her pregnancies were too difficult. She'd never been able to carry her babies to term. And now that she was older, how early would the child come? How would it affect Steven in the process? No, she couldn't have another child.

Steven rolled the car to where Nicole stood, glancing over her shoulder. Elizabeth opened the car door and approached her dear friend.

"I hear congrats are in order," Nicole said, hugging her. "I'm so happy for you both. I almost can't believe it. And now we have some shopping to do."

Elizabeth pushed her to arm's length.

"Shopping?" Nicole smiled and Elizabeth turned to Steven who stood by the hood of the car.

Steven shrugged, hiding a smile. "I wouldn't know where to begin." His gaze roamed to where Nicole looked only moments ago.

John, Mike, and Susan came through the sliding glass doors. It was like she'd been thrown back to her college days with all of them together. John was the first to approach, kissing Nicole's cheek. "Hey, honey."

Nicole smiled up at him. "Hey, babe. Ready to shop."

Mike chuckled. "Of course he is. He loves to shop. From what Susan told me, you both dropped some major cash yesterday."

John sighed, opening the back seat door for Nicole. "Please, don't remind me."

Susan threw her hands on her hips. "Mike, I told you no such thing. I can't believe you were listening to our conversation."

Mike held his hands up in the air as if to surrender. "You caught me." He leaned close to Susan, near enough to kiss her. "What are you going to do about it?" He winked.

Susan giggled and shook her head. "All these years and I still have no idea." Mike popped her a kiss on her cheek and wrapped an arm around her waist.

"And there lies the problem." John smirked as he slipped in next to his wife and closed the door.

Susan slid from Mike's embrace and hugged Elizabeth's neck. "I will certainly try to make the wedding but I still have a few more hours. I wouldn't want to miss it for the world." She pulled back and wiped her eyes. "I told the men where to take you and Nicole. Find yourself a beautiful dress." Before Elizabeth could reply her thank you, Susan turned her attention to Steven. "Keep Mike in line."

Steven laughed. "Mike, you following us?"

"I'll meet you there." Mike started through the garage as Susan waved good-bye while reentering the hospital.

Elizabeth climbed into the car and checked her cell phone. Still no word from Phillip or her sister. Hopefully everything was all right.

Thanks to John and Nicole, it wasn't long before laughter and the good ole days monopolized everyone's conversation. "You should have seen your face, Elizabeth," John was saying. "You jumped clear out of your skin when that first firework went off."

Elizabeth glanced at Steven and smiled, wishing she could recall it. At one time, Elizabeth was sure her memories had returned after her coma years ago, and most had, but from time to time, another memory tucked away in her consciousness would come to light. How she wished it now. She glanced out the car window.

Steven cupped her hand as if he understood and she felt her body relax to his touch. Then it happened. A memory found its way home. She captured the thought, the moment so long ago, replaying it over and over in her mind. The warm breeze against her face. Strolling across the intercoastal bridge. The deafening boom of the fireworks. A bright, star-like glimmer against the darkened night sky. Steven's kiss.

She closed her eyes, taking it all in, and the love she felt for Steven washed over her, stealing her breath. How many more memories were still lost to her? She wished she knew. But even if the memories never came, she was certain that whatever still hung in the balance of the unknown, God had always been there for her. Most importantly, He was there for her now and would remain faithful in the future.

Twenty minutes later, Steven pulled up to a bridal boutique where four mannequins stood stunningly dressed in sequin wedding gowns, peering out the glass windows. She smiled. Susan had exquisite taste.

On the way to the boutique, Steven sensed Elizabeth had become uneasy, and when she fell silent, he was drawn to touch her. Perhaps it was the past she didn't want to recall or maybe the fact they were rushing into marriage. Yet as he stopped in front of the shop, God's peace remained, confirming that he was doing the right thing by marrying Elizabeth.

Elizabeth kissed his hand and smiled up at him. "What will you do while I'm trying on gowns?"

"Anxiously wait for your return."

Her smile brightened.

Nicole opened the car door and paused before getting out. "John, why don't you say things like that to me?"

"Okay." John cleared his throat. He raised an arm, leaned close to Nicole, and placed a palm across his heart. He looked as if he was practicing a theatrical performance. "How thee has captured my heart, mind, and are wasting time when there's a wedding today. Let me count the ways."

Nicole smacked his arm. "Come on, Elizabeth."

Elizabeth slid from her seat, snatched her bag, and glanced at him. "If I hear from Phillip, I'll let you know." She closed the door and entered the boutique.

John stared at him oddly in the rearview mirror. "Elizabeth got mighty quiet. Do you think I said something wrong?"

"I know she's got a lot on her mind, the wedding I'm sure. We spoke about a few things this morning, the boys, how Luke will take the news of our wedding, and her concerns I wouldn't allow the Roberts to take their rightful place in her and the children's lives. I have a feeling there's more."

"I'm sure she'll share it with you when the time is right. Not like you, keeping your wedding plans a secret from her."

"Slightly different. We have only a few hours and I still need to get our rings from the safety deposit box."

"Won't she be surprised that you saved your rings after all this time. How about when Mike gets here, send him over to the bank. He's still listed on the account?"

Steven nodded. "Yes, and he's here."

"I'll check on the girls," John said as they exited the car.

Steven joined Mike at the front of the car and watched John enter the shop. His gaze caught a glimpse of Elizabeth as she passed by one of the mannequins and her smile warmed him. "Can you pick up the rings?"

"I can. The florist will have the flowers delivered in three hours so I'll need to hurry. The pastor from your church is free and said to call when you're ready since he lives in front of you on the hill."

Lord, this is really happening. Steven smiled. "Pretty convenient, don't you think?" He sought just one more glimpse of the woman he loved. "I need you to do me another favor. I know I haven't wanted to discuss the cancer and have almost been in denial...but I'm ready to meet your friend at the Moffitt Cancer Center. Can you get me in? I know I might have waited too—"

"I'll get you in."

"Oh, Elizabeth, this dress looks beautiful on you." Nicole bent and ran a slow finger down the edge of the gown in admiration, then quickly moved it across the platform where Elizabeth stood. "You look like you're going to a ball."

"And you shouldn't be bending so low, it can't be good for the baby."

Nicole waved her hand in the air. "I'm as

healthy as they come and so is this child." She palmed her abdomen. "He's got his own jungle gym in there, keeping me up all night, playing."

Elizabeth smiled and turned to the three-way mirror, noticing how the dress accentuated her hips and larger backside. "I remember the feelings of pregnancy so well. Miss them, actually." She'd much rather be trying on a maternity dress where there was room to breathe. Maybe she needed a larger size. She ran her hand over the transparent lace and cap sleeves.

She turned a bit and tilted her head, glancing at the side view of the gown. It certainly was pretty, gorgeous really. She wished her mother had been alive to help her decide. Would she have picked this dress for her? She let out a long sigh. "I don't know, Nicole."

When her friend didn't answer, Elizabeth glanced up to find Steven standing next to Nicole. His gaze roamed from where the gown rested on the edge of the platform, to the delicate lace across her chest, then lingered at her eyes.

"I know I wasn't supposed to see you, but I was looking for John and…" A grin spread across his face and his dark eyes sparkled. "You're breathtaking."

Warmth climbed to her cheeks. "Thank you," she said softly. She glanced quickly at Nicole who gave her a thumbs up behind Steven's shoulder, then returned her focus to Steven, fighting back a smile. "So you like?"

"More than like." Steven winked, reached into his pocket, pulled out his phone, and squinted at the screen. He answered quickly. "Phillip."

Elizabeth took a step toward Steven and Nicole rushed toward her. "You can't get down or you'll step all over your dress." She paused.

As if Steven read her mind, he walked to the edge of the platform and leaned in so she could listen. "How far are you?" he asked.

"We stopped in Valdosta but we're on our way now. Still looking at another three hours."

"Phillip, Elizabeth is standing right here. Let me give her the phone."

Phillip chuckled. "I had no doubt."

Steven handed her his cell and she eagerly grabbed it. "Hey, how's everything going?" Elizabeth lifted a corner of the gown slightly and walked a few steps toward the mirror.

"Everything is going well. Christopher is enjoying the drive. When we stopped by the house, Luke grabbed one of Christopher's CDs, and he's has been making a joyful noise ever since."

Elizabeth smiled at her older son's thoughtfulness. Luke knew the drive would be a difficult one for Christopher without his music, but he took care of his little brother. He had loved him fiercely ever since he was born. "How's Luke? Did you tell him why you were coming?"

"We did. He's been a little quiet." There was a pause. "God will work this out. Trust Him."

She hadn't been able to do anything but trust

God with her future, yet she didn't want the wedding to hurt her son in the process and her heart ached at the thought.

She placed the cell against her other ear. How many times had she drawn strength from God and Luke when she wanted to give up, stay in bed, and sleep? But she didn't give up; she fought to be the mother God called her to be and continue to be as she stood on the threshold of marriage. But was she marrying too quickly? She glanced up in the mirror to find Steven's reflection watching her. His handsome features were etched in sorrow, as if she'd spoken the words aloud. She was torn between the man she'd fallen in love with again after all these years and the son who held her heart.

"Elizabeth, did you hear what I said? God will work this out. Trust Him."

"I did." She took a long breath and admired the dress she wore and what it represented—a future certain to be filled with love, happiness in the midst of heartache, and a fulfillment that only God could have restored by bringing them together. And promises… Promises like the one she made to Steven yesterday, to stand by his side, and to love him regardless of their future. A commitment she planned to keep. "Tell the boys I love them and I'll see them soon."

Chapter Eighteen

Three hours later, after dropping John and Nicole off at his house, Steven and Elizabeth stood in line at the city hall in Monticello waiting to receive their marriage license while his friends and Mike made the final preparations for the wedding. Steven wanted everything to be perfect when she walked into their soon-to-be home. She would be surprised, no doubt, but it was Elizabeth's worried expression when speaking with Phillip earlier that he couldn't shake.

How would Luke take the news of their marriage? Would Luke accept him as his father? Perhaps if he and Elizabeth had more time together before they married... But time was running out, he felt it with every breath he took, and as the morning wore on, the peace he had surrendered to evaporated.

Elizabeth looked up at him, linking her arm through his. "You seem lost in thought."

Steven glanced at his watch. "Twenty minutes. We almost didn't make it."

She squeezed his arm as they took a step forward. "We're here now. Besides, we're next."

The young clerk pushed her black-framed glasses to the bridge of her nose and smiled up at them. "How may I help you?"

Elizabeth released her hold and Steven took out his wallet. "We'd like a marriage license."

The clerk raised a thin brow then glanced at the ornate clock on the wall. She slipped two forms onto the counter, one to Elizabeth and one to him. "Please fill these out while I ask you several questions." She handed them two pens. "Are you both of sound mind?"

Steven and Elizabeth glanced at each other and a sweet giggle slipped from her lips. Some might think not, but what did it matter. "We are." They said in unison.

The woman nodded, glancing at a form. She added a check mark. "Do you have a living spouse from an undissolved prior marriage?"

"No."

"Are either of you related in any way?"

"No," they said again.

"Have you completed premarital education within twelve months prior to the application for a marriage license?"

"No."

She scribbled a notation on the form. "Okay. Without the premarital counselling, that will be another thirty-five dollars." The clerk glanced over the forms they slid back to her. "All I need now are two valid forms of ID such as a driver's license, birth certificate, US passport, armed forces ID card, or resident alien ID card. Plus ninety-one dollars for the license."

Steven took out his wallet and placed a hundred dollar bill on the counter, along with his two forms of identification.

Elizabeth leaned into him, eyes wide. "Steven…I only have my driver's license and social security card. I didn't realize. My birth certificate is at home. In a filing cabinet with the boys'."

Elizabeth didn't need to say another word, his sinking heart was proof enough that the woman he loved, the woman he waited for all his life, would once again fail to be his wife. Elizabeth spoke to the clerk searching for another way to receive their license, but his hope fled.

"I'm sorry, but it's the law here in Jasper County. There's no waiting to be married, no blood test needed, but you have to have your birth certificate or another form of identification as I mentioned."

They stood there, motionless, staring at the woman. "Thank you," he finally said, taking a deep breath and turning to the door, Elizabeth close behind. He needed a few minutes to collect himself and let reality sink in. His throat tightened. Maybe he'd imagined God's peace this morning. Maybe this was a sign.

Suddenly he felt completely lost.

Steven placed his hand on the small of her back and escorted her to the car. He opened the door and she slid in. He took another long breath before he entered the driver's side. What were they going to do now? Phillip, Samantha, and the boys were on their way to see them marry. They were traveling all this way for nothing. He started the car and drove toward home.

Elizabeth placed her hand on his arm. "This doesn't change anything."

She was wrong, it changed everything. Elizabeth wouldn't be his to hold within his arms, to love through the night. He wouldn't feel the warmth of her body as he fell asleep, knowing that God's promise of a hope and a future could actually be tangible. Soon, perhaps tonight, Elizabeth would return to Miami. How quickly things could change.

Rounding the corner drive, Elizabeth pointed to Phillip's navy SUV parked in front of the house. Mike's black sedan was parked alongside. "They're here. Who else is here besides John and Nicole?"

"Mike." Steven parked the car and Elizabeth opened her door quickly. He reached over and held her arm before she could get out. He didn't want to speak the words, but everyone needed to know the marriage was off. "I'll tell them."

"We'll tell them together." She cupped his hand and squeezed. "Come on. Let's go see our boys." She slid from the car and walked quickly to the door. It opened instantly. Samantha stood on the other side with Christopher, who leapt into his mother's arms.

Steven joined them. "Samantha, it's good to see you again."

"It's wonderful to see you. May I give my soon-to-be brother-in-law a hug?" She hugged him close and whispered. "And we know that in all things God works for the good of those who love Him."

Oh, how he wanted to believe Samantha's words to be true.

After the death of his parents, he and his sister, as small children, were forced into an orphanage, but soon death claimed his sister too. Loneliness became his constant shadow. Even as an adult he struggled with the need to belong, to be loved, and here he was standing at the brink once again.

He looked away.

They entered the living room together and Elizabeth gasped. The room was simple but elegant, adorned with candlelight, bouquets of baby's breath, and white roses, her favorite. She turned, meeting his gaze. "Steven, this is beautiful." As if Christopher noticed him for the first time, he wiggled out of Elizabeth's arms and ran to him. "Sebeen!"

Steven knelt and Christopher instantly clung to his neck. "Sebeen. Miss uo." He planted a big, wet kiss on his cheek. Steven swallowed against the knot in his throat. *Lord, I love this little boy. I know You're his true Father and You'll care and love him as You did me, but please, don't let him grow up without knowing the love of an earthly father as I did. I want to be that man.*

Mike, dressed in a tuxedo and wearing the largest smile he'd ever seen, came to him. "Phillip and John are changing and the girls have everything ready for Elizabeth upstairs. Do you want me to call Pastor Bruce?"

Samantha smiled and linked her hand through Elizabeth's arm. "Ready?"

Elizabeth glanced at him, then looked to her sister. "I...um...I didn't have my birth certificate." Samantha's forehead creased and she gave her sister an odd expression as if she wasn't sure what was being said.

"We didn't get the marriage license," Steven said, feeling all eyes upon him, even Phillip and John who had entered the candlelit room. No one moved, nor did anyone say a word.

"You're not getting married?" Luke asked from the bottom of the stairwell. Luke made his way to his mother, slipping past Nicole and stopping an arm's distance away.

Elizabeth slid her hand from her sister and held out her arms to her son. He didn't move. "Not today it seems."

"When can we go home?"

"Luke." Phillip's kind yet strong voice filled the silence. "Whenever Steven and your mom say it's time, but not today, or for at least the next few days." Phillip smiled at Steven. "I just happen to have a document you might need. A birth certificate, perhaps?"

"You took it from the filing cabinet?" Elizabeth's face shone in surprise.

Steven's mind spun to grasp the meaning of what was happening. Christopher began jumping in his arms and Steven struggled to keep the little boy from falling to the hardwood floors. Luke turned and headed outside.

Samantha chuckled. "You should know by now how prepared my husband can be regarding certain matters, especially when they concern the heart." She looked to Nicole and nodded toward Phillip. "He's the romantic one."

Nicole turned to John and he shrugged his shoulders. "What?"

Elizabeth came to Steven and gave him a warm smile, then rested her hand on Christopher's. "I think we should speak with Luke. Will you join me?"

This was truly happening. They were marrying, not as he planned, but when had anything concerning Elizabeth ever gone as planned? "I'd be honored." Steven set Christopher on his feet and little fingers reached for him again.

Samantha snatched him up into her arms. "You come with me. After I change, I'll give you a bath. How does that sound?"

Christopher clapped. "Bubbles!"

Steven and Elizabeth headed in the direction Luke disappeared to, but once they were out of earshot from everyone, Steven stopped her. How could he tell her how amazing she was, never doubting that God brought them together and that a slip of paper wouldn't change anything. God brought Elizabeth into his life when he needed her the most.

Elizabeth looked into Steven's dark eyes so full of emotion. She wanted to run her hand along his jaw to soothe him but held back, not wanting to stop him from speaking. He doubted her. She sensed it at city hall, but did he doubt her still? Either way, she was becoming a bit anxious herself and wanted to start her life with Steven, to allow the children to come to know and love him as she had. She marveled at how his love unexpectedly swept through her heart, leaving her grateful as she stood on the eve of their wedding.

"Thank you." He finally spoke.

She reached up, her fingers touching his jaw, and her heart swelled. His words held a deeper meaning and perhaps he'd share them with her, but for now, the promise of their future waited for the rising sun. "Tomorrow."

"Tomorrow." Steven opened the door for her. Luke sat on a bench facing the woods, his shoulders slumped.

Elizabeth made her way to her son, feeling the temperature contrast from the house to the deck. The humidity was oppressive. She tucked her hair behind her ear. "We thought you might want some company." Steven waited for her to be seated then sat alongside her.

Luke sat up, rigid, saying nothing.

They sat quietly for a moment as she studied her son, contemplating how he might be feeling and what she might say, praying she didn't fail him. "I know this has come as a shock, finding out Steven and I are marrying, and you coming here." She took his small hand into hers. "We love each other and want to spend the rest of our lives together."

Luke glanced at Steven, then met her gaze. "But yesterday you said you didn't know if you loved him. Said you were scared to."

How would she explain? She thought she had time to explore her feelings for Steven, but learning the truth of his condition made her face them, and quickly. "God opened my eyes and my heart. I believe God's plan for us includes Steven in our lives."

Steven slid his palm around hers and began to speak as she smiled at their linked hands: Luke's, hers, and Steven's. Soon they'd be a family. "I know this is sudden, but I love your mom and I've come to love you and Christopher. I want to be there for you, to take care of you, provide for you."

"You don't have to be married to do those things."

"Okay, the truth. When I came to visit you and your mom, I had so much fun I didn't want to leave. Actually, I would have done anything to stay, but I felt I needed to walk away because I have cancer."

"You see, sweetheart," Elizabeth squeezed Luke's hand. "I felt the Lord telling me there was something wrong with Steven and I needed to find him."

Luke's brows wrinkled. "You don't seem

sick." He glanced between them. "How sick are you?"

Elizabeth looked to Steven for help. She didn't want to tell her son that the man she wanted him to love might die, leaving them as Chris had done. *Lord, please, how would I handle losing Steven? How would Luke if he begins to love him in return?* Should she hide the truth?

Steven answered for her. "One of my friends, Mike, he's inside the house, he's going to get me in to see a specialist. I've been putting it off for some time but now I want to go."

"Because of us?"

Steven nodded. "I've always wanted a family and you boys make me want to be your dad. And your mom..." He looked to her and smiled. "She captured my heart so long ago. I want to be her husband."

Luke's brow wrinkled again and questions fluttered across his face. Questions she was afraid to answer because he'd surely ask them. Her oldest was a deep thinker and sensitive to feelings of others around him. Could he read her now and sense her fear of hurting him?

Her son looked at Steven dead on. "Why marry my mom so fast? Are you pretty bad off or something? Like, going to die?"

The warm and loving smile Steven wore faded into a slight frown as he looked toward the woods. She didn't know what he saw there. Perhaps it was his answer, or the uncertainty of his future, but he stared for some time and pain gripped Elizabeth's chest as she watched distress cloud his eyes.

"I don't want to, Luke, but it's up to the Lord."

Her heart gave way to feelings and emotions that had all but died with Chris. But as much as she'd loved Chris, he was gone, and Steven was here. She ached to hold Steven. To love *him*. To give *him* a child. But would death tear them apart before they lived?

Chapter Nineteen

Early the next morning, before night gave way to the break of day, Steven sat on the same bench where he told Luke about his cancer and desperately tried to convince himself he wasn't as ill as the doctors had said. But the look of fear on the young boy's face pierced Steven's heart. Was it right of him to put his needs before Elizabeth and her children, forcing them to live though such heartache and pain once again? Regardless of the outcome of his treatment, it was a rough road ahead, but was he willing to hurt the ones he loved the most?

Steven stared at the trees shadowed in darkness, the peace of the early-morning hours settling around him. Insects vied to be heard while the small propane lamp he brought outside sizzled in the air. A single croak sounded to his right. He squinted in that direction and spied a toad. "Seems it's just you and me."

"Not quite."

Steven turned toward Elizabeth's voice, surprised she'd be up at this hour. "Everything all right?" She sank to the bench, the blanket he covered her with yesterday morning as a sign of love and commitment hanging over her shoulders. With all of the bedrooms in the house filled, Elizabeth and Christopher took his room while he moved into the smallest of six, the one he used mostly for storage. But it mattered little to him as long as Elizabeth and the boys were near.

"Yes, everything is fine. Christopher wanted a sip of water. I passed Nicole coming from the bathroom. It seems you're not the only one awake."

"Did Christopher fall back to sleep?"

"Soundly. Little snores drifted after me as I left the room."

He smiled, picturing the little tyke sound asleep in bed. If he'd been awake, he would have chased after his mother. Christopher's exuberance came to mind, but it was Luke's expression earlier in the day that filled his thoughts. His smile fell. "You do know the most important thing in my life is you, the boys, and your happiness?"

"I know," she said, leaning into him. "My happiness consists of obtaining a marriage license in a few hours."

He wrapped his arm around her, terrified to say the words plaguing his thoughts. She nestled her head against his chest. His mouth became dry and he swallowed against a lump in his throat.

"What is it, Steven?" she whispered. "You're too quiet."

He hesitated. Not because she didn't love him—he was certain she had or she wouldn't be with him now—but because the answer he feared was too real. "Are you sure you want to get married? You still have time to change your mind. Luke—"

"He's trying to take it all in. Figure things out. Give him time. I know he cares about you."

"I had to be honest with him about the cancer and I felt it needed to come from me."

"I know, and your honesty is one of the reasons I admire you. I admit though, I wasn't sure how to tell him. I was afraid even."

"Why?"

"It's hard for Luke to let people in. I was afraid he'd distance himself from you when I want him to love you like I do."

"Even if Luke distances himself, it won't stop me from loving him."

She sat up and gazed into his eyes. "There isn't anyone more aware of this than me." She reached up and cupped his face with her hand. "I want to be your wife, Steven. There are only a few things in this life I'm sure of—God, my family's love, and yours."

Steven pulled her into his arms, feeling the full impact of this moment as he held her close, stopping the waves of doubt once again.

"I love you, Steven. More than I ever thought possible."

And he'd love her to his last breath.

Elizabeth stared down at the marriage license

in her hands for the second time, unable to contain her happiness. If it hadn't shone on her face, then the kiss she planted on Steven's lips at city hall would have been a sure sign. The woman who refused to present them with a license yesterday chuckled at her excitement and wished them well. Now sitting in the passenger side of the car as Steven drove to her new home, his enthusiasm matched her own.

"Mike and Susan need to leave in an hour to make it to the hospital on time." He glanced at her. "Is that all right?"

"Will the pastor be there?"

"Mike texted me while we were waiting for the license and said he arrived."

She smiled up at him. "Well then, all I have to do is change."

When they arrived at the house, Steven rushed to her door and opened it. Taking her into his arms, he kissed her soundly. She touched her lips and giggled. Heavens, the man could kiss!

She recalled the other morning after they agreed to marry and how lost in his kisses she became. Her face warmed at the thought.

He leaned close as they climbed the back deck steps. "You're blushing. Should I call you the blushing bride?"

"Don't tease me." She pointed a finger at him. In an instant her feet came from beneath her as Steven lifted her into his arms. She gripped the marriage license tightly within her hand. "What on earth are you doing? Put me down."

"What does it look like? I'm carrying you over the threshold." And he did, as if she weighed a feather. He set her on her feet and drew her close. Steven bent and whispered, "Hurry. I can't wait another minute."

"Then you might need to release me." She countered.

"Just this once because I plan to never let you go again."

"I'm counting on it." She gave his cheek a kiss and left for the stairs, her heart full.

Fifteen minutes later, Elizabeth looked at herself in the mirror. Her sister stood by her side wearing an emerald gown, displaying her thin frame. "You look stunning as always."

"You look beautiful, Lizzy. Like a real princess."

She wrapped long strands of her hair around her finger, twirling the ends to give them a slight curl. "Does my makeup look all right? I don't have time for a touch-up."

"You're perfect."

"Hardly." Elizabeth said, insecurities creeping into her thoughts. She turned away from her reflection. "What happens if I'm not enough? What happens if…"

Her sister touched her bare arm. "Steven has loved you all these years. Nothing will be able to pull him away. Not even you."

Elizabeth nodded. "Thank you. Thank you for bringing the boys, for being here." She wiped her eyes with her fingers.

"I wouldn't be anywhere else. Now, don't smear your makeup." She smiled, collecting her hand. "Ready?"

Elizabeth inhaled and ran her free hand down the soft tulle of her gown. "As ready as I'll ever be."

Sam led her to the top of the stairwell, which hid her from the view of others, and stopped. "Once the music begins, you know what to do. Phillip will be waiting at the bottom of the stairs." Sam hugged her firmly and kissed her cheek, then descended the stairs.

"This is it," she whispered to herself, recalling Phillip's tears yesterday when she asked if he would walk her down the aisle. Phillip was only a few years older than she, but he'd come to be more than just a brother-in-law. The pain of losing Chris brought them closer and Phillip had become a rock for her, never stopped pointing her to Christ. She couldn't have imagined being married without Phillip's blessing or having him by her side.

The music from the living room drifted to her ears and she knew it was time. "Lord, please bless our marriage. Let it be full in years." She descended the stairs to find Phillip's smile and outstretched arm, waiting. She tucked her arm within his.

"You look lovely, Elizabeth," Phillip whispered and squeezed her hand.

"I'm nervous," she whispered in return, certain Steven regarded her as she moved toward him and the pastor. She had yet to look at Steven.

"I know. You're biting her lip." Her gaze jumped to his and he chuckled under his breath. "Just breathe."

"Mama!" Christopher called and Elizabeth looked to where he sat next to Sam, waving. She waved and blew him a kiss before meeting Steven.

"Who gives this woman to be wed?" Pastor Bruce asked.

"I do." Phillip said, unfolding his arm from hers. He kissed her cheek and tears filled her eyes. She watched as Phillip sat next to Luke. Steven edged up beside her in front of the pastor.

"Let us begin." Pastor Bruce grinned. "Dearly beloved, we are gathered here today for the joining of two lives, Steven Moore and Elizabeth Roberts…"

Elizabeth's bottom lip quivered and she bit down slightly. She glanced at Steven for the first time. Not only was he handsome, he was a man of integrity, of great devotion, but most importantly, a man of God.

He turned to her, moisture collecting in his eyes as he took the ring from the pastor and placed it in her palm. Her eyes widened. He had saved their rings after all these years. She slid Steven's ring on his finger and her heart swelled with love.

"Do you, Elizabeth, take Steven, to be your husband, to have and to hold from this day forward, for better or for worse, for richer, for poorer, in sickness and in health, to love and to cherish until death do you part."

"I do," she said against the tears in her throat.

Steven took her ring from the pastor, held her hand, then slid the ring on her finger.

Pastor Bruce closed his Bible. "Steven has asked to give his own vows to Elizabeth at this time."

Elizabeth looked at him with wide eyes. "I didn't know."

Steven met her gaze, love radiating from his dark eyes. A tear slipped down her cheek. He collected her other hand and placed it within his. "I promised God long ago that if He ever gave us a second chance of love, I would never let a day go by where you didn't know how deeply my love for you ran. In front of these witnesses, I, Steven, promise you, Elizabeth, to be your loving and faithful husband. To be by your side to share whatever comes our way. We will face it together. Whether it be happiness, I will rejoice with you, if in sorrow, I will be your comfort. I will forgive you as Christ has forgiven me, love you as Christ loves the church, and always remind you of the Lord's promises. For it is because of the Lord we live, and we are thankful He's restored our lives together. So from this day forward, I devote my life and my love to you until death do us part."

"Oh, Steven." Elizabeth placed her hand over her mouth, failing to keep her emotions in check. He took a step, closing the distance between them, and wiped her tears with his fingers.

"You may kiss your bride, Steven," Pastor Bruce announced.

Steven lifted her chin with his finger and

kissed her softly, lingering. When he pulled away, she yearned for him to hold her, for the opportunity to share how much his vows meant to her, for more of his kisses. She'd have to wait. Now was the time to share her joy with her friends and family.

Hopefully Luke shared in their joy.

Mike and Susan were the first to congratulate them. Susan hugged her then swiped at her tears while Mike and Steven shook hands. Susan unsnapped her purse and pulled out a tissue. "We are so happy for you." She dabbed at her cheeks.

"May I?" Mike asked, pulling Elizabeth into his arms for a quick hug. "I'm sorry for how secretive I had been about Steven's health. I hope you'll forgive me."

Steven clapped his shoulder. "And I'm sorry for how I reacted when she found out. I should have apologized to you sooner."

Elizabeth's smile grew. "It was God who brought me here, to Steven, to this moment. I'm not sorry for one second."

Steven placed an arm around her waist and kissed her temple. "I love you," he whispered, before turning his attention to Mike. "Can you grab a bite to eat before you leave?"

"I wish we could, but I'll be rushing to make my shift if we leave now. We'll be seeing the happy couple before too long I'm sure." Mike clasped Susan's hand and met her gaze. "Ready to go?"

Susan nodded, and while they said their good-byes, Elizabeth caught a glimpse of Luke and

Christopher on the other side of the cake table filling their plates next to Phillip and Sam.

Two hours later after John and Nicole left, Elizabeth plopped down next to Luke on the couch where he was playing a game on his phone, thankful to be back into a T-shirt and comfortable jeans. "You've been a little quiet. Do you want to talk about what's on your mind?"

"Who said I was thinking about anything?"

She cocked her head to the side and smirked. "Luke James Roberts—"

Luke dropped the phone to his lap. "You know, I sound like a bank robber in the olden days when you call me that. Why did you and dad decide to call me Luke James anyway?"

Elizabeth could sense her son didn't want to share what was really on his mind, or perhaps speaking about Chris was the only way he knew how. She said a quick prayer for her son and for words to bring him comfort for the weeks ahead. No matter how hard he tried to hide it, her marrying Steven was difficult for him.

"Actually, it was your father's idea to call you after his great-grandfather, Henry James."

"But that sounds like Grandpop's name."

"And there's a reason, your grandpop is named after him. The name James is a family name. You never know, maybe one day you'll name your son James." She leaned into his shoulder.

"That's pretty cool."

"And you probably didn't know this about your brother, but I named him Christopher Henry James Roberts. I used the family name James, Henry after your grandpop, then Christopher after your father."

"So you couldn't decide what to name him?" Luke smiled.

"Precisely." She elbowed him. "How old are you anyway, finding out my secret."

He shrugged. "Without dad it's hard to make decisions."

Elizabeth thought about this for a moment. What was her son struggling with? What type of decisions does an eleven-year-old boy have to make? "Can I help?"

"Maybe later." Luke jumped to his feet.

Elizabeth sat ramrod straight. "Where are you going?"

"Outside. Uncle Phillip said he'd take me fishing. He also said you and Steven were leaving for the night and since it's getting late, I want to hurry."

Elizabeth stared after him. What had happened? And where were she and Steven going? As far as she knew, they had no honeymoon plans. Actually, she hadn't thought past the wedding.

"Hey," Sam said, sitting across from her in an oversize leather chair. Her hair still held soft ringlets that cascaded down her back and over her shoulders. She tucked several strands of brown hair behind her ear.

"Luke just informed me that Steven and I are leaving tonight for our honeymoon. I thought we were planning to stay here in Monticello. Would you happen to know anything about it? And speaking of Steven, have you seen him? After John and Nicole left, he went upstairs to change and then disappeared."

"You haven't seen him? That's strange."

Elizabeth studied her sister, a hint of a smile registered on her face. They were up to something and she hated not knowing. "What do ya'll have up your sleeves?"

"Who? Me?" Sam touched her chest in mock surprise. She was never good at keeping up pretenses.

Elizabeth laughed. "All right. Where's this husband of mine?"

Sam rose from the couch, took the stairs, and came back a moment later with a travel bag she'd left at her home in Florida. "I've packed you a few things, new things."

Elizabeth met her sister in the large foyer. She took the bag and looked to the front door. "Where am I going? And what about the children?"

"Christopher is asleep, and you heard Luke, he's fishing. We have everything under control." Sam pushed her to the door and opened it. "When you walk down the steps, turn to your left and follow the walkway."

Elizabeth glanced in the direction her sister indicated. She knew what this meant, yet was she ready? Marriage yes, but this? Her mouth grew dry. She turned back to her sister.

Fear must have shown on her face for Sam hugged her. "There is no fear in love, because perfect love casts out fear. You'll see." She pulled her at arm's length. "Now go to your husband, he's waiting."

As Elizabeth took each step down the lighted walkway toward a home nestled within the woods, her fear grew and multiplied along with her insecurities. She had taken comfort that there was to be no honeymoon, how wrong she'd been. Not that she didn't want to be with Steven romantically. She did, very much so, but would she disappoint him? Her twenty-year-old thin body had vanished and in its place, stretch marks and wrinkles filled its spaces. Would she be able to keep his attention after the initial honeymoon was over? By the time she reached the front door, her heart was too heavy. She couldn't ring the doorbell.

She had to tell Steven the distress she felt no matter how difficult sharing her fears would be. She had learned from her time with Chris how important honesty was in any marriage, and how quickly one could fall apart if it wasn't protected. She wasn't willing to allow anyone or anything to come between her and Steven, even if she had to lay her heart bare.

The door opened and Elizabeth startled.

Steven's smile faded and the look of concern on his face pierced her. "Elizabeth."

Unexpected tears filled her eyes.

Chapter Twenty

Steven drew Elizabeth inside and closed the door behind them. He took her bag and dropped it where they stood. Whatever upset his wife, his heart ached at the look in her eyes. Was it fear? "It's all right," he said, pulling her into his arms. He stroked her hair in hopes of bringing her comfort. He never imagined his wedding vows to comfort his wife in sorrow would begin on their honeymoon night.

"Let's go into the living room and sit down." Steven led her to the couch then slid beside her. She gave him a weary glance, leaning her head against his chest. He tucked her silk-like tresses over her shoulder.

Once again he thought of how their relationship over the years had never been predictable, or in Steven's timing. Perhaps tonight was no different. No matter how much he wanted to be with his wife, if they didn't consummate their marriage, he'd hold her close and cherish their first night together as husband and wife. The rest would come in time.

She lifted her head and began to look around.

"Would you like to show me around?" She looked to the high, vaulted ceilings, then something must have caught her eye because the corners of her mouth lifted slightly.

"What?" He couldn't help but smile. She was so beautiful. He drank in the sight of her, and the tiny freckle on her lip beckoned to be kissed.

She turned to him. "The picture. The one of the silver music box. I have it still." She rose and stood in front of the black and white print hanging on the wall. "It's on a table in the condo. You gave it to me."

Steven's brows furrowed. Her last statement sounded like... "Do you not remember?"

She glanced at her hands for a moment before meeting his gaze. "Maybe I should have told you sooner. Most of my memories have returned, but there are a few that seem a bit hazy. Like I remember you giving it to me, but I can't recall the occasion."

Odd how after all this time such an admission could bring a jolt of sadness, even though Elizabeth now stood in front of him as his wife. "It was my wedding present to you. I gave it to you early, the day after your parent's accident, in hopes it could bring a smile to your face."

Elizabeth held out her hand to him and he went to her, needing her reassuring touch. "And it did, even when I couldn't remember, it brought joy to my heart." She wrapped his arm around her and they both stared at the photo she took. "I don't enjoy photography like I once did. I believe I still have an eye for it, but the desire is no longer there."

His chin rested on the top of her head. Her hair smelled of outdoors and mixed berries. Kissing her hair, he inhaled once again. "What else has changed?"

Her body rested against him. "I've become an introvert. I'd rather stay in the middle of the woods with my family than be anywhere else."

They never discussed where they'd live after they married, but he had hoped it would be here, in the home he always imagined filled with love and children, which never came to fruition. "Speaking of the woods and family, where would you like to live? We can live here or somewhere else if you'd like. I'm not asking you to give up your home by any means, but I don't think I could live in Chris's..."

She turned in his arms and met his gaze. "I would never ask you to. Besides, I'd much rather stay here. From the first time I visited this place twelve years ago, I could picture myself here with you, and a home full of children."

Her announcement stilled him and the air seemed to have been sucked from the room. *Lord, you put the desire in my heart to build this house, but I thought it was for Jess and Steven. Was it for Elizabeth and our children? Will we adopt as we have always dreamed?"*

"Steven, you look pale." She touched his cheek with the back of her hand, then his forehead. "Are you all right?"

He recovered quickly, forcing a smile. "The room seems a little warm all of a sudden." He released her and checked the thermostat, dropping it down a notch.

"Are you sure you're all right?"

"Fine, now let me show you around." He took her by the waist and guided her through the open layout of the home, first the chefs' kitchen with stainless steel appliances, and finally the master bedroom he planned for them to share. Earlier in the day he'd carried a bouquet of flowers from their wedding and placed them on a nightstand by the bed.

Elizabeth fingered the soft petals. "I love white roses. You hadn't forgotten."

"You're not a woman that's easily forgotten." The Lord knew he tried, more times than he could remember. Perhaps God didn't want him to forget.

Elizabeth leaned down and smelled her beautiful bouquet. From the moment she stepped into the house, Steven began loving her and she took comfort in his presence no matter how tangled a mess her emotions. She didn't know how this evening would end, but before it went any farther, she needed to be honest and share her fears and insecurities.

She inhaled another breath of the sweet aroma, and then turned to face her husband. He stood a few yards away. The color in his face had returned but his eyes grew darker as he watched her, a yearning passed over his gaze. She walked to the bed unsure of herself, unsure of what to do next. She sat on the edge of the bed and patted the mattress next to her. "There's something I need to share with you."

Steven took slow, deliberate steps and she guessed he was trying to decipher her feelings, but how could he when she wasn't sure of them herself. They sat together hand in hand and he waited for her to speak. She tried to say the words but they wouldn't come. They sat in uncomfortable silence.

Steven lifted her hand to his mouth and pressed a gentle kiss to her knuckles. "I'm willing to wait..."

And he would, she knew, but hearing him say the words only drew her more to him. "I'm scared, Steven, not only of sharing this bed, but of something coming between us."

"Nothing could ever come between us."

"I used to think that with Chris and me." She looked down at their joined hands and swallowed. She forged on. "We need to be honest with each other, about everything, regardless. We can't be afraid to hurt each other by the way we think or feel."

"Of course."

"I'm also talking about your cancer. I want to know, Steven. I don't want you to hide anything from me and then by chance have me find something out through Mike."

Steven released her hand and stood. He walked to the large window that looked out toward the main house. "For the last two years, Elizabeth, I've been somewhat in denial about my cancer. I've fought to keep the thoughts away, especially at the prospect that..."

...*that you're dying*. Elizabeth rose from the

bed and walked to him, her heart aching. She couldn't lose him. "I need this," she begged. "I need you to love me enough to tell me."

Steven turned from the window, meeting her gaze. "What do you want me to tell you—that I'm frightened? That I've waited my entire life to love you freely, to make you my wife, only to realize I'm scared to death of losing you again."

Elizabeth cupped his cheek. "Yes."

Steven placed his hand over hers.

She swallowed against her tears. "And I'm so frightened to lose you, to death, to another woman. What happens if I'm not enough for you, that after all this time you'll regret marrying me?"

"I promise you, Elizabeth, as long as God breathes life into my lungs, you will always be enough. I will never stray. There will never be a hint of regret on my lips or in my heart. Today you became my wife. You have no idea how happy you've made me. You are all I'll ever need or want."

There were no words to express how she felt so she allowed her heart to lead. She slipped her hand into his and walked him to the bed in a silent invitation.

Steven ran his thumb along her jaw, across her lips and gazed into her eyes before claiming the first kiss of many, gently as if it were a privilege.

Chapter Twenty-One

Steven rolled over and took in the sight of his wife's hair as it fell across her bare back onto the bed. His gaze traveled to her hips where the sheet began. What they shared during the last two days overwhelmed him, but it was God who amazed him. Their marriage was not only physical, but spiritual. They were one, and that oneness brought glory to their Creator.

He smiled. The urge to wake his wife grew. Instead, he climbed out of bed, dressed, and headed into the kitchen. He glanced at their shoes by the back door, enjoying the memory of holding hands as they strolled through the woods, reminiscing, kissing, and talking about the children. The pleasure on her face when she heard the trickle of water at the creek beyond the house still fazed him. He watched as she ran her fingers through the stream, the way the sunlight peeked through the trees and shone around her. With every movement she made, his senses came alive, anew, as if he was discovering what it meant to breathe, to live, to love for the first time.

"Good morning."

Steven looked up to find Elizabeth wrapped in a sheet, standing in the bedroom doorway. "I thought I'd shower before we head to the house. I know Sam and Phillip wanted to leave early to head back."

He forced himself to stay put.

"What are you doing?"

What was he doing besides standing in the kitchen looking like a goof, doing absolutely nothing but daydreaming about her. "Nothing." He continued to force himself to stay put.

She took a step through the doorway, her hair draped to one side, her lips turned into a perfect frown. "Is everything all right?"

He was on his honeymoon for a few more hours. He didn't need willpower. Steven marched over to Elizabeth, swooped her up into his arms, and kissed her with all the passion he felt.

"The woods are so beautiful. I love it." Elizabeth sat on the sofa across from Phillip and Samantha. "In a strange way, I feel closer to God here, like I'm standing in His very presence."

Steven thought so too. He gave Elizabeth's hand a gentle squeeze. "It's one of the reasons I built on this property."

"That's the way I feel when I travel to Goma." Phillip set Christopher down from his lap. The little boy ran from the room. "In a couple of years when Jeremiah is older, we plan to go back."

Elizabeth's grip tensed at this. "What for? I thought you weren't going back. You said that this was the last time."

Phillip gave Elizabeth a reassuring smile. "God holds our futures as well as those poor children in His hands. Who would I be if I let fear steal the joy God has for me?" He looked to Samantha and she smiled in return. "We want to adopt another child. Maybe two this time. Juwonya is older, almost an adult now, and we still want little ones running around the house. As many as God will give us."

That was exactly the way Steven felt. He glanced at Elizabeth from the corner of his eye. Was it still Elizabeth's dream to adopt as it was his? How he missed holding and caring for infants, the only reason he missed the hospital.

Steven shook the thought from his mind. The reality was, he wasn't sure how much time he had, months, years. It would be wrong to adopt. Having another child was out of the question. He would never purposely leave Elizabeth to raise another child alone.

Phillip stood and yawned slightly. "We should be getting on the road before I get too relaxed." He glanced around. "Where are those boys?"

Samantha stood and followed her husband. "I'll start putting our bags in the car."

"I'll get the suitcases." Steven rose. "Besides, your husband might need a little help. I have a feeling Christopher is hiding to keep you here longer."

Samantha watched Elizabeth climb the stairs before turning to him. "Your home is lovely, but it's a mansion. It might take us a week." She leaned into him. "Now, if my sister gives you a hard time, you know where to reach me." She gave him a hug as Phillip strolled into the living room, Christopher hanging sideways off his shoulder. "Phillip and I are so happy for you both."

"Thank you, Samantha, it means a lot, especially for all that you both have done to make our wedding possible."

"It was our pleasure," Phillip tilted his head meeting Christopher eye to eye. "You be a good boy for your daddy and mommy." Christopher's happy smile widened and he jerked his head in a yes.

"Good." Phillip set his nephew down on his feet and planted a kiss on his forehead.

Elizabeth descended the stairs with Luke in tow, his hand shoved in his pockets. Her face shone with irritation, which then vanished as she moved toward her sister. "Oh, Sam, I'm going to miss you so much."

Steven lifted two of the suitcases while Phillip gathered the other two. "Luke, can you grab your aunt and uncle a few waters from the fridge so they'll have something to drink until they decide to stop?"

Luke glanced between him and Phillip, then with a sigh, dragged himself into the kitchen.

Phillip and Steven reached the back deck and Phillip stopped him. "Like I told Elizabeth, Luke will be fine. He'll need time to adjust. That's all." Phillip glanced back to the house. Luke was nowhere in sight. "Come on, Luke. We need to go." He met Steven's gaze one final time and whispered, "He's a wonderful boy. Don't let him fool you." Luke appeared in the doorway so they continued to the car.

Saying good-bye was difficult on Elizabeth, but not as much as it was on Luke. Steven observed how Luke acted when he thought no one was looking, how he wiped his eyes or how his fingers turned white from the pressure with which he hugged Phillip.

As they drove away, Steven's heart hurt for the boy. His entire life had changed within a week. What could he do to help him adjust? What did a family do to bond? He was married for such a short time before his wife and son died, he didn't know. "So…what do we want to do tonight? Luke, have any ideas?"

Luke's voice broke. "Be left alone." He ran into the house.

Elizabeth shifted Christopher on her hip and started to go after him, but Steven took Christopher from her arms. "Let him go. He has a lot to adjust to."

"He knows better, Steven."

"I know."

She nodded and when they entered the house, a door from one of the upstairs bedrooms slammed shut. She inhaled a long breath.

Elizabeth knocked lightly on Luke's door in

case he was asleep, although it was early in the afternoon. With no answer, she cracked the door and peeked in. Luke lay on his side, a blanket covering him. He still wore his shoes from earlier in the day. She wanted to hold him, take away any fears or pain he might be feeling. She wanted to understand what he was going through. As she gingerly closed the door, she prayed for wisdom and for her son to speak to her.

"Luke's asleep?" Steven patted the couch next to him as she descended the stairs, his arm resting across Christopher's sleeping form. A smile fluttered over her little boy's face.

She looked to Steven. *Yes, son, dreams do come true.* She sunk into the sofa beside him and leaned her head against his shoulder. "I'm not sure what Phillip and my sister did to the kids, but they're tuckered out. You know, I'm kinda tuckered out myself."

"Then close your eyes and rest."

"I might take you up on your offer." She yawned, but as soon as her eyes closed, the doorbell rang, then a hard knock on the door followed. She jumped up. "Steven?"

Steven scooted Christopher onto the couch. "Stay here." He hurried to the door and swung it wide.

A young man she guessed was in his early twenties stood at the entrance, worry marring his face. "Please." He grabbed Steven's shirt with both hands. "Somethin' is wrong. The midwife told me to hurry."

Elizabeth froze where she stood as Steven ran past. A moment later he hurried out the door carrying a bag. The man followed quickly behind him, leaving her stunned. She peeked outside. Dust billowed in the air as the cars raced along the driveway's rocky trail. She slowly closed the door, yet she was anything but calm. She palmed her chest, willing her heart to settle. Movement to her right caught her attention. Luke looked on from the stairwell.

"What's going on?"

Her hand fell to her side. "I'm not sure. How long have you been standing there?"

Luke made his way down the stairs and sat in a double sized leather chair. "Heard a noise." He shrugged. "Wanted to see what was going on. Who was that?"

"I'm not sure," she glanced at the door once again, "but he made it sound urgent. The man needed a doctor. I'm assuming it has to do with the birth of his child."

"A baby? Steven's a baby doctor? I thought you said he helps babies who are born too early, like Christopher."

"I guess he does more than I know, but yes, he does."

"So he's still a doctor even if he doesn't work anymore."

"He is, and a very good doctor, too. He has saved many lives."

"I bet he hasn't saved everyone."

Luke's remark stilled her. He had no idea how

close his comment came. She never shared much about his sister, Katherine, mostly because she didn't want to relive the hurt of losing her, and then when Chris died, she didn't want to think about death or deal with the memories. God used her family to help her through. Maybe she could help Luke through this time by helping him to understand who Steven is and how much their past intertwined by God's hand. "Luke, let's pray for the safety of the baby Steven's trying to help, then I'd like to share something with you."

Elizabeth held out her hands to Luke and he scooted to the edge of the chair. Hand in hand they prayed. "Dear, Father, we ask for the safety of this newborn child. Give Steven wisdom. Give the mother strength. Direct and guide them, for we pray these things in your name's sake. Amen."

Luke released her hands and sat back into the chair. "What is it you want to tell me?"

Elizabeth said a quick prayer of her own. "Do you remember when I told you Steven and I knew each other in college?"

He nodded. "Yeah."

"Well, we were boyfriend and girlfriend. We even planned to get married."

Luke leaned forward. "You didn't marry him? Why?"

"I was scared. I ran away. Then sometime later I met your dad. We got married and I became pregnant."

"With, Katherine, my sister."

"Yes, but before it was time for her to be born, I had a terrible accident that caused me to go into a coma. Do you know what a coma is?"

"Mom, how old do you think I am?"

"Of course you do." She took a breath and pressed on. "Well, Katherine was born while I was in the coma. She had to go to a special place in the hospital for small children called NICU. There was a doctor who took care of Katherine, watched over her, made sure she ate, helped her to grow like she was supposed to. I didn't know at the time, but the doctor was Steven."

"Steven said he knew dad. That he came to the hospital when I was born."

"Yes, Steven was there as well when you were born. Your dad knew Steven as well."

"Were they friends?"

How could she explain? Give me the words, Lord. "They weren't really friends to begin with. I believe they held a great respect for each other, and having respect for someone can eventually bring on friendship. I do believe though over the years, both your father and Steven thought highly of each other."

"Mom, can I ask you a question?"

"Sure."

"I know this might be hard for you since you don't talk about her much, but how did Katherine die?"

The despair of losing Katherine swept over her and she shivered. "She had a breathing problem and Steven couldn't save her."

"Steven was there? What did dad do?"

"What could he do? There was nothing anyone could do." She closed her eyes for a moment, fighting back the pain she seldom visited, and said a silent prayer for the child Steven was bringing into the world. *Please, Lord, keep that child safe.*

Her son's arms wrapped around her neck and she opened her eyes to see the loving child she knew. "I'm sorry, mom."

She hugged him tight. "I love you, Luke. There is no one or nothing that can ever take my love away from you."

He sniffled and squeezed her close in return. "I miss dad."

"I know you do and I miss him too."

He looked at her then, eyes searching her face. "You do?"

"Of course, but like what had happened with Katherine, there was nothing I could do. Nothing anyone could have done. But I do know as we're sitting here, talking about Katherine and your father, they're up in heaven, waiting for us to one day join them. But until then, we need to keep on living by loving other people."

"Like Steven."

"Yes, like Steven. I'm not sure how you feel about him, but as you mentioned to me before, my heart has enough room inside to love both your dad and Steven. You know what? I think Steven feels the same way about you. Did you know he had a little boy who died, too? Steven still loves him, but his heart is big enough to love you and Christopher. That's one *big* heart if you ask me."

Luke ran his fingers through his hair just like Chris used to do. "I'll try to love him, but all I can do now is respect him like dad did."

"Fair enough." The front door swung open. She glanced up to Steven's weary expression. Dread filled her belly. She went to him quickly. "What happened?"

"The umbilical cord was wrapped around the baby's neck. I don't know how long the mother had been pushing or how long the baby had been without air. When I got her out, she wasn't breathing. I couldn't let her die." His voice cracked with emotion. "I brought her back...but it wasn't me...it was God."

She clung to him and him to her, both in their own way experiencing Katherine's death all over again. It wasn't until later when the house was still that Steven shared when he lost Katherine and how a part of him died with her. Elizabeth hadn't known the pain he felt or how he'd blamed himself for her death even though he had done all he could. But there, within their shared tears, they found comfort and the lost pieces of their hearts.

Chapter Twenty-Two

Falling in and out of sleep, Steven rolled over seeking Elizabeth's warmth only to be met with resistance. Something hard and bony pressed against his chest. He opened one eye to find Christopher sleeping upside down right between him and Elizabeth. His small foot shifted to Steven's ribs. Deep joy enveloped Steven as he watched his wife and son sleep. The rise and fall of their chests, the way Elizabeth's mouth parted and how light her lashes were without makeup, the way Christopher sucked his thumb. How wonderful it felt to think this sweet child had missed him and couldn't wait until morning.

Elizabeth stirred and his gaze returned to her. She smiled lazily, her eyes blinked then closed. "Good morning," she whispered, moving closer only to find, as he had, a heel poking her stomach. Shock registered on her face.

He chuckled. "I don't mind."

"He's never done this at home."

Steven ran a finger along her forehead, smoothing out the wrinkles. "Perhaps he missed us.

He is in a new place. Maybe he needed to go to the bathroom." Steven immediately looked down at the sheet around Christopher's sleeping form. "Let's hope it wasn't the bathroom."

"You know, I've potty trained him and he can do it, but with us not being home, he's disinterested. Maybe we can get him into a routine. Want to help?"

"Did you say hitting balls in the front yard? Sure. I'm there."

Elizabeth chuckled. "Oh, I see. And there's no way to convince you otherwise?"

"I didn't say that…I think I can be convinced at the right price." He wiggled his brows.

"So we're bartering now, are we?"

"Let me tell you a little secret." Steven whispered and Elizabeth inched as close as she could with Christopher in-between. "For your ears only, but I have a thing for a certain blonde with exceptional turquoise eyes. If you find her, keep her close because she is my weakness. I'd do anything for her."

"I see. Thank you for your wise counsel." She bowed her head slightly and giggled. "Do you remember that time in college when we played Zechariah and Elizabeth and how awkward I looked with that pillow under my dress? I was simply pitiful as the mother of John the Baptist."

Steven rolled over and propped his hands behind his head. They'd been cast together and it was the first time they'd spoken to each other. He recalled her short blonde hair and how her beauty had captivated him. Later that year, Mike had set them up on a double date with John and Nicole and did he fall in love with her, hard. "Yeah, you were something else all right."

Elizabeth reached over and hit his arm. "What does that mean?"

"You were beautiful then as you are now, more so now."

"I'm not so sure about that. I was—"

Steven shifted to face her and ran his thumb slowly over her mouth. "Trust me. *I* should know." Steven glanced down at Christopher still sleeping between them, wishing now the little guy was in his own bed. "I think this conversation will need to resume later tonight."

Elizabeth smiled and her eyes sparkled. "I look forward to our conversation and our continued walk down memory lane."

"So do I, Mrs. Moore."

She threw the sheet to the side, rose and fingered her hair. "What shall we do today?"

"What do you think about fishing?"

"Sounds like fun. Luke loves to fish."

"I thought he might by the way his attention is constantly fixated on the water. If I had a bat and a ball, we could practice his hitting." He moved from the bed to the dresser and grabbed a shirt. "When do you want to head back to Miami? I think if Luke had his things, it would be a better transition for him instead of playing limbo between two houses."

"I'm not ready to leave. I like being secluded

from the world out here. Do you think we can get a few things for Luke and Christopher? I still have the gift card you gave me. I can always—"

Steven grabbed her waist and pulled her into his arms, lips almost touching. "You listen, wife of mine. Everything, and I mean everything that is mine is yours. You can do as you please. Tomorrow we'll go to the bank and add you on the account, and then we can go shopping for a few things. How does a bat and a few balls sound?" He kissed her gently, wanting to savor every second with this woman. "What do you say?" He lifted her chin with his finger and ran a trail of kisses along her jaw.

"Sebeen kiss Mommy. Me want kiss."

Steven stilled, his heart racing. "Tonight," he whispered in her ear. Christopher now bounced on the bed and held out his arms for him. Elizabeth's smile vanished and she shook her head, but before she could speak, he lifted the little boy into his arms. "Let's not jump on the bed. You can fall and get hurt. You don't want to fall and get hurt do you?"

Christopher nodded then shook his head. "No. Fall down."

Elizabeth gave a long sigh. "That's right. We don't want you to get hurt, okay. No jumping on the bed." She gathered her things and headed into the bathroom.

Steven set Christopher on his feet. "Let's get something to eat. What do you say? Hungry?" Christopher shouted *Eat!* as he ran from the room. Steven slipped his shirt on and entered the living room where Luke sat on the couch with his phone. "Hey, buddy, you ready to eat?"

Luke didn't glance up. "Yeah."

Steven paused. "Want to go fishing today?"

He shrugged, eyes never leaving his phone.

"Great." Steven ignored the I-don't-care attitude and entered the kitchen. The boy did care, he'd seen it when they first met, the times he watched his ball games, and the day they spent together at the house. Luke had begun to let him in, but how could he reach him when he not only closed the door, but slammed it shut?

The phone rang and Steven answered. "Hello."

"Hey, it's me." Mike sounded serious. "I called my friend at Moffitt. He's on vacation but said he'd squeeze you in after he returns."

Steven swallowed the knot in his throat. He'd been suppressing the fear nipping at his happiness. Why couldn't he avoid it altogether and enjoy his life with Elizabeth, this dream he was living in? He didn't want to think about anything except grabbing hold of these moments forever.

"Steven? Did you hear me?"

"Um…yeah. I heard you. When is the appointment?"

"A few weeks. The first of June."

He should be grateful, it was what he wanted, but he wasn't ready to face reality when he was sure of what the outcome would be. "Thanks, Mike."

"Steven, you're doing the right thing, for

Elizabeth and those boys."

He leaned into the counter and closed his eyes. "I don't want to think about this, not today."

"I know, buddy. I understand."

There was a long pause. Steven opened his eyes and looked at the fridge. "Hey, I gotta go. I was about to make breakfast."

"Sure thing. I'm heading to radiology. Talk to you later. And Steven?"

"Yeah?"

"I'm praying."

"Thanks." Steven hung up to find Elizabeth watching him. He forced a smile. "You know what? I think I'll head down to the fast food place that opened a couple of weeks ago. Is a breakfast platter fine for you and the boys?"

Something passed over her eyes but he blinked and it was gone. "That would be nice."

Steven went into the bedroom, changed into a pair of beige slacks, and grabbed the keys from his dresser, all while rethinking his promise to Elizabeth. How could he be open with his feelings and the fears once again plaguing him when he didn't want to face them himself?

The boys scurried out toward the water with fishing poles in hand. Elizabeth intertwined her fingers with Steven's as they strode side by side, following in the children's footsteps.

"I love you and the boys." Emotion strained

his voice.

She smiled, fighting against the rising questions. "They're wonderful, and so are you, but I'm a bit biased." Her gaze followed the children as they neared the water, Christopher stopping at the edge. She glanced up at Steven, his saddened expression stopped her. "Who called earlier? Something changed after you received that call."

His gaze seemed to trail after the children as if he wished he was there now, instead of answering her questions.

"Steven." He faced her. His brows dipped slightly. She looked him in the eye, needing to know the truth no matter the outcome. "Was it Mike? He wasn't able to get you an appointment?"

"No, he got me an appointment. It's in three weeks."

"This is great news." She took a step to him but his dark eyes flashed with concern. Or was it worry? "Steven, I'm here. You can talk to me." She continued, recalling his wedding vows. "'I will be by your side to share whatever comes our way. We will face it together whether it be happiness, I will rejoice with you, if in sorrow, I will be your comfort.'"

He closed the space between them. "I meant them. Every last word. I love you, Elizabeth, more than I could ever express."

"Share with me." She yearned, searching his eyes, eyes that drew her, strong, unrelenting, unbridled love, and fear shown clearly within those dark orbs.

His voice was nothing but a whisper, but his arms solid as he took her in an embrace. "You're my home. My life. What happens if they tell me there's no hope, that it's only a matter of time? I'm scared, Elizabeth. I'm scared to lose you."

Her heart raced and a memory of a time she too had given up hope came rushing back. Steven's words washed over her once again as they held each other close. "'Even though I walk through the valley of the shadow of death, I will fear no evil, for You are with me; Your rod and staff, they comfort me.'"

Chapter Twenty-Three

Elizabeth heard Christopher squeal in laughter from the other room. She said 'amen' and rose from her knees, wiping her tears from her cheek. Their time in Monticello was coming to an end and Steven had amazed her over these last three weeks, how he tried to help potty train Christopher or fished with Luke down at the pond. Steven's love for her children—their children, led her to her knees in thanksgiving more times than she could count, not only for Steven, but for all of them as a family. Today, they'd return to Miami where they'd drop off the children, then head to Moffitt the next morning.

Her gaze caught on the black suitcases waiting to be loaded by the bed, Christopher's blanket draped across. She lifted the blanket in her hand and walked out to the living room. "I think I have everything ready."

Steven looked up from the floor fighting back...laughter? Christopher peeked at her from behind his back.

Elizabeth planted her hands on her hips and pretended not to see her little boy. "Now, where's

Christopher?"

Christopher giggled and covered his mouth with his hand. Steven's wide smile warmed her. She pointed to Christopher. "There you are!" He ran and she chased after him, snagging him up in her arms. She planted kisses on his soft cheeks.

Steven rose and planted his own kiss on Christopher's forehead. "I'll load the car after I tell Luke we're about to head out." He climbed the stairs and Elizabeth spun her little boy in circles.

"Mommy, potty."

Elizabeth stopped quickly and Christopher giggled as he wobbled to the bathroom. She hurried to help him undress and scooted him to his potty chair. She turned on the water, which seemed to help, and leaned against the sink.

He began to hum. This was going to take a while.

Steven popped his head in. "Good job, Christopher! I'm so proud of you!"

"Do you need me?" Elizabeth asked.

"No, I was heading to the room to grab our bags when I heard the humming." He gave her a knowing smile. "Luke's getting the last of his things together."

"Sounds good. If you need me to do anything—"

Steven winked. "I know where you'll be."

She chuckled to herself and turned to the sink, looking at the happiness radiating from her rosy cheeks. She wasn't ready to go but she wouldn't admit it to Steven. She let out a small sigh. The last few weeks had been bliss, except for Luke's cold behavior toward Steven. Her husband had been nothing but understanding, telling her Luke would come around when he was ready. She hoped it was sooner rather than later, because once they visited Moffitt, things would change for them.

She glanced at Christopher who still hummed. "Did you go, sweetie?"

He shook his head. "Done."

"But you didn't go."

"Sebeen, help."

"He can't help right now, he's outside getting ready for our trip."

"He ishing?"

"No, sweetie. He's not fishing. He's putting the suitcases in the car. We're going to see Uncle Phillip and Aunt Sam. Are you excited?"

"I go ishing."

She chuckled. "You have one thing on your mind."

"Mo-o-o-om," Luke called.

Christopher leaned down and touched his toes, sat up, and repeated the motion.

Luke called her again. "I'm going to see what Brother needs. Christopher, you stay here and go potty. I'll be back in a minute." She entered the living room, but Luke was nowhere in sight. She climbed the stairs to his room where he lay on the bed playing once again with his phone. She inhaled a deep breath and released it slowly. "You could have come down the stairs and found me. I left Christopher on the potty alone."

"Are we going home?"

Elizabeth tucked her hair behind her ear, processing his question to find a possible hidden meaning. "We'll go back to the house when the moving trucks arrive, but we'll be staying with Uncle Phillip and Aunt Sam when we're there."

Luke flung his phone to the bed and crossed his arms. "But I don't want to move. Why can't Steven move in with us instead of us moving? I have no friends here. No baseball. And our family will be so far away."

"We've already been over this, Luke. Steven said we could live anywhere, but I want to live here, in this house. This is where we belong. You have to trust me on this." She pointed to his bags. "Please, take those down and give them to Steven. He's out there loading the car."

Luke sighed. He rose from the bed, and shoved his phone into his pocket before threading his arms through the straps of his backpack. He lifted his suitcase. "I trust you, mom. I just don't want to be here." Luke's shoulders slumped as they descended the stairs and walked through the living room.

As she hurried back to Christopher, she noticed the humming had stopped. Perhaps he'd done his business. She hoped he hadn't made a mess wiping. She entered the bathroom and Christopher was nowhere in sight, pants still laying on the floor.

Elizabeth spun on her heels and caught Luke

going out the door. "Have you seen Christopher?"

He took a couple of steps back into the house. "No. Why?"

"I left him in the bathroom when you called me." She tucked her hair behind her ears and began searching. "Help me find him. I'll check the bottom floor, you check upstairs."

Luke dropped his stuff at the front door and yelled for Christopher as he climbed the stairs.

Elizabeth called out to her son as she dashed through the house, first to her bedroom then to the guest room with no reply.

Luke met her at the bottom of the stairwell. "He's not there."

Her stomach began to churn and her gut told her she needed to hurry. Panic made her clumsy as she tripped over Luke's stuff on her way out the door and onto the deck. "Steven!" she yelled, standing to her feet.

Steven bounded onto the deck, concern marred his features. "What it is?"

"Christopher. He's missing. He was in the bathroom. Luke called me so I went upstairs. When I came back he was gone."

"We searched the house. He's not there," Luke said from behind her.

Elizabeth turned pale. "He asked to go fishing. You don't think?" She shook her head. "No. He wouldn't have gone without us."

Steven turned down the path that led to the lake, pushing the brush to the side as he ran. Luke's quick footsteps pounded after him. Steven continued to scan the ground for any sign of Christopher that showed he might have come this way.

Nothing.

Once he broke through the trees, his gaze searched the area, still seeing nothing. The pond was over a mile, the water, still and quiet. "Christopher!" *Oh, Lord. Guide me. Direct me. He could be anywhere.*

A few feet away on the ground lay Christopher's blanket. He yanked it from the dirt and stood, eyes trained toward the water once again.

Luke began to yell out his brother's name. Elizabeth went to the edge of the pond and stared into the murky water.

Steven's gaze scanned the area. And there, crouched down on the small bridge several yards away, was Christopher.

Elizabeth must have seen him at the same time for she yelled, "Stay put, Christopher! Don't move!"

Christopher looked up and smiled. He stood and waved, but the sun glimmered into Steven's eyes and for a moment he couldn't see him. Steven sprinted, fear setting in. A cloud's shadow fell over him and within an instant, Christopher had disappeared from the bridge. It was a race against time.

Reaching the bridge, Steven jumped into the murky, shallow water, and swiped his hand against the water's floor. Nothing.

He reached in again and snagged Christopher, then thrust him out of the water, bringing him to his chest. No response.

"You need to do CPR!" Luke yelled from the bank.

"Luke, go call 911."

"Not until you start CPR. Are you trying to kill my brother like you did my sister?"

Stunned, Steven reached the pond's bank and laid Christopher on his back and began compressions. *Lord*...Steven counted. He sensed Elizabeth's presence.

Steven checked Christopher's airways, and began two rescue breaths.

Christopher choked. A full cry pierced the air.

Elizabeth jumped to her son's side and clasped him to her chest, tears streaming down her face. Steven sat on the ground, terror still racing through him as he caught his breath. What would have happened if he lost another one of Elizabeth's children? Lost this little boy he loved? Steven looked for Luke. He was gone.

Christopher's cries, now whimpers, began to settle and his breathing was becoming normal as he rested his head against Elizabeth. She gripped him close. No one moved. No one said a word. The only sound was a siren wailing through the trees as an ambulance approached over the dam.

Elizabeth couldn't remember a longer day, not since the day Katherine had passed. Her insides grew cold at the sight of Christopher's lifeless body.

She glanced to the back seat to make sure it wasn't a dream. He was alive, asleep in his car seat. If it hadn't been for Steven...

She didn't want to think about what might have happened, but the hospital had no difficulty reminding them about the importance of water safety. After Christopher was released from the hospital, they walked to the car, and she relished Steven's protective arm as much as the way he carried Christopher asleep on his shoulder. All she wanted to do was to go home, but it was the start of their long journey to Miami.

Eight hours later, the image of her son's limp body in Steven's arms played in her mind, as did the way Steven had changed back into the confident Dr. Moore once he stepped foot into the hospital. He was in his element and his presence radiated self-assurance, drawing the attention of the doctor in charge as well as the nurses. People flocked to him, always had.

Elizabeth took Steven's hand within hers. She contemplated what was running through his thoughts as he drove. Yes, her husband, Steven, Dr. Moore was a strong man physically, spiritually, confident in his abilities as a doctor, and compassionate like no one she'd ever known, but this was the same man who doubted himself, feared death, and desired nothing else but to be loved. She was one of the few who truly knew this man, whom he allowed in, and she was blessed to be loved by him. Her cheeks grew hot remembering the way Luke spoke to Steven at the bridge. If she'd known Luke would use the past against Steven, she'd have thought twice about telling him the circumstances of Katherine's death. What she'd intended as a tool to help her son gain a better understanding of his new father had instead became a weapon.

"Mom, I need to stop," Luke whispered over her shoulder from the back seat.

Steven released her hand, turned on the right signal, and entered the other lane. "Can you make it two more exits? I saw a sign for a hotel a couple of miles ahead. We'll stop for the night."

Luke hesitated. "Yeah."

"Are you sure?" she asked Steven. "That will put us—"

"It's been a long day and we're all tired. A good night's rest will do us good."

She couldn't disagree, but tomorrow's meeting with Mike's friend at Moffitt was too important to miss. And Steven knew it.

Chapter Twenty-Four

Steven released Elizabeth's hand as they stepped into Moffitt, the cool air stealing his breath. Or perhaps it was facing reality head on. Since the day of their wedding, he'd lived in a dream state, holding on to every precious moment, but now as he stood at the nurse's desk, his stomach rolled and dread filled him.

"I'm Steven Moore. I have an appointment with Dr. Middleton."

The nurse glanced down at the computer screen. "Yes," she said, handing him a clipboard with several papers attached. "Please fill these out and return them when you're finished."

"Would you happen to know if this is a consultation only or will I be sent for testing?"

"Every patient is different so I really can't say. You can ask Dr. Middleton when you see him."

Steven nodded. "Thank you. I will." He turned and Elizabeth gave him a reassuring smile that did little to help his nerves. If truth be known, if he could have asked her to stay behind without hurting her, he would have. Life was about to change for them both and there was no way he could protect his wife. But first he needed to process the news of his cancer, then deal with the outcome one way or the other.

Elizabeth looked toward the semi-empty waiting room and pointed to a spot near the row of windows. Instead, Steven took the nearest chair. Elizabeth slid into a seat alongside him as he began filling out the paperwork. She placed her bag on the floor. He glanced at her, wishing he could see her face, but her long hair got in the way. *I love her, Lord. Help her to understand. I have to do this alone.*

After completing the paperwork, Steven returned to the nurse's desk. "All finished."

"Great." The nurse took the clipboard. "They should be calling you shortly."

"Thank you." Steven took a long breath and returned to his seat. He gazed into Elizabeth's beautiful eyes. A worried expression crossed her features and he fought to find the words he wanted to say. "Elizabeth, there's something I need to tell you."

Her forehead wrinkled.

"Mr. Moore."

Steven heard the nurse's summons but ignored it. He was drawn to his wife, desiring to hold her, to kiss her fears away.

"Mr. Moore." The nurse called again.

Elizabeth rose. "We have to go. You can tell me later."

Steven stood and looked to the nurse. "Can I have a minute?" She nodded. He turned his attention back to Elizabeth.

She touched his arm. "What is it, Steven?"

"I need you to stay here."

Frowning, she shook her head. "I'm going with you."

"I need to do this alone, Elizabeth. Please," he whispered.

Her lips tightened but her eyes pleaded with him. He resisted. He was strong enough to handle almost anything, but standing with the woman he loved and knowing he might die sooner rather than later was more than he could bear.

Her hand slid from his arm. "Go ahead. I'll wait for you here."

He forced a smile he didn't feel as his thank you, then turned to the nurse who waited by the open door. "How are you today, Mr. Moore?"

"Fine." Yet he felt anything but fine. He was being led down a hall where he'd soon know what his future held.

No. He was definitely not fine.

Elizabeth's gaze followed Steven as he trailed the nurse down the hall. The door closed behind them. She bit the inside of her cheek to hold back the uneasiness of the past two days and the emotions lingering in the back of her throat. It never occurred to her that Steven wouldn't want her with him. She was his helpmate, his wife. She was supposed to be there for him in all things, good and bad. Isn't that what they promised each other?

She sat back in the chair and ran her fingers over her forehead, soothing out the beginnings of a tension headache. Steven loved her, there was no doubt, but why didn't he want her with him? She took her phone from her bag and dialed her sister. *Voice mail.*

"Hey, it's me. I guess you took the kids to Linda and Henry's for a swim. I was checking to see how things were going. Steven's with the doctor. He didn't want me to go with him, Sam. He asked me to stay behind. I'm scared he's going to shut me out." She paused, fighting not to break down emotionally in the waiting room. "Okay, I'll call you later."

Elizabeth hung up and tossed her phone back into her bag. She stood and walked to the row of windows looking over the hospital grounds, seeing nothing. Absentmindedly, she grabbed a magazine from a table and carried it over to her chair. She plopped down and flipped through the pages, her mind racing with thoughts of what Steven and Dr. Middleton were discussing.

"I hope you don't mind me saying," a shaky voice said, "but you're new to the whole cancer thing, aren't you?"

Elizabeth's hands stilled and she glanced up at a gentleman with white hair who sat three chairs over. She hadn't noticed him until now. "How did you know?"

"Well," he gave her a reassuring smile, "my wife usually comes with me and when she does, she brings things to occupy her time. You know," he shrugged his thin shoulders, "something to read, to do. If she doesn't have her nose stuck in a book, it's in a crossword puzzle she picked up at a yard sale."

"Am I that obvious?"

"A little."

"I wish I had a novel or crossword puzzle right about now." She lifted the magazine slightly from her lap. "This isn't holding my attention." She tossed it into the chair Steven had occupied.

"Let me introduce myself. I'm David Barns."

"Nice to meet you, David. I'm Elizabeth Rob…Moore. Elizabeth Moore." The older gentleman's brows furrowed at the fumble with her name and heat crawled up her neck. It was the first time she'd actually said it to another person. She rushed to explain. "My husband and I have only been married a few weeks. Almost a month, but who's counting."

"Newlyweds. Well, congratulations to you both. I remember the day I met my Cynthia." He had a faraway look in his eyes, but hearing her mother's name brought tears to the back of Elizabeth's throat. How she wished she were here now, comforting her, praying for her and Steven.

"…We were high school sweethearts. Married right before I joined to fight in the Korean War. I wanted to enlist in the navy during WWII, but I was too young. Good thing, too. I wouldn't have met my Cynthia."

"I'm sorry she wasn't able to come with you

today. It sounds as if you miss her."

The corners of his mouth lifted. "She's the loveliest woman I know. Supportive too. Been comin' with me over the last several years for every appointment or treatment. She was upset she had to stay home but she's got a stomach virus. No sense in her gettin' worse or givin' it to someone else. Besides, I'm only havin' a PET scan." He leaned over the arm of the chair. "How about your husband? What's he here for?"

"He's meeting with a Dr. Middleton for the first time today. My husband has stage IV cancer. Melanoma." She looked down at her folded hands. "I only wish he wanted me to go back with him to speak with the doctor. I have no idea what's going on. I have no idea how to help him." She shook her head. "Sorry. I shouldn't burden you with my concerns when—"

He held up his hand. "Nonsense. One thing you learn when you or someone you love has cancer is to allow people to share what's on their minds. When I first found out I had cancer, I kept to myself, didn't know how to handle the news, worried to leave my Cynthia behind. And if you don't mind me sayin' it sounds to me your husband might need time to take things in."

"How did your wife handle being shut out?"

"Well, I'm not right sure I shut her out, but she waited for me to share. She stood by me. She sat here in this waiting room time after time. Love isn't only words, but actions, and sometimes they speak louder than words ever can."

A woman's voice called out. "Mr. Barns."

They both turned toward the nurse. Mr. Barns stood and turned back to Elizabeth with a smile. "Just think, you weren't only here for your husband, but to keep an old man company."

"Thank you for saying that, Mr. Barns."

"It's David. And you're welcome." He headed toward the nurse, and just like it did with her husband, the door closed behind them.

Steven found Elizabeth in the waiting room with a tall cup he was sure was hot chocolate in one hand, and a Bible in the other, her eyes focused on a page. It amazed him how her faith had grown in the twelve years they were apart. Seeing her like this now brought him strength. He was certain his wife was praying on his behalf, for them both.

She didn't notice him walk up. "Hey."

Elizabeth looked up wide-eyed at him, closed her Bible, and shoved it in her bag. "What did the doctor say?" She stood and collected her purse.

"I'll tell you on the way." He'd fully intended to, but he barely breathed a word on their way back to Phillip and Sam's or when they agreed to stop since it was getting late. What could he say? He didn't know anything more than when he walked into Moffitt hours earlier.

Steven walked with Elizabeth to their hotel room and opened the door, then placed their overnight bag on the couch. "I think I'll take a shower."

"Steven," Elizabeth said, stopping him. She touched his arm, uncertainty reflected in her eyes, mirroring his own heart. "Talk to me. I need to know. I have the right to know."

Her touch sent his mind reeling through the doctor's words and what they meant. Were they ready for a battle? To fight this cancer head on with an experimental trial? He moved away from her touch and hurt flashed across her face. "I don't know anything, Elizabeth. All I did were tests and they should come back next week." He walked through their room and entered the bathroom, closing the door behind him.

Steven leaned on the counter and looked at his reflection in the mirror, but his mind couldn't focus. He didn't want to deal with his illness, or even utter the words. How could he fight something he didn't want to exist?

Twenty minutes later, Elizabeth bit her lip, fighting back her tears. *God, I don't know what to do. I feel so lost, helpless.* She pulled the towel from her hair and laid it on the bathroom counter. Her fingers worked their way through the tangles in her wet hair while she collected herself before seeing Steven. She tightened her robe around her waist. Cold air hit her face as she stepped from the bathroom. She shivered.

"It's cold in here." She found the thermostat and pushed the temperature up ten degrees. "Are you trying to freeze us?" No answer. The room was empty. "Steven," she whispered, "where did you go?"

After dressing for bed, she called her sister. It was wonderful to know the boys were fine but that was thirty minutes ago and she still hadn't heard a word from Steven. Elizabeth paced the length of the room. Why would he leave without saying a word?

She checked her cell where it lay on the dresser once more. No call, no text. She turned the thermostat back down the ten degrees and used the hotel note pad to fan her face. If she didn't know better, she'd think she had a fever. Frustration was more like it, and plenty of it. She huffed and crossed her arms against her chest.

A noise sounded at the door and she turned. Steven walked in with a thin white grocery bag in hand. "You left without a word. I came out of the bathroom, talking to you. No. To myself. Shivering in my robe."

Steven smiled. "I would have loved to have seen that." He set the bag on the small table against the wall.

She pointed a finger at him. "You're not getting off that easy, flashing that gorgeous smile of yours." He took several steps toward her and she backed away. "You might be able to draw doctors, nurses, or whomever you please with one look, but your charms don't work on me."

"Really."

"Yes. Really. You have some explaining to do.

You left me in the shower and didn't say good-bye." Elizabeth wanted to dig in her heels, but how could she when he looked at her like that, half mischievous, half vulnerable. The vulnerable side won her over as he walked back to the table and pulled out two pints of ice cream from the plastic bag.

"After my shower, I felt restless. I needed a late night snack."

"At midnight?"

He shrugged. "Seemed like a perfect time. I kept driving until I found your favorite. Sugar free too." He held out a carton of mint chocolate chip.

She shook her head, taking the carton and plastic spoon he handed her. "What am I going to do with you?"

"Eat ice cream until 1 a.m. After that, it's up to you." He wiggled his eyebrows.

Elizabeth smiled and elbowed him in the chest.

Steven kissed her forehead then led her to the couch. "I want to share what the doctor said."

Her heart lightened and the tension in her shoulders eased slightly. Once seated on the sofa, she lifted the lid from the ice cream and Steven took it from her, setting both their lids on the coffee table in front of them.

He pulled her close. "I go back next week to find out the result. The doctor briefly spoke about an experimental trial that I might be a good candidate for, but he'll know more once the results come back. It feels like I have a week to be me, to live the way I want to, and what I want…is to spend every moment with you and the children. What do you say about going to the beach for the week?" He scooped out a spoonful of ice cream.

"Where would we go? It might be hard to find a place when it's so close to summer, and to find a place for all of us on such short notice. And do you think it's a good idea for you to be in the sun?"

"Not to worry. What do you say?"

Elizabeth took her own bite of ice cream and enjoyed the coolness of the mint on her tongue, even if the thought of going back to the beach made her uneasy for several reasons. She'd avoided the beach for years. Too many memories, and Chris was in every one, especially their last night together as husband and wife. And now her new husband had stage IV melanoma cancer. She glanced into the ice cream container. Her thoughts left a bitter taste on her tongue. *Could this be our last time together at the beach?* She gave herself an inward kick. This was about Steven and what he wanted. "Sure."

Chapter Twenty-Five

Steven pulled into the condo parking lot and slowed as a guard exited the security house with a clipboard in hand. Steven checked the rearview mirror to make sure Phillip had followed after the last turn.

Steven rolled his window down. "We're staying at the Reynolds' place. The SUV behind us is with us as well. The name's Steven Moore."

The guard checked the clipboard then handed him two pieces of paper with numbers attached. "These are your parking passes. Please keep them on your vehicle's dash at all times or your car may be towed."

"Not a problem." Steven slipped the number card on his dash then gave the papers to Elizabeth. "Appreciate it."

The guard opened the gate. "Have a good stay."

Steven pulled into the gated community and smiled inwardly as he parked. He never expected Phillip and Samantha to accept his invitation to join them, but they did, and he was ecstatic for the opportunity to get to know Elizabeth's family better. Perhaps this might help Luke come to terms with the fact Steven was now part of their family.

Elizabeth cupped his hand. "What are you thinking?"

"I'm glad Phillip and Samantha agreed to come, even if it's only for a couple of days. How about you wake up our little boy and I'll find us a luggage cart." He glanced around and opened his door. Luke and Juwonya slipped out of Phillip's car.

Phillip came around to him and gazed up at the thirty plus floors. "Thanks for the invite."

"Anytime. Reynolds has asked me on several occasions if I wanted to use the place but I've never accepted until now. I'm heading to find a luggage cart. You need one?"

"Count me in. Samantha packs like she'll be here a few weeks."

"Must run in the family." Steven chuckled as they grabbed the luggage carts at the lobby entrance. "So how did the drive go with Jeremiah?"

"Better than we expected. He slept most of the time. By the way, I hope you didn't mind that Luke wanted to ride with us."

"Not at all. Maybe giving him some room is what he needs to accept my marriage to his mother. Maybe seeing us all together might help as well. Honestly, I don't know."

"Give him time to adjust and give him your love. I believe that's all he'll need."

Steven took Phillip's words to heart as they

unloaded the vehicles and found their way to the condo. Luke hadn't said two words to him since their drive to Miami, but whatever it was the boy needed, Steven was willing to give, and unconditional love was no exception.

"Oh, Steven!" Elizabeth called to him as he deposited their things in the master suite. He joined her in front of four sliding glass doors overlooking the ocean. "This view is breathtaking."

Christopher, now fully awake, pressed his face against the glass. "Come here." Steven caught Christopher up in his arms so he could get a better view. "It's beautiful, isn't it? God made the ocean."

Samantha came and stood alongside her sister. "The thirty-fourth floor definitely gives you a different perspective than the third or fourth. I know where I'm having my devotion time in the morning." She pulled open one of the sliding glass doors and moaned. "I could live out here. Phillip! Come look at this view."

"Did you call?" Phillip joined Samantha on the balcony with Luke and Juwonya close behind.

Christopher squirmed out of Steven's hands, but before Steven let him go, he knelt. "Christopher, you may not climb on the patio furniture, the railing, or you won't be able to go outside."

Elizabeth leaned in. "Do you understand what Steven is saying?" Christopher nodded then ran to the others through the sliding glass doors. She straightened. "Do you think he'll listen?"

"Do you?"

She shook her head. "No."

"I didn't think so, but if he sees we mean what we say, he'll get the point." Immediately after he spoke the last word, Christopher climbed up onto the table and Phillip snatched him up.

Elizabeth huffed. "I guess our united front starts now." She stepped into the balcony. "Christopher, what did we just say, young man? No climbing on the table or chairs."

Steven followed, taking Christopher from Phillip. "Time to go inside." He carried Christopher to where he and his brother would be sharing a room. Steven didn't know how Elizabeth was able to keep up with him by herself for so long—one near-death experience was enough for him.

Ignoring Christopher's pout and watery eyes, Steven set the little boy on his bed. He and Elizabeth sat alongside him. The fear of losing this little child just yesterday washed over him once again. "Christopher, you need to listen to Mommy and Daddy. Chairs are for sitting. Tables are for eating. You can't climb on them."

Christopher tilted his head and looked to Elizabeth. His pout vanished. "Mama. Mommy. Sebeen. Daddy?"

Elizabeth smiled. "Yes, sweetheart. Steven is your daddy. You need to listen to your daddy. Okay?"

Steven paused, taken back by Christopher's words and the encouraging nod Elizabeth was giving him.

Christopher lunged into Steven with his arms flung wide, barely spanning his chest. "Wuv Daddy."

Overtaken with emotion, Steven couldn't speak. He held Christopher close and kissed the top of his head as he did with his own son so many years ago. Steven closed his eyes. *Lord, thank you.*

Christopher wiggled out of his embrace and hugged Elizabeth. She quickly began kissing his cheeks then the rest of his face. He giggled, "Top. Top. Ickle. Ickle."

Steven reached over and started tickling Elizabeth. She let out a laugh and squirmed. Christopher joined in and before they knew it, they had an audience. Luke stood there silent. The ever-present frown deepened. "Want to join us, Luke?"

The boy glanced away and thumbed the air from where he came. "No. I was wondering about dinner. Can we have pizza? Uncle Phillip told me to ask you."

"Sure. I like pizza. How about after dinner we head down to the pier and go fishing? What do you say?"

Luke's gaze returned to him. "Really? Is Christopher coming?"

Steven thought about it for a moment. It hadn't crossed his mind, but after two days of Christopher's antics, it was best to leave him behind. "I was thinking about the two of us. It might be a little difficult fishing with him, but of course, if Phillip or Juwonya would like to come, I don't see why not."

"Can I ask them?" His voice raised a notch

and his face brightened.

"Sure. Go right ahead." Luke vaulted from the room and Steven turned to Elizabeth who was grinning. "He was actually smiling. I can't believe it."

Christopher stood on the bed, showing a full set of baby teeth, clapping his palms on both sides of Steven's face.

Steven's eyes widened. "Are you smiling, too?"

Christopher gave him an exaggerated nod.

Elizabeth's laughter filled not only the room, but Steven's heart. He prayed for his joy to never end.

"Ickle, Daddy. Ickle, Daddy."

Elizabeth tucked Christopher in his bed and closed the door slightly so the light from the kitchen wouldn't disturb him as he slept. She joined her sister on the couch. "He's out like a light."

Sam took a sip of her coffee and moaned. "Nothing like a nightcap before bed."

"I don't see how you can drink coffee before bed."

"Caffeine doesn't affect me anymore. So." She lowered her mug to her lap. "I hear that a certain little boy is calling Steven 'Daddy.'"

Elizabeth sat up. "Can you believe it? Out of nowhere."

"My guess is that Christopher wanted a daddy of his own, and with how taken he was with Steven, it came naturally." She took another sip from her mug. "Christopher adores Steven, but not only that, Steven adores you, Lizzy. I see the small touches he gives you, the glances you give him, the smiles between you two. It does my heart good to see you so happy."

"I am, so incredibly happy, but what about next week, after we find out the news of his cancer? I'm scared, Sam. I can't lose him. My children can't lose him."

Sam covered her hand. "God will help you through whatever your future holds."

"I know. I only wish we knew."

"What would you do?"

"Fight the cancer. Live to the fullest."

"Then live to the fullest. Fight the cancer. Bathe your husband in prayer. Be thankful for your time together, because *none* of us knows the time or date God will call us to home."

"I know you're right..."

"Then pray, Elizabeth."

Steven glanced down the boardwalk where Phillip had taken Juwonya, giving him and Luke some time alone. In the last few hours, clouds had rolled in and the sky darkened as Steven baited his hook. It had been years since he fished off the pier, but they were having perfect weather for it. "Can I help?" He squatted near Luke who insisted on baiting his own hook.

Luke's fingers fumbled. "I've got it." He

frowned, pinching the bait in half, both pieces of shrimp falling to the boardwalk. "I don't know why I can't do it." He sighed as he picked up both halves.

"Sometimes we have to admit we can't do things on our own and ask for help."

Luke didn't respond, so Steven cast his line out to the ocean. Before long, Steven reeled in a fish, and Luke's expression turned grim.

Steven pretended it was a monster and allowed the fish to have its lead, fighting what might be nothing more than the size of his own bait.

Luke's eyes lit as he watched the line being reeled in and out. "How big do you think it is?"

"Not too big. I'm just tiring him out." Steven smiled. At least he had the boy's attention. "Do you want to finish reeling him in?"

"Sure! If you don't mind?"

"Not at all," Steven assured, handing him his rod. Immediately, he went to working on Luke's rod, adding fresh shrimp to the hook. Luke struggled to reel in the fish but fought him in, and to Steven's surprise, it looked like a two-pound Spanish mackerel. "Wow, Luke!" Steven grabbed the line and set the fish on the ground.

"It's a big one!"

"It sure is." Steven snatched his cell from his pocket. "Stand next to the fish and I'll take your picture." Luke's eyes widened along with his smile. "Now, do you think you can hold the line up so I can get another shot?" Luke did as Steven asked and pride radiated from his face.

"Hey, great fish!" Juwonya called, running toward them. Phillip followed close behind. "We haven't caught anything yet."

Phillip patted Luke on the back and then set his and Juwonya's fishing equipment down against the railing. "You might have to show us how. Here. Let me take a picture with you and Steven."

"Sure," Luke said, readjusting his hold on the line. "Gotta hurry though. He's heavy." Steven said nothing as he handed Phillip his phone and stood next to Luke. Phillip took several shots and afterward, Luke looked up at him. "Can we put him back in the water now? I don't want him to die. His family would miss him."

Steven swallowed against the wave of emotions growing in this throat. Would Steven be able to help the boy heal from losing his father? Would God take Steven away before he had the chance? "We'll do it right now." Steven bent and unhooked the fish. "Do you want to help me throw him back in?"

"No. I wouldn't want to drop him. I want to make sure he gets in the water okay."

Steven caught Phillip's gaze as he turned and released the mackerel back into the water. A small splash could be heard and Luke ran to the rail, eyes searching the water. "He's home now."

Luke gave him a hesitant smile, grabbing his fishing pole. "Thank you."

"Hey, I want to catch one, too!" Juwonya lifted her rod and bag of shrimp, handing it to Phillip.

"Just because I'm a girl, doesn't mean I can't catch a fish."

Phillip chuckled. "Yes, but it looks to me like Luke doesn't need me to help him bait his hook."

Steven and Luke glanced at each other and smiled before going back to fishing. Steven threw his line out.

"Sometimes, Cuz," Luke threw his line out alongside Steven's, "we have to admit we can't do things on our own and ask for help." He shrugged his shoulders. "Just sayin'."

Juwonya let out an exasperated breath and planted her hands on her hips. "Oh, hush."

Steven bit back a chuckle and glanced at Luke again. One thing for sure, the boy was listening to what he was saying, but could he hear how much Steven loved him? Would he truly let him in?

Chapter Twenty-Six

Steven turned over in bed, a hint of bacon in the air causing him to lift his gaze to Elizabeth lying next to him. She had mentioned how Phillip liked to cook, how he was an early riser, and how bacon was always on the breakfast menu. Phillip had said as much, too, but as Steven squinted over his wife's shoulder toward the clock on the nightstand, five in the morning was even a bit early for him. It hadn't been long ago his shifts at the hospital required five o'clock mornings, and yet, it seemed a lifetime ago. Everything seemed like a lifetime ago, but his unending love for Elizabeth and how it continued to exist through the test of time.

His gaze followed the length of the sheet to the curve of her body. He moved closer and draped his arm over her, tucking her to himself. She let out a light snore as she settled against his chest, a sound which continually brought him comfort, reassuring him he wasn't alone after all these years. God did indeed satisfy the desires of man's heart. He couldn't imagine ever deserving such a life, or loving another woman more.

He tried not to wake her as he gently kissed her hair and inhaled the faint fruity smell that lingered from her shampoo, but she stirred slightly.

"Good morning," she whispered.

"Good morning." He smiled as he trailed his fingers down her arm. "How did you sleep?"

She inhaled a long breath. "Wonderfully. I hope you still like bacon." He could hear the smile in her voice.

"I do, but not as much as you."

She rolled over, and the corners of her eyes wrinkled as she smiled at him. "Good thing. How long have you been awake?"

"Not long."

"Have you heard from the children? Christopher doesn't seem to be in our bed this morning."

"No. I suppose our fishing trip last night kept everyone up later than normal."

She ran her fingers through his hair, and for a moment, he shut his eyes, enjoying her touch. "I could tell Luke had a wonderful time. He was different than when he left."

Steven thought for a moment before meeting her gaze. "He was, wasn't he? This trip is good, giving us time for just Luke and me without interruptions."

She smiled. "Hopefully like us."

Elizabeth lifted her face to the warm sun as

seagulls flew overhead. She rubbed sunscreen on her arms while admiring the beauty of the afternoon, thankful the rain showers had finally passed. Only the salty film from the ocean lingered in the air.

She spotted Sam waving from the water. She was about to call out to her sister but thought better of it. She set the sunscreen down and waved in return, glancing at Jeremiah's sleeping form in his little sun tent.

Elizabeth glanced down the shoreline, her gaze caught on a couple running side by side, a scene she recalled creating with Chris so long ago. There were things in her life she cherished now—her children, Steven, her family—but there were also her memories of Chris. Now as she looked out at the vast ocean, she remembered their cruise and how much they loved each other, but also how God had begun to be real in her life. It had been a hard road, but now as she looked back, she was thankful. Thankful for Chris, her children, and the family God had given her, but most importantly, the woman she'd become by God's mercy and grace.

Sam plopped down beside her on the towel. "How's Jeremiah been?" She untwisted her black bathing suit strap then readjusted the canopy covering her son's sleeping form.

"He's slept the entire time."

"After the lunch he had, no doubt. He must be going through a growing spurt." She pointed to the waves. "Do you want to go in?"

"I'm happy just to sit. It gives me time to

think."

"About?"

Elizabeth felt a little embarrassed to say she was thinking of Chris even if there was no reason to be. "Well, about Chris. Our cruise." She shrugged. "The last time I was at the beach was with Chris."

Sam's eyes widened. "I had no idea. Your favorite place in the entire world is at the beach. How come you've not been back?"

"It was too hard and I wasn't ready. My last night with Chris was at the condo. The night we had Christopher." She inhaled a long breath. "I've missed being here. I've missed the salt water in the air. The way it seems to cover my skin. The sand between my toes. Water splashing against my calves. The sound of the waves. But with all that, I don't miss it like I thought I would. Honestly, I'd rather be back in Georgia, with the tall pines, seeing the deer come up to the house from the woods." She looked back out at the ocean. Steven jumped a wave, holding Christopher in his arms. Christopher held Steven's neck in what looked to be a death grip, but he was laughing. She smiled.

"I can tell. You're glowing. Or is it because of Steven?"

Warmth ran up Elizabeth's neck and she was sure she was blushing. "Both."

"Here comes Luke."

Luke ran toward them, sloshing sand every which way.

"Whoa!" Sam held up a hand. "Watch the

sand. Jeremiah is asleep under the tent."

Luke quickly slowed to a stop. He came around to Elizabeth. "Steven wants me to get you." He held out his hand for her to take.

Elizabeth grinned. "All right then." She clasped Luke's hand and they walked to where the waves broke along the shore. She lifted her free hand and shielded her eyes from the sun. "Did you want me?"

Steven's smile grew. "Yes, out here with us. Isn't that right boys?"

Luke tightened his hold and pulled her into the water. They went out the short distance to where Steven and Christopher wave jumped moments ago. "Want to jump with us, Mom? You have to hear Christopher's laugh. It's awesome. But you gotta wait for a good wave. It's the only time he does it."

Elizabeth pushed her fingers through the smaller waves as she tiptoed along the sandy bottom. "I was thinking about dinner—"

Steven tucked a few strands of hair behind her ear. "Were you really?"

She laughed. "No, but it's good to know what we might want to eat."

Luke swam between them and pinched Christopher's toes. "Shrimp. Not raw like when we went fishing yesterday, but cooked."

Steven raised a brow at Luke. "You like shrimp?"

"Yep. Don't you?" Luke turned from Steven and pointed at an upcoming wave.

"I sure do. Then shrimp it is." Steven poked Christopher in the belly. "Do you like shrimp?"

Luke shouted. "Here it comes, Mom."

The wave came in one fine swoop, washing over her even though she jumped. Christopher's shrill laughter tickled her, but what tickled her more was the smile on Luke's face as he grabbed onto Steven's arm coming through the wave.

Steven sat on the edge of the bed while Elizabeth stood on her knees behind him and squeezed lotion into the palm of her hand. "I'm sorry your skin is tender."

"I didn't think we were out in the sun too long. What good is sunscreen?" The inflection in Steven's voice pained her, knowing they shouldn't have been in the sun in the worst time of the day. Maybe she should have tried to change his mind about spending time at the beach. Steven sighed. "I knew better."

She ran her fingers in a circular pattern gently down his back, not missing the long, pink, jagged scar along the back of his neck. Another reminder of what the sun had cost him, and now would cost both of them.

I need you. She bit her lip, steadying her wavering thoughts. "Did you notice the way Luke clung to you when you both were jumping the waves? How he laughed? How Christopher laughed?"

Still facing the door, he reached back and covered her hand on his shoulder. "Yes, but I also noticed you. How radiant you looked, your smile, your laughter. I was able to make my family happy today, and honestly, Elizabeth, I wouldn't have missed it for the world."

Neither would I. A tear slid down her cheek and she wiped it away with her sleeve, thankful Steven wasn't facing her. "Let's get you a shirt." She pulled her hand from his and searched through Steven's dresser drawer, taking out the crimson retro T-shirt he bought yesterday at the souvenir shop. Not exactly beachy, but scrolled across the chest read Panama City Beach, Florida. She'd bought one for herself in pink while Luke picked out a blue one and Christopher a green. Tonight they'd all look like tourists in their matching tees.

She turned and leaned against the dresser. "How about this one?" She draped his T-shirt against her chest, covering the one she wore and tipped her chin up. "I think it's perfect."

He gave her an amused look before taking her into his arms. "Indeed." He kissed her chin, cheek, and hovered over her mouth. "I love you."

"And I love you."

"Mommy. Daddy. In." Christopher's voice sounded from the opposite side of the door.

Steven gave her lips a quick peck and half smiled. "I'm being summoned." He grabbed his shirt and slipped it on, then took the keys and phone from the dresser.

Elizabeth swung the door open and Christopher fell into the room, his hands and knees hitting the hardwood floors. "Oh, sweetheart." She lifted the pouty-faced boy into her arms. Steven stood alongside her, his gaze sweeping over Christopher. She felt Steven's body relax. "Were you leaning against the door?"

Christopher gave her a hard nod and pointed to his elbow. "Ouch."

"You want me to kiss your boo boo?" She leaned toward him, but Christopher turned to Steven and his pout grew.

"Daddy. Kiss."

Steven kissed Christopher's elbow and the little boy's pout immediately faded into a smile. "Let's go eat!"

Everyone left the condo and headed toward their cars. Luke climbed into their vehicle with Juwonya, convincing her to try shrimp for the first time.

"You'll like it the way I eat it," Luke assured her.

Elizabeth held her breath, afraid she was imagining what she was seeing. Luke chose to be with them. Her eyes met Steven's and they grinned at each other. Once they entered the restaurant, Steven opened his mouth to say something but the waitress stepped toward them.

"How many in your party?"

"Seven." Steven pointed to Christopher who held his hand. "We'll need a booster seat for one."

"Right this way." The waitress led them through a large room of diners, weaving their way down several steps to the table with an open view of the ocean. She placed menus on the table.

Steven pulled out Elizabeth's chair then set Christopher in his seat and pushed him up to the table. "Don't fall." He seated himself next to Christopher whose small hands reached for the children's menu and crayons.

"Beautiful view," Sam observed when the waitress returned with a booster seat.

After the waitress took their order, Christopher, now seated a bit higher, leaned both elbows on the table. "Eat pockcorn."

Phillip chuckled. "A boy after my own heart. It's not popcorn, but shrimp, popcorn shrimp." Phillip turned to Elizabeth. "Before I forget, while we were on our way here, Eric called and wanted to confirm your phone number. I told him we were following you and on our way to eat dinner. I told him I'd have you call, but he mentioned it wasn't anything that couldn't wait. Said he'd call you tomorrow."

She questioned why Eric would want to speak with her but came up blank. The last time Eric contacted her had to do with Steven. She looked to her husband. "Do you know what Eric wanted?"

He shook his head. "No, but if you'd feel better, call him. We'll wait for you to eat."

Elizabeth reached for her bag, until she glimpsed their waitress plus another, carrying trays.

"Eric said it wasn't important and with all that talk about shrimp, I'm not letting mine get cold. Isn't that right, Luke?"

"Right, Mom." Luke and Juwonya lifted their gazes from studying the dessert menu. "Hot fried shrimp, then later a cool-down with this ice cream chocolate drizzle cake." He pointed to the cake's photo.

Sam giggled. "No doubt Phillip is your uncle. Oh, here's our food." The waitresses placed the platters on the table and Christopher clapped his hands. Sam turned to Phillip who popped a shrimp in his mouth. "What time do we need to leave tomorrow?"

Phillip cut open his potato. "Before lunch, that way we can head to the bookstore for a few hours to check on things." He pointed to Juwonya who sat across from him. "How's the shrimp?"

Juwonya smiled, pulling the tail of the shrimp from her mouth. "One word. Yum!"

Elizabeth ate a bite of her scampi, savoring the garlic butter on her tongue. "Sam, how's it going with Lindsey?"

"Mommy, bread." Christopher pointed to the out-of-reach basket of garlic rolls the waitress placed in front of him.

Sam reached over and handed him a roll. "Lindsey, she's a keeper. I told Timothy he had nothing to worry about and she proved me right, but I understand why he was concerned since this is her first job."

Phillip took a sip of his soda and set it on the paper coaster. "She's a quick learner, plus it's great to have an extra hand. Our family business is growing, even Sarah had mentioned helping out once a week to help with merchandising."

Elizabeth missed the bookstore, the feel and smell of the books, her customers, most of whom she knew by name, and the hustle and bustle of the sale. But as she told Sam on the beach, her store, the sand and waves were no longer a part of her. It seemed a verse from Ecclesiastes had blossomed to truth in her life. *To every thing there is a season, and a time to every purpose under the heaven.* She still enjoyed those things, but it didn't define her as it once had and it was no longer her passion—the Lord and her family were her passion.

Steven leaned toward her. "Good?"

"Very." The way he gazed into her eyes—soft, full of love—stirred her heart. "Very good," she said, knowing full well he was speaking about their dinner, yet her answer had everything to do with the man sitting beside her.

Steven's phone rang and he gave her a regretful look, as if he planned to say something in response. He pulled his cell from his pocket and frowned. "I need to take this." He rose from the table without meeting her gaze and headed toward the front of the restaurant.

Elizabeth tried to focus on the conversation between Phillip and Juwonya but it became too difficult with Steven's expression fresh in her mind.

Who had called him? Eric? Did he want to speak with Steven about the same thing he called her for? Eric didn't know they married last month, perhaps it had to do with Steven. Yet, he said he didn't know why Eric had called. But if it wasn't Eric…then who?

Elizabeth continued to eat, though her hunger fled the moment Steven avoided her gaze and left the restaurant. After two rolls, and a handful of shrimp, she drank her soda, anxiety setting in sip after sip. Where was Steven?

She glanced at the door where a large group had entered. "I'm going to see what's taking Steven so long." Elizabeth rose from her seat and placed her napkin on the table. At the front door, she squeezed her way through a group of teenagers and exited. She looked to her right as a car whizzed by, then turned to the left and spotted Steven. No phone to his ear, he paced, hands in his pockets, near an empty lot where a sand dune stood a few yards away. His head hung low, but he looked up as she approached.

"Hi." She forced a smile, but there was no response. She stood in the dim moonlight and interlaced their fingers. "Steven. What is it?"

He stared at their joined hands. "We have to leave in the morning."

"Why?" Long seconds dragged on. *Talk to me Steven.* "I thought we're staying for the week."

Steven's forehead knitted and though he might not have noticed, his grip tightened ever so slightly. "The phone call…it was Mike's friend from Moffitt. The results came back."

Lord, please. Her heart whispered, afraid to hear the news, determined not to show it. She cupped his cheek and he met her gaze. "What did he say?"

"He wants to see me tomorrow. Said to make plans to stay."

Chapter Twenty-Seven

More than seven hours had passed since Steven and Elizabeth left the children with Phillip and Samantha and headed north. Steven hated leaving the boys, especially after the last few days they'd spent together. Luke seemed to avoid him once he heard they were leaving.

Now, anger and fear waged war as he sat across from the doctor. Cancer was taking everything from him and he felt completely hopeless. Worst of all, Elizabeth occupied the chair next to him. He never considered himself a weak man. Never meant to cause her pain, but as he glanced at his wife's rigid posture, and watched her bite her bottom lip in obvious distress, he knew he was the weakest of all, forcing the woman he loved to go through this with him. They shouldn't have married. She would have found someone else. But heaven help him, he needed her like the earth needed the sunrise, pushing away the darkness into the very corners of the world. He needed her touch, her love, and she had awakened the man he'd once been. He wasn't giving up, but it was that same anger and fear that made him want to fight this cancer because the thought of losing Elizabeth all over again would kill him faster than cancer ever would.

Steven made the introductions between Elizabeth and Dr. Middleton, and once he finished, the doctor opened a file on his desk. His kind gaze met Steven's. "I spoke with several doctors about your case and I believe I have a plan, including the trial study I spoke with you about last week."

Steven nodded though he wasn't ready for what was coming next. He doubted anyone would be ready. "I guess I'm surprised to have heard from you so soon."

"Yes, well, I could have waited, but I received the results back and had already spoken with a handful of doctors, and I felt there was no need to wait to start treatments. The sooner we start, the better it will be for you," he glanced to Elizabeth, "your wife, and for your family."

"What did the test show?" Elizabeth asked.

"The PET scan showed the cancer had indeed spread to the lymph nodes as your husband is aware. At this stage of cancer, bordering between stage III and stage IV—"

Steven felt the air leave his lungs. He could barely breathe as he leaned forward in his chair. "How...how is that possible? This entire time...I've been told I'm at stage IV."

"I wish I could say for certain, but we have some of the newest technology in cancer research and according to our tests, it's not progressed to stage IV at this time. This is one of the reasons I called you so quickly."

Elizabeth looked to Steven with wide eyes then back to the doctor. "So what does this mean?"

Doctor Middleton folded his hands on top of his desk. "Your husband and I spoke about his previous surgeries. His last surgery several months ago was called a lymph node dissection. With this type of surgery, the doctor tries to remove as many cancer-infected lymph nodes as possible. Since this has already been done, I'd like to move on to radiation."

Though still processing the news, Steven understood now why the doctor had asked him to be prepared to stay. "You'd like me to start radiation."

"Yes, tomorrow. If you're ready. The treatments will be for three consecutive days, then you'll return the following week for three more days. You'll do this for four weeks. Once your radiation is completed, we'll wait a month before beginning your clinical trial."

Elizabeth reached over, grabbed Steven's hand and intertwined their fingers. There was nothing to think about and so much to live for. "I'm ready."

"Great." The doctor took out several forms and handed it to him. They discussed in depth Steven's health plan, treatments, the clinical trial, and information concerning their risks if she became pregnant. By the time they checked into their hotel, ate dinner, and their heads hit the pillow, the long day had caught up with him.

"How are you doing?" Elizabeth snuggled up beside him.

He pulled her close and kissed the top of her head. "A lot to think about, but better now with you in my arms."

Elizabeth tilted her chin up and her hair moved along his arm. "What's on your mind?"

Steven ran his fingers through her silky hair and rubbed a few strands together, lifting it to his nose. Did he really want to go where his thoughts had taken him? How agreeing to the terms of the clinical trial took away their ability to have children, and without hesitation, Elizabeth signed the contract first. Had she not wanted any more children? "The day has caught up with me. I'm surprised you're not snoring yet."

"I don't know if I should turn over or ignore the comment altogether because I don't snore."

He chuckled, running his fingers down her arms. "Of course you don't."

"And just so you know, I'm ignoring you because I'm comfortable."

Minutes passed. Steven suspected Elizabeth had fallen asleep when long snorts filled the room. He chuckled to himself and kissed the top of her head again. "I never said you snored like a pig. It's quieter. Gentle."

"More like this." She snorted a sound like a car engine with a problem, puttering off and on.

"Getting closer."

She lifted her head. "Hey."

He smiled, easing her head back to his chest. "How about I describe how it soothes me? Your snore is a lovely sound, actually. It reminds me I'm not alone. It reminds me of God's promises and how He has brought me the perfect helper. You."

"I want to be, Steven. I want to encourage and support you in any way I can."

"Is that why you signed the clinical trial contract so quickly? I don't know how long this trial will go on, but it means we may never have a child."

"Signing it was our only option. I want to spend the rest of my life loving you, feeling you next to me. I want to grow old with you, Steven. If I have to give up having a child for you, I choose you."

Steven knew she was right, yet… "Is it wrong I still want you to be the mother of my children?"

She lifted slightly on her elbow and cupped his cheek. "And I will be. I am. We have two boys who love you. I know it's not the same, but they are *your* children."

And how he loved Luke and Christopher as if they were his flesh and blood, but the hope to have a child of his own with Elizabeth had not faded. Was it wrong to desire more than God had given him? Was it wrong to hope?

"Maybe it's the way God intended so we'd adopt like we've always wanted. I don't know what the right answer is, but anything is worth giving up to save you."

She was willing to give up anything for him,

to save him. *Lord, You're using her, aren't You? To remind me of Your love for me?* He covered his hand with his own and closed his eyes. "I told myself I didn't want you to become pregnant and then leave you like..."

"Like Chris," she finished his sentence. "I admit, it was one of the most difficult times in my life, the joy of giving birth to Christopher and the emptiness of not having Chris by my side to share our son's life..." Her voice trembled. "But God was with me."

He held her close, feeling a tear drop to his chest. "I'm sorry, Elizabeth."

"No. I'm sorry." She wiped her face. "I think I'm a little tired. I'm sure I'll be snoring in a few minutes."

"Then rest." His eyes closed and he absorbed her warmth as he clung to her.

God, be with us.

Steven's voice whispered through Elizabeth's dream. Or was it a dream? She felt the warmth of his hand as he pushed back the hair from her face. "My Lizzy," he whispered the name he claimed for her so long ago. "So beautiful." His fingers ran down her cheek.

Elizabeth's eyes slowly opened. "I was dreaming...about you." She gave him a sleepy smile.

"I take it by your grin it was a good dream."

"Yes."

Steven turned to the nightstand so she could only see his profile, but his expression seemed preoccupied. She rolled over and faced him. He collected his keys and phone and stuffed them into his pocket.

"Where are you going?"

"I'll be back soon."

She reached for her phone on the nightstand closest to her and checked the time. They should be leaving now. She threw the covers to the other side of the bed and leapt to the floor.

"Elizabeth."

She bit her lip to keep her tongue under control. He'd planned to leave her in this hotel while he received his first treatment? He had another thing coming! Hardheaded! That's what he was—a romantic, hardheaded man! She opened her suitcase and grabbed the first thing she touched.

"Elizabeth. I thought—"

"You thought wrong." She bit her tongue once again and hard as she quickly dressed. Within minutes she was ready, tossing her toothbrush and toothpaste into her bag. She'd brush her teeth and comb her hair after he left for his treatment. "You're not stopping me from going."

Steven opened the hotel door. He led her to the car and opened her door without a word.

Coming around to his side, he slid into his seat and looked at her. "What are you going to do while you're there? Here, you can watch TV, swim, eat breakfast, there are so many things."

"I'm going so you might as well stop trying to convince me otherwise. If I have to sit in the waiting room all day, I will. Nothing is more important than being there for you. I love you. Don't you understand that? I'm not going to let you do this alone. Now, can we go before you're late?"

After they started down the road, Elizabeth held out her hand. "I need your hand."

He wrapped his fingers around hers. "Bossy this morning, are we?"

"I haven't had my coffee."

"You don't drink coffee."

"It's what Sam always says." She shrugged her shoulders. "Sounded right."

"Do me a favor? While I have my treatments, please eat. I get concerned when you miss a meal or your snacks."

"If you promise me we won't go through this again tomorrow, next week, or next month?"

He nodded. "Deal."

Twenty minutes later, Steven stood tall, handsome, smiling, seemingly in command while he signed in at the desk and spoke with the nurses. Elizabeth on the other hand was a rattled mess. Literally. A film covered her teeth and her hair hadn't been brushed. She had no idea what she looked like and she still couldn't get over the idea Steven had planned to leave her behind. The hurry-up-and-get-out-the-door mad dash caused her stomach to become nauseous and now she didn't feel so well.

Steven sat beside her and his soft, chocolate

colored eyes searched her face. "You look a little peaked. Do you need me to get you something to eat?" He stood.

"I'm fine. Sit down. We need to pray."

Steven returned to his chair and clasped her palm. "Are you sure you don't want some coffee?"

She elbowed him before bowing her head. "Dear, Lord, please be with Steven today especially during his radiation. Let the treatment go directly into the cancer cells completely missing his good cells. Heal his body from this cancer, Lord. Do a miracle in his life, our lives, and in our children's lives. You are our Hope and our Healer, Lord. Give us strength whatever comes our way. Amen."

Steven brought her fingers to his mouth and kissed her knuckles. "I should've woken you. I'm thankful you're here."

"Mr. Moore," a nurse called. "If you're ready, we'll take you back now."

Steven squeezed her hand then rose from his chair.

I hate this! Her heart cried out. She needed a moment longer with Steven to reassure her everything would be all right, but it wasn't and there was nothing she could do. "I love you."

"And I love you." He turned and followed the nurse down the hallway before the door closed behind them.

She was beginning to hate closed doors.

Her phone rang and she fumbled through her purse to find it. "Hello."

"Elizabeth?"

She glanced at her phone's screen. "Eric. Hi." She leaned on the chair's armrest and closed her eyes. "Sorry I missed your call."

"Did you have a nice dinner?"

"We did." *Until Dr. Middleton called.*

"The reason why I was calling was to see if your boys would like to be shepherds in our upcoming Christmas in July choir performance."

Relief filled her there wasn't another emergency to attend to. "Thank you for asking, but I'm sorry we won't be able to make it. This might come as a surprise but Steven and I married last month."

He chuckled. "Actually, Elizabeth, it's not a surprise at all. I'm happy for you both."

"Thank you. We're very happy." She sat up quickly. "Eric, I need your help. A few months back there was a new family that had joined our church, and if I'm not mistaken, the husband is a realtor. Can you get me in contact with him? I want to sell my house."

"You want to sell?"

It did seem odd after everything she did to try to save her house and years of prayers not to lose it, but now it was the right thing to do no matter how difficult it might be to let go. "I do."

"Where are you living now?"

"We're staying near Moffitt, the cancer center, for the time being while Steven receives radiation, but he has a beautiful place in Georgia we're calling home."

"It's wonderful to hear, Elizabeth, especially that he's sought out treatment. It's obvious he did it for you. Whatever you both need, I'm here."

"Thank you, Eric. And one more thing. Pray for us. This is going to be a long journey and one of the reasons I want to sell the house. Steven showed me love by paying off my home and I want to show him love by doing the opposite, selling. The next phase of his treatment is expensive and selling the house will cover some of the cost."

"I understand. I'll let you know something by the end of the day. Also, I'll add you both to the church prayer list."

"I'd appreciate that very much."

"Take care, Elizabeth. I'll talk to you soon."

Leaning back in her chair, she tucked her cell back into her purse. A woman sitting across from her stared. Self-consciously, Elizabeth touched her hair. She scanned the waiting room and her gaze caught on a restroom sign. First thing, clean up, then keep her promise to her husband.

Chapter Twenty-Eight

Two days later, Elizabeth sat in the hospital's waiting room chairs, exhaustion pulling at her in every which way, but Steven fared worse. He slept, yet hadn't felt rested. He had also recognized that after his treatments, the sheer heaviness of his body made his movements more difficult. She began taking extra care of herself because the worse his fatigue seemed, the more he focused on her health, as if cancer was contagious and she'd contract it by his nearness.

She lifted her cell from her lap and checked her email. She'd been waiting to hear from the realtor to confirm their meeting on Thursday. She wanted a 'for sale' sign in her front yard by Friday, packing to begin by Saturday. She had yet to tell Steven what she had planned and wanted to share it with him on the way back to Miami. Hopefully Luke would understand. It was going to be difficult for them both but what mattered was getting the ball rolling so by month's end, they'd be officially moved into their home in Monticello. From there, they'd have a month before his clinical trial began and she wanted nothing to stand in their way of living as a family.

She smiled. The realtor sent word he'd meet with her tomorrow at two o'clock.

"You look happy."

Steven's voice made her smile widen. She met his gaze, noticing the dark circles beneath his glassy eyes. "Let's go see our boys." She collected her things, stuffing her cell into her bag. They walked hand in hand through the waiting room and down to the parking lot.

"It will be nice to have a few days off before my next treatment. Maybe I'll be able to rest." As they neared the driver's side door, Steven slowed to a stop. "Are you sure you want to drive?"

She'd offered to drive to Moffitt this morning when Steven mentioned his weariness. "I enjoy being behind the wheel. Besides, it's an easy shot."

He nodded and moved around to the passenger's side.

Several minutes into the drive, Steven's eyes closed. Elizabeth had hoped to share her plans for selling the house but it could wait; she didn't want to disrupt his sleep. Instead, she thought of what to box up and what to give away. But the more she thought on it, the more difficult the decisions became. Sixteen years of memories were wrapped up in the house Chris had bought her as a wedding present. That home had seen difficult times, but also wonderful times with children. It was a home built on love.

Elizabeth veered onto Interstate 75, toward her past, planning for her family's future. When the time came, she'd leave the past behind.

Three hours later and nearing Miami, her phone vibrated. She looked to Steven's sleeping form and hurriedly answered her sister's call. "Hey."

"Lizzy, I wanted to let you know we're at your house. The kids wanted to swim."

"I'm glad you called. We were heading your way. We'll be there in fifteen."

"See you then."

Elizabeth ended the call.

Steven sighed. "So I take it we're close. I only meant to close my eyes."

"You were more tired than you thought. We're heading to our house. We'll be there soon." *Our house. But it's not ours.* "Steven, I wanted to speak with you about something."

"Sounds serious."

She tightened her grip on the steering wheel. "I've made an appointment with a realtor tomorrow. I'm selling the house." She felt Steven's gaze before glancing his way. "I think it's the right thing to do."

"For whom?"

"For our family."

He remained silent for a few moments. "I don't want you to regret selling. Are you sure you want to do this?"

No. It's going to be hard, but I'm doing this for us. "It's time to move on."

Steven slumped into a porch chair illuminated

by the setting sun. In the pool, Phillip wrestled with a laughing Luke. Elizabeth had yet to include Luke in her plan to sell the house. Surely, the boy wouldn't take to the idea willingly. His world had already turned upside down when his dad was ripped from him. Would this cause the rift between him and Steven to grow?

Steven rose from the chair, lifted the grill's lid, and flipped the hamburgers. Flames leaped to lick the grease from the sides of the meat. He turned the grill to medium heat and called to Phillip. "How does everyone like their burgers?"

Phillip pushed through the water towards him. "I prefer mine with a thin pink center but everyone else likes theirs completely done."

Luke swam to the edge of the pool alongside Phillip. "Steven, are you going to swim?"

Steven closed the lid and hung the spatula off the grill. If only he had the strength. "Maybe later."

Phillip splashed Luke. "Someone has to watch our food if I'm in the pool with you. You wouldn't want your mom cooking."

Somehow Phillip must have sensed that Steven didn't have the energy to swim as the day crept on, so when Phillip handed him the spatula and asked if he minded grilling, Steven didn't hesitate. He wanted to feel useful, be a part, and yet still take it easy. He was doing just that as Elizabeth, Samantha, and Christopher, who no longer wore their bathing suits, ambled through the patio carrying paper plates, plastic silverware, and napkins. Christopher left a napkin trail behind him as he went.

Steven followed, snatching up flowered napkins from the ground. "Here you go, buddy."

Christopher angled his head and pointed to the pool. "Me in pool now, Daddy?"

Steven's heart melted at Christopher's words. "Mommy has already given you a bath and changed you into pajamas. You'll have to wait until tomorrow." He lifted Christopher into his arms and carried him to the table, setting him into a chair. "Let me check on the food. Elizabeth, can you grab me a plate? The burgers should be done."

"Sure." Elizabeth hurried inside and came right back out with a yellow ceramic platter. "Here you go."

He took the plate and leaned over to give her a small peck on the cheek. "Thank you."

"For what?"

Where should he begin? How she loved him. The support she continually showed him through this cancer. For the times she wanted to press him to talk—he could see it in her expressions—yet didn't ask, only stayed by his side and comforted him. The way she prayed for them and as a family. How could he tell her how blessed he was having her as his wife? "For being you."

She gave him a smirk. "I hope that's a compliment."

"It's meant to be," he said quietly. "I love you, Elizabeth. I only wish I knew how to show you."

She cupped his cheek. "Make no mistake, Mr.

Moore. You've left no doubt in my mind to the length or depth of your love." Her palm slid to his chest. "You might want to take those hamburgers off."

Steven quickly opened the lid to the grill and scooped the burgers onto the plate Elizabeth held out for him. "I'm glad I put Phillip's burger on the top rack. There might be a little pink."

"I'm sure they'll be fine. Besides, it's good to see someone else cook like me." She winked, leaving him smiling in her wake.

As Elizabeth claimed her chair, Steven scanned the potato salad, chips, condiments, and burgers on the red and white checkered tablecloth. Hopefully his stomach agreed it was time to eat. He sat next to Christopher who raised his hand. "Me, pray."

"Of course." Phillip encouraged, cupping his hands together as Christopher had done. Everyone followed.

"Tank God fo food. Tank God fo Mommy, Daddy, brater. Amen." Christopher crawled up on his knees and stuffed his hand into one of the chip bowls like a torpedo. Broken chips flew from the bowl to the table.

"Since we're all together," Elizabeth began. "I want to share some news with you."

Samantha leaned forward. "Are you pregnant?"

Steven's heart jumped. He turned to his wife whose cheeks now reddened to a beautiful pink. She met his gaze and he saw regret in her turquoise eyes.

"I'm not," she whispered, then continued to tell them about her plans to sell the house. Luke set his burger down, his expression a mirror image of how Steven felt inside—of something precious being taken away in an instant. A house. A child. They both held great meaning and left a void so deep, so real, Steven understood.

"… the realtor will be here at nine in the morning." Elizabeth continued until Luke stood from the patio chair and ran into the house.

"I'll go." Steven rose and headed to where he suspected Luke had gone. Steven knocked on the bedroom door. Should he open the door or wait? "May I come in?" He leaned against the doorframe, trying to think what he'd say. Luke had given up so much and now he'd be forced to leave the only home he'd ever known. "I know this is going to be hard on you, and I had hoped my fishing buddy might feel like talking about it."

Steven listened closely but heard nothing except for blaring silence. Silence he had desperately wanted them to overcome. "Do you remember what you told Juwonya on the pier the other day? We have to admit we can't do things on our own and ask for help? I'm asking, Luke. I need your help because I can't do this on my own."

Moments passed. Steven's body slumped and his head rested against the door. He had failed. No matter how much he loved Luke or how hard he tried, he wasn't able to reach him.

Footfalls sounded. Steven stood upright and

the door opened.

Luke met his gaze. "Why would you need my help? You're a grown-up. Grown-ups don't need help with anything. They just make the decisions and the kids have to follow." He turned and walked across his room then plopped on his bed.

Taking this as an invitation, Steven entered Luke's room and sat on the edge of his bed. "It's a myth, you know."

"What is?"

"Adults really don't have all the answers. Some of the time we're so afraid to make decisions or mistakes, we don't even try. This is where your mom and I are different. No, we both don't have all the answers, but she's not afraid to make mistakes or try. She wants to do what's best for everyone in the long run, for our future. She's a fighter and her faith in the Lord is what sustains her."

"So what about you? You said you're different than mom?"

"My faith right now is strained because of my health and I don't want to think about the future. And that's where I need your help. I want you to help me not to be afraid."

Luke frowned. "Afraid? Afraid of what?"

Steven let out a long breath. "Afraid of the future. Afraid I might not be around to love your mom, you, or Christopher. But did you know that when we're together, as a family, I'm less scared? I feel stronger and I'm reminded of God's love for me. I'm not alone."

Luke ran his hand over his sheets and pulled a blanket to his chest.

"I know this might not be making much sense, but I want you to know if you feel afraid because of all the changes in your life or the ones about to take place, I understand. I just hope you know you're not alone."

"But I am alone. Nobody cares how I feel about anything."

"Your mom cares greatly about how you feel. She loves you more than her own life. And I wouldn't be sitting here if I didn't care. But most importantly, God cares. I know you know this. I also know it's been difficult for you and for that I'm sorry."

Luke seemed to be taking in his words so Steven waited quietly once again.

"I'm sorry, too." Luke lowered his voice. "For what I said at the pond."

If Steven hadn't been intently waiting for the boy to respond, he would have missed his meaning all together. Was he apologizing for what happened at the pond with Christopher?

"I didn't mean it."

"I know."

"You saved my brother." Luke looked him in the eye. "Is it okay to be scared? Afraid people I love will die?"

"Yes, it's okay."

"Do you think God is okay with my feelings, too?"

"Yes, God knows our hearts better than we

know ourselves and nothing you can say, think, or do will ever change how much He loves you. But now you know why I need your help. We need to love each other. We need to be a family. We need to pray for each other because God is the only One who takes away our fears. Do you think you can do that even if you're scared of the future?

"I'll try."

Steven placed an arm around his shoulders. "You're a wonderful boy and I'm proud of you."

Tears formed in Luke's eyes. "Dad use to tell me that."

Steven fought the moisture from filling his own eyes. "He was right, you know, and I'm proud to be a part of your family."

Luke nodded and brushed away a fallen tear.

Steven rose. "I'm hungry. Do you want to go back and eat?"

"I'm starved." Luke jumped up and wiped his face with his sleeve. "Do you remember the baseball cards you bought me?"

"I do." They descended the stairs.

"I never finished opening the packs." He shrugged. "Do you want to finish?"

Steven smiled. "You bet."

For several minutes Steven replayed his conversation with Luke. A turning point in their relationship at last. He and Luke exited the house where Elizabeth was reclining in a chair on the patio with her hand resting on her abdomen.

Samantha's earlier question about Elizabeth

being pregnant blindsided him yet again. He desired a child of his own, prayed God would bless them. And for a blink of an eye, he could picture Elizabeth with his child.

A dream.

Chapter Twenty-Nine

Elizabeth sat on her bedroom floor, knee deep in family photo albums, DVD's Chris had made over the years, and cards he and Luke had given her. Tears rolled down her cheeks as she unfolded a letter Chris had given her for their anniversary a few years ago. She ran her finger along the masculine script.

Sweetheart,

She smiled at the way he always addressed his letters.

I can't tell you how surprised I was the other night to find you waiting for me at the pool with a candlelight dinner. I had never danced in the moonlight before...

Neither had she. She touched her lips recalling their kiss.

She couldn't do this. She shouldn't be doing this.

Elizabeth pushed everything from her lap and stood quickly, moving to the window. She drew back the curtains. Several street lamps in the cul-de-sac blazed into the night, reflecting off the gentle rain.

She shouldn't have left Steven's side for a second night in a row to finish this torturous walk into the past, but she didn't want him to see her like this, like she'd knew she'd be, crying over her dead husband.

She wiped her face with the back of her hand and yet it did little good. She glanced down to the yard where the 'for sale' sign stood. She prayed the house would sell quickly. This move was tearing her apart.

Elizabeth spun and grabbed an empty box by the closet and begun filling it with memories, one by one. The more it filled, the more tears streaked down her face. By the time the photo albums reached the top, she began filling another, then another. She wanted to burn them to stop the pain. She bit back a gasp at her thoughts.

"I'm sorry, Chris. I didn't mean it." She hiccupped.

She glanced up to the ceiling. "Lord, what is wrong with me? Why am I falling apart?"

She needed to lie down if only for a few minutes. She climbed into her bed and yanked the throw by her feet into her arms, yet remained on top of the comforter. She let out a long breath trying to control her breathing and hiccupped instead.

She'd been working hard for the last few days, perhaps too hard. Even Steven had mentioned it in passing, but it had to be done. She closed her eyes and envisioned Steven still helping her box up her many books, how he'd enjoyed playing with the children, and the meals he cooked them for dinner.

She wiped her cheeks with the blanket and

hiccupped once again, but her breathing was evening out. The calming effect Steven possessed by the mere thought of him could never be denied, nor could their love for each other. Then why did she feel so broken?

Her eyes became heavy. She wanted to be with Steven, to fall asleep in his arms, but he seemed so far away.

Steven startled from a dream and felt for his wife alongside him. He reached farther and rose up to nothing but an empty bed. He blinked, willing his eyes to focus within the darkened room. Katherine's room.

Sweat beaded his face and body. He threw the covers back and stood from the bed. "Elizabeth?" A glow from the street light trickled into the room, just enough to show she wasn't with him.

Steven flung a shirt over his head and started down the hall, stopping first in Christopher's room. With no sign of her, Steven strode into the room and placed a gentle hand on Christopher's small form. Hoping not to wake him, Steven bowed his head. "Lord, protect this child. Help him to love and to know You at an early age. Allow me to see him grow into the man You'll call him to be." Quietly exiting the room, Steven proceeded to Luke's room and prayed a similar prayer, but praised God for the growth of their newfound relationship and family.

At the end of the hall, light seeped beneath the door of the bedroom Chris and Elizabeth had shared.

Since he'd been at the house, he had yet to enter. Although he knew she spent time here, he never wanted to intrude. But tonight he needed to see that she was all right.

Steven opened the door and walked in, his gaze scanning the bedroom. Boxes, some stacked seven high, stood like building blocks along the floor. He caught the sound of a light hiccup and wove his way through the clutter to find Elizabeth asleep on the bed.

Red blotches covered her face and from what he could tell, her eyes seemed swollen. He glanced back at the scattered mess along the floor.

Steven went to the hallway closet, pulled down two quilts and returned, laying one over his wife and tossing the other onto the oversized chair next to the bed.

He placed a protective hand on her hip and his heart ached. "Lord," he begged under his breath. "I know this is a difficult time. Please give her peace."

She moaned.

He took a step back and glimpsed several pictures face-up on the floor. He couldn't see them clearly but as he approached, there were more than pictures. Letters, cards, homemade gifts of cupcake-liner flowers and a cotton ball snowman drew him to his knees. This was where she'd sat, he was sure. He lifted the snowman for a moment and smiled at Luke's missing coal button. He set it down and picked up a letter that rested on top of a pile of pictures. His pulse quickened at the sight of Chris's note to

Elizabeth. *She was missing him.* Tempted to read the letter, he set the note back down and hesitated before rising to his feet. He wouldn't intrude on her past. He turned off the light and settled into the oversized chair next to his wife.

Some things were sacred.

"Would you like to wake up and eat something?"

Elizabeth's head pounded. She reached up and rubbed her forehead, trying to clear her mind. "Chris?"

Within a moment's pause, she realized what she'd done. She forced her eyes open and sat up, taking hold of Steven's arm. "I'm so sorry, Steven. Last night…I was going through—"

"I understand." Love shone on his face. "You were thinking of him when you fell asleep so it's only natural to think of him this morning."

She shook her head. "No. He wasn't who I thought of as I fell asleep—it was you. I had been crying and gotten myself so upset I couldn't sleep, but when I thought of you, our love for each other, I could finally close my eyes."

He covered her hand that rested on his arm. "You don't need to sell."

She noticed for the first time the blanket partly covering her. "Thank you for the blanket."

"You're welcome." Steven tipped her chin with his finger and met her gaze. "You don't need to sell."

"I do. After I leave, I can't come back. It's too hard."

"Is there anything I can do?"

What hadn't he done but be supportive in every way? "Feed me? I'm starved."

He grinned and clasped her hand. "Come on. Breakfast is waiting."

Elizabeth stood and the room spun. She clutched Steven's hand.

Steven caught her against him. "Elizabeth, what's the matter?" His words came out panicked, drawing her attention to his face.

"It's got to be my sugar. I didn't eat any snacks last night."

His features softened. "Your sugar must have dropped." He led her out of the bedroom and down the stairwell to the kitchen where the children were eating.

She separated from Steven and took a chair next to Luke. With luck, he wouldn't suspect she wasn't feeling well. Christopher pushed his plate away and climbed down from his seat into her lap. "What's for breakfast? It smells and looks great." She ran her fingers through Christopher's blond hair.

Luke shoveled a spoonful of eggs into his mouth. "Mom, can I go to Ryan's house? He's going to the batting cages later."

She looked to Steven who placed a plate of food and a glass of orange juice in front of her. *Drink,* he mouthed. She lifted the glass and enjoyed the cool, tangy liquid on her tongue.

Steven took Christopher from her lap and held him. "Beka called this morning. She was surprised that I answered." The corners of his mouth rose slightly.

Elizabeth chuckled before taking a small bite of scrambled eggs, ignoring the nausea. "I take it she interrogated you?"

He winked. "I was able to handle her. I told her we were married. She's after you now."

"Thanks." She picked out a sausage piece and placed it in her mouth, taking an extra breath. She'd felt this way before, three times to be exact. *Could she be pregnant?*

"Mom, can I?"

Elizabeth looked to her son. "What?"

Steven set Christopher on his feet and the little boy scurried out through the kitchen. "I'll take him to Ryan's. Luke said he knows the way but it's up to you."

"Yes, of course, it's fine."

Luke jumped up from his chair, shoveling the rest of his food into his mouth on his way to the sink. "I'll grab my stuff."

Elizabeth watched her son leave, unsure if she should tell Steven her thoughts. "I should check my sugar." She stood.

Steven held out his hand. "You eat. I'll get it."

Alone, Elizabeth leaned back in her chair and rubbed her temples. *Could she be pregnant? Of course she could.* She stood and paced, then opened the cabinet, taking out headache medicine. Grabbing a glass, she filled it with water and swallowed the tablets. *She needed a pregnancy test.*

Steven entered the kitchen with her glucose monitor in hand. "It's all ready to check your sugar."

She walked to the counter and pricked her finger, then added the blood to the strip. A second later, there was a beep. "My sugar is a bit too low." *So it was her sugar.* The possibility of having Steven's child, even for a moment, clashed hope and disappointment together like cymbals, vibrating through her heart.

"Elizabeth, are you all right?"

She nodded. "Yes. Yes. I am fine. Are you leaving now for Beka's?"

"Would you'd rather I wait?"

"No. I'll be fine. Besides, he misses Ryan. This will be good for him."

Steven gathered her in his arms. "Do me a favor. While I'm gone, please rest."

She smiled up at him. "You know I can't resist anything you ask of me, but with you gone, Christopher will need my attention."

He leaned close to her ear. "I'm taking him with me. No excuses."

She giggled at his closeness. "No excuses, but I want a kiss to seal the deal."

"You drive a hard bargain, Mrs. Moore, and one I'd gladly accept." He pressed a kiss to one corner of her mouth, then the other, before hitting his mark. His kisses were gentle, thorough.

She clung to him and tears pricked her eyes.

He held her close and rubbed her back. "Are you sure you're all right?"

No. "Yes."

Chapter Thirty

Two weeks later, after Steven's third set of radiation treatments, Elizabeth once again drove back to her sister's while Steven slept in the seat next to her. And weariness claimed her like never before. She'd made a doctor's appointment for tomorrow in hopes of finding out the cause of her fatigue. Her sugar had leveled out and two pregnancy tests told her she definitely wasn't pregnant. Still, her nausea grew. She hadn't told Steven. No need to worry him when his own fatigue was worsening. She had to stay well to take care of him. They had extra help with the boys since moving in with Phillip and Sam. They'd had little choice with a serious offer on the house. The closing was set for the day after tomorrow. Things had moved so quickly with the house that she'd had little time to think of the past and what signing the contract meant. Today though, driving from Moffitt gave her plenty of time and reassured her she'd been doing the right thing all along. Thankfully, Steven had sent most of her things from the house to storage while movers had taken the rest to Monticello. Mike had called to let Steven know everything had arrived.

Next week was Steven's last set of radiation treatments and then they'd be home, really home, and she couldn't wait.

Elizabeth pulled into her sister's driveway and Steven yawned. "We're here?" His head rested against the car seat. She ran her fingers through his hair and his eyes closed again. A deep moan came from within his throat. "I love you."

She cupped his cheek. "And I love you."

They remained motionless for several more minutes before Steven opened his eyes and smiled at her, that smile that made it difficult to breathe. "Next week, we'll be home."

"I can't wait to start our lives together."

His brows dipped slightly. "From the first moment you stepped into my life to this very moment, here and now…our lives together have already started. I've cherished each moment with you."

"Steven…"

He took her hand and pressed a kiss to her palm. "I think I'll go in and take a short nap."

Her body tensed as he slid from the car. An alarm went off within her as she followed after him. Steven usually slept in the car after his treatments, but never once after he saw the boys. He'd made sure to spend time with Luke opening baseball cards. It was something they enjoyed together and they both looked forward to. Elizabeth suspected he did so more for Luke's sake, a way of showing him that Steven was fine.

Steven knocked on the front door and Luke's ready smile greeted them. How would her son handle the change? But most importantly, was her husband all right?

Luke held several baseball cards in one hand and pointed into the house as they made their way to the living room. "Ryan's here. We opened a few packs because he has to go home soon, but I saved us a few to open together. I even traded him for a couple of rookie cards we needed."

They entered the living room where everyone had gathered. Phillip and Sam smiled up at them from the couch.

Beka quickly got to her feet and hugged her neck. "About time I caught up with the happy couple." She looked to Steven. "I knew I had a good feeling about you."

Steven smiled. "Likewise."

Luke held the cards out for Steven and he took them.

Was it her imagination or did Steven grow weaker right before her? His vibrant dark eyes seemed to dull as he shuffled through each baseball card. "Good job. Your collection is shaping up," he said, glancing toward the bedroom. "Excuse me, everyone, but I think I'll go lie down for a bit. Beka, good to see you."

"Great to see you, Steven."

Her husband made a beeline for the room and she barely had time to close the door behind them before he fell into bed, shoes and all. "At least let me remove your shoes." After placing his shoes by the closet, she returned to his side and leaned over him. "How are you feeling?"

"Tired," he sighed.

"I gathered. What else?"

"Extremely tired." He pushed back the hair that fell in her face and tucked the strands behind her ear. "Wake me in an hour and I'll be good as new."

She pressed her lips to his and he sighed again. She pulled back quickly. "Did that hurt?"

"No. I was enjoying my kiss." He reached up and brought her back to him, kissing her soundly.

She giggled against his mouth. "I thought you were tired."

"You give me super strength." He pulled her close and nuzzled her hair. "You feel and smell wonderful."

She said nothing, but listened to the beating of her husband's heart. The sound wooed her to relax and the worry and tension she had bottled inside began to drain away. "I should say good-bye to Beka."

"You should." He mumbled the words.

She closed her eyes and all the things she felt she needed to do filled her mind. She pushed back her to-do list and began to praise the Lord for her husband and family instead. Somewhere within her prayer, sleep carried her away.

Steven rolled over to find the bed empty and

the memory of his dream hit him full force. "Elizabeth," he called, sitting up quickly.

Elizabeth rushed from the bathroom fully dressed. "I'm right here. What's wrong?"

He blinked twice, trying to comprehend her words, yet relief surged through him upon seeing her with wet hair and holding a brush. *She'd been in the shower.*

Elizabeth came and sat on the bed. "Steven?"

"I'm fine. I was concerned about you. It must have been a dream."

Her shoulders relaxed. "More like a nightmare the way you shouted my name."

He screamed out for her? A nightmare. How right she was. "What time is it?"

"Seven in the morning. We slept through the night."

"No, Sleeping Beauty, you slept. I got up close to bedtime and put the boys to bed. Luke and I opened the packs of baseball cards he mentioned earlier. I stayed up for another hour talking with Phillip and Samantha before coming to bed."

Her brows dipped slightly. "Why didn't you wake me?"

"You needed your sleep. I know you haven't been feeling well lately even if you haven't mentioned it." He placed a hand over hers. "I want you to make an appointment to see the doctor. Will you do it for me? I'd feel better knowing everything checks out."

Something passed over her eyes and she

looked at their hands.

"What aren't you telling me, Elizabeth?"

"I've already made an appointment."

"When?"

"I called last week."

He lifted her chin with his finger so their eyes met. "I meant, when is your appointment? Why didn't you tell me you were feeling worse?"

"I didn't want to worry you. I know you've been concerned the last few weeks with this move and my working hard into the night, but all that's over now." She cupped his face. "Tomorrow I sign the papers to sell the house. In no time, I'll be feeling more like myself."

Since his radiation started, Steven had a difficult time concentrating on more than one thing at a time, and right now his wife was much too distracting regardless that she was fully dressed. The smell of her hair. The fullness of her lips…

Steven stood from the bed. "So when is your appointment? Or have you already been? Are you hiding something from me?"

Elizabeth went to him, but Steven took a step back. Her turquoise eyes reflected hurt and possibly frustration. "Yes, I should have told you and for that I'm sorry. My appointment is this morning."

"This morning?" It was beginning to make sense. His wife was dressed and showered so early. "When were you going to tell me?" She didn't answer.

Steven opened the dresser and pulled out a

navy blue shirt and a pair of khakis and hurried to dress. He jammed his feet into his shoes and turned to her. "You asked me to tell you about my cancer. I need to know what's going on with you. Don't you think I have the right to know as well?"

"Can't you understand why I didn't? You have to take care of yourself. I didn't want to worry you if there's nothing wrong. It could be as simple as needing a little B12 or another vitamin supplement."

"Why? Have you been depressed? Lacking in energy before the move?"

She threw her hands to her hips. "No, Doctor Moore, I have not."

"Okay, good." He nodded. "But we'll still have them check when they do your blood work." Steven grabbed the keys from the dresser.

She turned away and headed back toward the bathroom, shaking her head. "I don't know what I'm going to do with you."

Steven watched her disappear behind the wall, but he had a few ideas. He smiled. "Tell me. What were you going to do with the kids?"

"Remember, I mentioned I was taking them to Henry and Linda's. Since the children were going to be with them for the afternoon, I decided to make an appointment to see the doctor."

She came out of the bathroom and took her purse from the bench at the end of the bed. "The children are almost ready. Phillip is feeding them cereal."

Steven grasped the door handle before she

could. "You asked me not to shut you out. I'm asking the same of you."

"Forgive me." She kissed his cheek. "I won't."

Why in the world did she insist on Steven staying in the waiting area? Thirty minutes in this stark white room had brought the tension seeping into her neck.

She focused on the brown examining table, the two grey chairs flanking the other wall. She had already counted the lights, the colors in the flooring, anything to take her mind off the worry and the nausea that grew worse with each passing minute. She opened her purse, pulled out her cell, and texted Steven. *Miss you.*

Miss you. Has the doctor returned?

No. I'm just sitting here.

Are you all right?

I don't know. I don't know what's wrong with me, Steven. Please don't be upset. I thought I might have been pregnant but wasn't.

There was a long pause and Elizabeth stared at her phone waiting for his response.

None came.

She closed her eyes and shook her head. She should have told him. Steven's voice sounded down the hall and drew near.

"She's right in here." A nurse spoke and the door opened. "You have a visitor." She smiled at her then at Steven before closing the door behind her.

Steven took the chair beside her. "You're not alone in this."

"I know."

"You can lean on me. Share whatever is on your mind, however you're feeling. I'm not fragile. I won't break."

"I know." But did she, really? Was she allowing his cancer to change the way she looked at him, the man who had always represented strength to her. "I took two pregnancy tests a week apart. They both came back negative. I didn't tell you because I didn't want you to be disappointed, but I also wasn't sure how I felt."

He collected her hand and ran his thumb over her knuckles in a circular motion. "You didn't want to be pregnant?"

"Actually, I was afraid to hope. To be able to give you a child—our child. I knew if I wasn't, the opportunity of us having a baby of our own is very slim. Then I thought perhaps it was for the best since my pregnancies are never to full term and I land on bedrest for weeks at a time. The chance of me miscarrying is very high."

"Have you miscarried before?"

"After Luke. Before Christopher."

"I'm sorry."

"It was hard. I went in for an ultrasound to see the baby's sex and blood was coming from the sac. Two days later I miscarried and had a D&C." She took a deep breath and leaned her head on Steven's shoulder.

He wrapped his arm around her waist. "I had mixed feelings myself, knowing you could become pregnant since you weren't on birth control. I wanted you to become pregnant, but I was afraid if something happened to me…"

"With the cancer."

He nodded. "I didn't want to leave you alone to raise our child."

Like what she'd experienced with Chris. "I'm thankful for Christopher every day and I would be just as thankful if God had given us a child." She let out a yawn. "Do you think they forgot about us?"

He kissed her hair and rested his head against hers. "I spoke with the nurse. They sent the blood work to the lab but they're waiting for the results of one test."

"Do you know what it's for?" Just then the doctor knocked on the door and entered, followed by a nurse. Elizabeth sat up. "What did you find out?"

"You have low progesterone and your HCG levels are low. You'll need to make an appointment with your OB/GYN, but in the meantime, with your history, I'm prescribing you progesterone pills for two weeks."

Steven smiled. "Are you saying what I think you're saying?"

"Isn't this why you both came? Didn't you know?"

Elizabeth rose and looked between Steven and the doctor, feeling lost in translation. "Would someone please explain what's going on?"

"You're pregnant." The doctor was matter-of-fact. "I'd suggest you start taking the progesterone pills today if possible. With your history and your levels being so low, you're at a high risk for a miscarriage."

She frowned. "How is that possible?" She glanced at Steven for understanding. "I took two pregnancy tests and they came back negative."

Steven took her hand once again and kissed her knuckles where he'd lovingly rubbed a moment ago. "Your HCG level isn't high enough for a pregnancy test to detect, but a blood test is able to read your HCG more clearly."

"How far along am I?" She looked to the doctor.

"I'd say about four to six weeks. Your OB/GYN will be able to tell you more."

"I'm pregnant." The words rolled off her tongue. She placed her hand on her midsection and looked to Steven. "We're going to have a baby."

The doctor chuckled. "I'll leave you two alone."

Steven's eyes lit and his smile threatened to melt her right where she stood.

Chapter Thirty-One

Steven awoke and peered at his wife next to him. He blinked. She was watching him with a faraway look in her eyes. He turned on his side and nestled his head against the pillow, facing her.

"I'm pregnant," she said, as if she heard the news for the first time.

He couldn't help but grin. "So I've heard."

"I wonder if she'll have blonde hair or dark hair like yours."

"She?" Steven raised an eyebrow. Had he ever told her he'd prayed she'd have another daughter? He couldn't recall. He rose up on one elbow and fingered the soft tendrils of hair that lay across her chest. "What happens if it's a boy?"

She pushed him back down and snuggled into his arms. "Whether boy or girl—however our child will look, they will be just the way God made them to be."

He rested his hands on her abdomen, anticipating the day he'd be able to feel their child's movements.

She inhaled a big breath. "I'm selling the

house today."

Obviously, she'd been awake for some time with a lot on her mind. He waited for her to say more but when she didn't, he pressed her to continue. "Are you ready?"

"Mostly. God's given me peace and it's time to move on." She covered his hands with her own. "I think our baby is a sign of God's blessing. Don't you?"

"A wonderful sign."

A muffled sound came from the other side of the door. "I think we have company." She twisted and smiled at him. "We haven't had a chance to talk about it, but do we want to tell the boys or wait until I see the OB/GYN next week?"

More than ready. Before Steven could respond, the door swung open and Christopher ran full speed toward them. His body slammed into the bed and he gripped the sheets with both hands. He fought to climb up and when Steven reached over to help, a triumphant smile shone on Christopher's face. "I here!"

"Yes, you are." Steven laughed.

Christopher walked on his knees across the bed, falling to his hands once before he wiggled his way beside them to a sitting position. "Morrring."

"Good morning to you." Elizabeth tried to comb down Christopher's hair with her fingers while looking at Steven. *Well?* she mouthed. As if giving him football signs from the sidelines of a game, she alternately nodded, shook her head then shrugged her shoulders.

Steven answered her secret code with his own nod and a smile. Her own smile grew wide as she turned back to Christopher. "Daddy and Mommy have something very special to tell you and your brother."

Christopher pointed to the door. "Brater, eat."

Steven rose from the bed and stuck his head out of the bedroom door. Luke sat at the kitchen bar, shoving a spoon filled with some sort of fruity cereal into his mouth. "Luke, can you come here for a minute?" Luke rose from his chair quickly and joined the rest of them on the bed. Steven sat down and Christopher climbed into his lap.

Elizabeth put her arm around Luke's shoulders. "Steven and I have something we want to share with you."

Luke sat upright and his hazel eyes lit. "We're not selling the house?"

"Oh, no, Luke. That's not the news I was about to tell you." Elizabeth shook her head slightly and glanced at Steven. "I'm still meeting with the lawyer in a few hours."

Luke's shoulders slumped. "Then what's the news?"

Elizabeth glanced at Steven, reached for his hand. Steven took hers immediately. "We found out yesterday that I'm pregnant."

Luke said nothing, but looked at the bed as if he'd found something there that amazed him. Christopher however bounced from Steven's lap and into Elizabeth's. She let out a slight moan and hugged him to her chest.

"Christopher, come here. I want to show you something." Steven said, holding out his arms for the boy. Christopher jumped out of her lap and came to Steven. He plopped his little bottom in his lap and Steven pointed to Elizabeth's stomach. "Christopher, you have to be careful with Mommy, she has a baby in her tummy. Be careful sitting in Mommy's lap. Go slow."

Christopher crawled over to Elizabeth and she grinned at him. He pointed to her stomach. "Baby." He returned to her lap at a much slower pace.

"When is the baby coming?" Luke eyed his younger brother but showed no emotion.

"We'll know more when we see the doctor next week, but we think the baby's due date will be around the beginning of March." Steven waited for a reaction, anything to help him understand how Luke had processed the news. Still nothing.

"Steven and I are leaving soon, but what would you like to do when we return?"

"I'd like to go to Dad's grave."

Steven cringed, though this was what he'd been waiting for—a sign to the boy's feelings. Luke didn't want to leave his home, his family, or his dad. "Then we will."

Luke glanced at Steven. "Thank you." He rose from the bed and ambled out of the room.

"Elizabeth, we just need your signature on this last page and everything will be finalized." Eric, her lawyer and friend, accompanied his words with a reassuring smile. When she and Steven visited the house she'd shared with Chris for the last time, not a single tear moistened her eyes. Not so now. She could barely see the line for her signature.

Steven leaned close. "You don't have to do this."

Oh, how she loved this man by her side, always supportive and loving her in every way. He told her yet again she didn't need to sell, they were fine financially, but she couldn't imagine the amount of money his treatments would take. Selling the house was another way she could love him and bring their new family closer together.

Peace settled over her, like it had this morning when she watched Steven sleep. She wiped her cheek with her left hand, gripped the pen with her right, and scrawled her name across the line. She set the pen down and pushed the last sheet of the contract across the table to Eric.

Eric gave her the same reassuring smile he had a moment ago and added the sheet to the others. She received a bank check and the buyers of her home received the keys. After everything had been exchanged, both families stood, and both couples went their separate ways.

The rain clouds that filled the skies when they entered Eric's office now drizzled ever so slightly. "Elizabeth. Steven." Eric ran out to them with an umbrella. "I know you plan to leave for Georgia after this last set of treatments. I might not see you both for some time, but I hope you'll keep in touch. I'll be praying for you."

"Of course." Elizabeth hugged his neck. "Thank you for everything."

"You're family." Eric said, releasing her and shaking Steven's hand. "Don't ever forget."

"We won't."

Eric nodded and ran back toward his building while she and Steven headed home to face another obstacle—visiting Chris's grave.

The rain fell harder as Steven pulled up to the cemetery where Chris and Katherine were buried. His efforts to persuade Elizabeth to wait for a night when it wasn't so wet proved useless. She'd been adamant about keeping her word to Luke. Not even his warnings about catching cold in the rain dampened the passion in her eyes. This wasn't just for Luke.

He opened Elizabeth's door and held an oversized golf umbrella over her. Luke exited the other side of the car and fiddled with another umbrella they'd borrowed from Phillip and Sam. Thankfully Elizabeth had agreed to leave Christopher with them.

Steven put his arm around Elizabeth's waist and pulled her close to shield her from the downpour. Luke led the way ahead of them. "It's pretty humid,"

Elizabeth stated as they continued down a winding path.

Luke turned back and waited until they caught up. "I want us to go together." He looked up at Steven. "Is that okay?"

"That's more than okay." Thankfulness flooded Steven's heart. "I'd be honored."

Elizabeth and Luke stepped between the two loved ones' graves. Steven stood back, waiting to comfort or strengthen his family if needed.

Luke knelt in the mud and grass at his father's headstone. "Dad, we're moving and I don't know when I'll be back. Mom reminds me you're not here. I know you're in heaven but I still wanted to come." Luke's head fell. "I love you," he whispered.

Steven's heart ached. He handed Elizabeth the umbrella and knelt beside Luke in the rain. "Your dad loves you, and one day you'll see him again."

Luke looked to Steven with tears in his eyes. "I feel like I'm leaving him behind."

"How can you leave him behind when he's in your heart? It doesn't matter which state you live in, Luke, or which college you attend…he'll always be with you because you'll take his memory wherever you go."

Was it the rain or a tear that slid down the boy's cheek? He swiped it away. "Do you really think so?"

"I do." Steven said, resisting the urge to hug him. *Oh, Lord, give me the words to comfort Your child.* "But do you know who else will be with you no matter where you go?"

"The Lord?"

"Yes. The Lord will never leave you, Luke. He will be your comfort and help with anything you will face, like a new school, new friends, or a new brother and sister who will probably get into your things." Luke's mouth lifted slightly. "You are never alone, and we, together as a family, will help each other in the future."

Luke gave a small nod.

Steven placed a palm on Luke's shoulder. "We'll be right over here." Luke nodded again and Steven stood. Elizabeth reached out to him and he joined her under the umbrella. Steven ran his fingers through his hair. "I don't want to get you wet."

"Rain never bothered me." She held out the umbrella for him to hold and they walked a few steps, stopping at Katherine's headstone. Elizabeth knelt and Steven followed, holding the umbrella steady.

She ran her fingers over her daughter's name, pressing out the rain that had collected in the depressions. "I miss you and your daddy." Her voice broke and Steven pressed in close to assure her the words he'd spoken to Luke were meant for her as well.

She continued, "I think about you both so often, more so lately since I've been going through our things at the house. I sold the house today." She took a long breath and glanced toward Chris's headstone where Luke still knelt, her eyes filling with tears. "You have given me such wonderful children,

Chris, and God has given our family a future." She palmed her stomach and glanced up at Steven and smiled through her tears. "We are so blessed."

God's awesomeness nearly overwhelmed him as they knelt at the graves. The Lord had indeed given them a wonderful future, to cherish, to love each other with joy and thanksgiving every day of their lives. Tears filled Steven's eyes and he didn't bother to wipe them away.

Elizabeth rose, sniffed, and took a couple steps back to gaze at both graves. Luke came to her side and they hugged. "Ready, Luke?"

"Yeah…I think I'm ready now."

Chapter Thirty-Two

Elizabeth hesitated at the closed bedroom door. Her heart pumped violently within her chest. As soon as Steven stepped into the shower, Elizabeth had sprung into action, asking Sam to take the kids from the house. She had to convince her husband to allow her to travel with him to his last radiation treatment. She wanted, needed, to be at Moffitt with him.

Her hand rested on the knob, her heart racing. Exhaling, she pushed open the door to find her bare-chested husband packing a suitcase. Her pulse increased, but was it because of the man standing before her, or because he was leaving within minutes? Either way, she closed the door behind her and with much determination, pushed her way through the room, stopping in front of him. "I'm going with you."

Steven dropped a shirt into the suitcase. "Elizabeth." He touched her cheek with his hand and ran his thumb down her jaw. Without permission her eyes closed and his mouth found hers. The kiss lingered, and afterward she almost wept in his arms as he held her close.

"You don't want me to stay. Your kiss was proof enough."

He ran his thumb over her lips. "I need you here. I need to know you're safe."

"I will be safe, but I want to come with you."

Steven intertwined their fingers. "You have your appointment with the doctor. I wish I could go with you to hear our child's heartbeat. It's killing me that I can't, but you have to stay for me and the baby. And I have to be at Moffitt for you and our family. I hope you understand. Believe me, Elizabeth, I'd give anything to stay with you."

She nodded in agreement although she felt anything but agreeable at the moment. She loved her husband and wanted to continue to be by his side every step of the way with his treatments. Couldn't they find a way?

"I guess I should finish getting ready." Steven made no move to release her. Instead, he kissed her again.

Her heart stuttered as he put space between them. "Can you stay just a little bit longer? Everyone has left. It's just us for another hour."

He quirked a dark brow and smiled. "Just the two of us?"

Oh, how he looked at her. "Yes."

He gently kissed her cheek, her jaw, and her body leaned into his yet again, enjoying the warmth of his breath against her face. "I'm going to miss you."

Breathless in her husband's arms, she decided right then and there she'd find a way to be with him at Moffitt. "And I'll miss you."

Three days later, Elizabeth entered the doctor's office and went straight to the receptionist's window. She'd explained to her OB/GYN, Carmen, about Steven's condition and her need to be with him while he received his last radiation treatment. In full agreement, Carmen arranged for Elizabeth to be at the office an hour before opening for her examination. She glanced at the ticking clock, sensing time slipping by as she waited.

A nurse opened the window and smiled. "Elizabeth. Good to see you. Meet me on the other side of the door and we'll get started."

"Thank you." Elizabeth took a deep breath and hurried to the door. It opened before she could turn the handle. The nurse escorted her down the hall and entered the examining room where Carmen was turning on the ultrasound machine.

"Elizabeth, I'm so happy for you. Let's get started so you can surprise that new husband of yours."

Once Elizabeth was ready for the exam, the coolness of the table against her back sent a shiver up her spine. Carmen squeezed a clear gel on the probe. "Here we go," she said.

Elizabeth narrowed her eyes in on the ultrasound screen. She couldn't tell anything.

Carmen typed on the keyboard attached to the screen. "You're still rather early, a little over six weeks, but we'll be able to hear the heart beat today."

"I wish Steven could hear it as well. It was really difficult for him not being here."

Carmen squeezed her hand. "Then let's tape it for him." She leaned down for a moment and sat back up. "Ready?"

She nodded. There was a long pause as Carmen moved the probe.

Elizabeth bit her lip. *Had she lost the baby?* And then, she heard it. A pulsating sound filled the silent room and tears filled her eyes.

"Your baby's heartbeat. It sounds healthy." Carmen left the probe there a little longer. "Make sure you continue with your progesterone until it's finished. Once you're in Georgia, you'll need to see another OB/GYN as soon as possible since you're considered a high-risk pregnancy. Make sure they monitor you regularly because you'll possibly be on bedrest like with your other pregnancies." Carmen moved the probe and Elizabeth felt lost in the quietness of the room.

After Carmen typed a few more notes, she gave Elizabeth two hot cloths. "Everything looks good."

Elizabeth climbed down from the table and readied herself to leave. "Did you have a chance to calculate my estimated due date?"

"Yes, I almost forgot." She handed her a DVD. "Around March sixth, and remember Elizabeth, if you have any questions, you can always call me. I might not be able to deliver in Georgia, but I certainly can give you advice."

"Thank you for delivering my children and always being there for me over the years."

"Anytime." Carmen smiled. "Don't forget to tell your husband hello for me and congrats."

"I will." Elizabeth gripped the DVD Carmen had given her and made her way down the hall and through the waiting room with one thing on her mind—to surprise Steven.

She exited the garage elevator and neared her car to find Phillip and Sam waiting for her with the boys. She took out her keys, unlocked the car doors, and opened the trunk.

"So?" Sam reached her first. "How is everything?"

Elizabeth's smile widened at the memory of Carmen's words. "Everything looks good. The heartbeat sounds healthy."

"How wonderful." Her sister linked her arm around hers as they walked to where Phillip was lifting her bags out of their SUV.

"What did the doctor say?" Concern shone in Phillip's eyes as he set the last suitcase down.

Elizabeth touched his arm. "Everything is good. Thank you for praying."

Phillip grinned. "Always. Even when you're in Georgia."

"You'd better." She hugged him for a long moment and when she pulled back, she was certain moisture filled his eyes. He bent down and grabbed a suitcase and took it to her car.

Luke climbed out of the car. "Are we going to make it in time?"

Elizabeth tilted her head. "Are you worried we won't?"

"Yeah." He shrugged. "I'll take Christopher to our car." He hurried off.

"Looks like someone's coming around." Sam pulled Elizabeth into a hug. "We'll be praying for you and expect us before the baby comes. I have a feeling you might need several extra hands in the months to come."

"Do you want me to have Eric draw up a contract? Because if my past pregnancies are any indication of what's to come, I'm holding you to it."

Sam chuckled. "We'll be there."

With one final hug, Elizabeth said good-bye to her sister and brother-in-law and headed toward the interstate. Wouldn't Steven be surprised to see them.

Steven rested in a chair for a few minutes with his eyes closed. This was the last of his radiation treatment. He'd done it. He finished. And he'd do it again if it meant fighting to live one more day to see Elizabeth and his family. Her pregnancy still had him on cloud nine. Perhaps if he'd listened to their child's heartbeat, the fear of Elizabeth not being able to carry their child to term might have sunk in, but it also meant that every step in this life called for faith. Faith that God would heal him. Faith that God would protect his family and his developing child. Faith that no matter how many times Steven began to waver and doubt God, He remained faithful.

"Mr. Moore?" A nurse touched his shoulder and he opened his eyes. "How are you feeling?"

He smiled. "Wonderful."

She grinned. "It must be your last radiation treatment?"

"It is." He stood and collected his things.

"Then make sure you ring the bell before you leave. Congratulations."

Steven had witnessed other patients ringing the bell in the lobby. An accomplishment, a sign radiation treatments had been completed. It was his turn and he couldn't wait. "Thank you. I certainly will."

As Steven walked through the hallway his thoughts turned to Elizabeth once again. How was she? The boys? How was their baby? An ache to see her, to hold her, filled him. He'd missed her terribly these last three days. Every day when he'd finished his treatments and Elizabeth wasn't waiting in the lobby as she had all the times before, he'd returned to an empty hotel room, only to find he couldn't get her out of his mind. Her laugh, her tenderness, seeing her pray, watching her sleep, the way she felt against him. Within a few hours his wife would be in his arms again and it wasn't soon enough.

Steven entered the waiting room and movement in the corner of his eye caught his attention. A little boy came running at him. "Christopher?" Steven knelt to catch the little tyke running as fast as his legs would allow.

"Daddy!" Christopher wrapped his small hands around Steven's neck.

Steven's pulse quickened as he glanced in the direction Christopher came. There, walking toward him, his wife smiled a mischievous grin. Luke stepped out from behind Elizabeth and he too smiled as they neared.

"I can't believe it." Steven hugged his family then stepped back. "How long have you been here?"

Luke answered first. "About thirty minutes."

"You didn't have to come all this way."

Elizabeth cupped his cheek. "Yes, we did. We wanted to be with you and see you ring the bell before we head to our new home in Georgia."

"You have everything?"

"Everything but you." Luke shrugged and stuffed his hand in his pockets. "I need someone to open baseball cards with and show me how to improve my batting average."

Steven's heart swelled. *God is truly a God of restoration.* "Let's go make some music."

Steven strode across the waiting room and approached the brass bell. Grasping the rope, he met Elizabeth's gaze. As if understanding his thoughts, she smiled and nodded in agreement.

Together, with joined hands, they all rang the bell.

Epilogue

Twenty Months Later

"Go, Luke! Go!" Steven lunged from the bleachers, his gaze trailing Luke as he rounded first base. The outfielder in left field scooped up the baseball and threw it toward second. Luke slid over second base. *Safe!*

Luke stood, brushed himself off, and got into position to race for third. As the pitcher wound up, he rocked back and forth on each foot, anticipating his friend's hit.

Steven looked to the scoreboard. Three balls. Two outs. Tied at the bottom of the ninth.

Pete took a practice swing and then gave Luke an exaggerated nod. Steven had seen them run through this move on several occasions. Pete had precise accuracy, but Luke had to run hard.

Pete stepped up to the plate.

This is it.

The windup. The pitch. The hit.

Steven watched as the ball sailed down the first base line into right field.

Luke rounded third.

The right fielder snatched the ball from the ground and threw to the first baseman, who fired the ball toward home.

The first base umpire called Pete safe moments before Luke slid headfirst over home plate, the ball a second too late.

The Cardinals won!

Steven cupped his hands to his mouth. "Whoo! Go, Cardinals!" He looked to Elizabeth. "They did it!" She was smiling up at him from the bleachers.

"They won." He returned to his seat alongside her.

She leaned into him. "I thought for a minute you might hop over the fence and join them."

"That bad, huh?"

She chuckled and those beautiful eyes of hers sparkled. "No. It's wonderful."

"I'm so proud of him, Elizabeth. He's come such a long way."

"He has…but so have you."

Steven wrapped an arm around her, pulling her close. He glanced down at their one-year-old daughter, Anna Mae. Her eyes fluttered slightly as she slept. Her dark hair resembled his, and her eyes, when she was awake, were much like Elizabeth's, stunning, giving him such a sense of awe.

Luke ran up to them. "Mom. Steven. Can Pete and the guys come over and use the batting cages?"

Steven looked to Elizabeth. The batting cages

he'd built last year were a hit in more ways than one. He wanted to continue Chris's tradition to help Luke improve in a game he loved, but most importantly, to remember his dad.

Elizabeth returned his look with a nod. "Sure. I can make some brownies. We have plenty of chips and drinks."

Steven stood. "Let the coach know in case he wants to come. The entire team is invited."

Luke smiled. "Thanks!" His cleats pounded the concrete as he ran off. Luke stopped in front of the coach and a moment later, the coach met Steven's gaze with a smile and a wave.

"Are you sure we have enough food?" Steven took Anna Mae from Elizabeth.

"The way my men eat, are you kidding me?" Elizabeth shook her head and rose from the bleachers. "I have a secret stash just for the occasion."

"Did you plan this?"

She wiggled her brows then laid a light pink blanket over his shoulder. "I had a feeling he might ask." She rearranged her purse and baby bag in the storage area of the stroller. Steven placed Anna Mae in the reclining seat and tucked the blanket along her small frame. They walked together to the grassy area where a mound of dirt attracted the younger children. "Christopher. We're going, sweetheart."

"Five more minutes?"

Steven waved for him to come. "Sorry, buddy, but we're leaving now. The team is coming home with us." Christopher descended from the top of the hill, sand pouring from his clothes the whole way. Steven ruffled his blond hair and fine grains of sand rained to the ground.

As they neared the house, Steven slowed to a stop at the mailbox, grabbed the mail, and handed the letters to Elizabeth before continuing up their driveway. She shuffled through the mail while Luke poked his head between the front seats. "Pete's car is right behind us."

Steven drove over the dam, seeing Pete and the coach's car in the rearview mirror. He parked in front of the house and Luke burst from the car, followed closely by Christopher. "It won't be long before Luke brings Christopher back to us." He slid from the car and opened the back door, waving at Pete's parents and the coach as they drove down to the batting cages.

Anna Mae smiled up at him, kicking her legs. Elizabeth, still in the front seat, gripped a white envelope. Before he could ask about it, she hurried straight from the car into the house.

"Hey, sweetie. You ready?" Steven unbuckled Anna Mae's car seat straps and carried her into the house. He set his keys on the kitchen bar and placed Anna Mae in her play saucer. "I'm going to find mommy. I'll be back in a minute."

He found Elizabeth on the edge of their bed, thoughtful, her brows knitting together. She stared down at her hands that held tight to the white envelope.

"What do you have there?" He sat beside her

on the edge of the bed. She inhaled and slowly passed the letter to him.

From Moffitt. "My results from my PET scan?"

"Probably."

Steven flipped the envelope over and saw the edge had already been cut open. He glanced at her.

She wrung her fingers. "I couldn't decide if I wanted to read it."

Steven covered her hand with his. "God is in control." He paused a moment before sliding the paper out. He unfolded the letter and Elizabeth leaned in. Tears blurred his vision before he reached the end.

"Oh, Steven." Elizabeth covered her mouth. Tears filled her eyes and ran down her cheeks. "They found *nothing*."

He couldn't speak. Dazed, he looked down at the letter again and reread the words. "...your PET scan came back clear. There is no sign of cancer..."

"Mom, Christopher—" Luke stopped at the door, worry and grief filling his eyes. "What's happened? Your cancer—"

What must he think with both of them in tears? Steven stood quickly.

"It's gone." He handed Luke the letter to read for himself.

Luke's hand shook as he read. "It's gone? It's really gone?"

Elizabeth rose and wiped her face. "Yes, sweetheart, the cancer is gone. God has healed, Steven."

Moisture filled Luke's eyes and he threw his arms around Steven. "I was so afraid you'd leave me, too, like Dad."

So was I. Steven's heart swelled and he held his son close for the first time. Somewhere in the house, a door opened and closed, warning him the moment was ending. He kissed the top of Luke's head before releasing him.

"Hey, Luke!" Pete called. "Where are you?"

"I'm coming." Luke smiled at Steven and wiped his face quickly. "Are the tears gone?"

"They're gone." Steven grinned. "Go have fun. We'll call you when everything is ready."

Elizabeth intertwined their hands as Luke left the room. Anna Mae's babbling grew louder. "I hear someone calling us."

They walked back to the living room where Anna Mae rocked back and forth with joy at the sight of them. Elizabeth picked her up. "Hey there, sweetie, I'll bring you into the kitchen."

"You can start the brownies. I'll get the chips and drinks." Steven moved the play saucer to the kitchen. He grabbed four different types of chips from the pantry and set them on the counter, then paused to watch Elizabeth set Anna Mae back in the saucer. From his soul, he cried out praise and thanksgiving. Elizabeth was his Ruth, this was his dream, the life God had restored to him when he was lost, without hope, and his faith was shaken.

Truly, nothing is impossible with God. Nothing.

Acknowledgements

To Mary Hamilton, Jennifer Slattery, Pam Hillman, and Joanne Sher, thank you for your wonderful insight and feedback on this novel. I'm blessed by you and your friendship!

To my husband--my friend and companion. I'm so thankful for your love and support as God deepens my faith in this journey. I couldn't do this without you.

A special thanks to Cyn Rogalski who named Steven and Elizabeth's daughter, Anna Mae. Thank you for sharing your mother's name with me and my readers. God bless you.

About the Author

Tanya Eavenson is an international bestselling and award-winning inspirational romance author. She enjoys spending time with her husband and their three children. Her favorite pastime is grabbing a cup of coffee, eating chocolate, and reading a good book. You can find her at her website.
www.tanyaeavenson.com

<h1 style="text-align:center">Books by Tanya</h1>

Unending Love Series

Unconditional

Elizabeth wants to forget. Chris wants to save his marriage. Can they trust God with their future and find a love that's unconditional?

Restored

Unwilling to deal with his prognosis, Dr. Steven Moore retreats to a happier time in his past—to the woman who once stole his heart, never suspecting she might offer hope for his future.

Gaining Love Series

To Gain a Mommy

When Hope Michaels decides to face her past, she unknowingly purchases the house across the street from her former fiancé—the man her twin sister married, then widowed. Fire Captain Carl McGuire can put out any flame, except for the one Hope sparks within him—some things never change.

To Gain a Valentine

As Valentine's Day approaches, will Patrick and Amabelle miss out on the love they've always desired? Or will their love take flight under the stars on this very special night?

To Gain a Bodyguard

Undercover ICE agent Madi Reynolds has spent years infiltrating a human-trafficking ring, but when her life is threatened, she is forced to walk away and advised to leave the country. War Veteran and ICE agent Brice Johnson faces the biggest assignment of his life—protect the woman he loves.